Negative Reaction

Lori Roberts Herbst

Editor: Lisa Mathews, Kill Your Darlings Editing Services

Cover Designer: Molly Burton, Cozy Cover Designs

ISBN-13: 978-1-7362593-9-9

The Callie Cassidy Mystery series

Suitable for Framing, Book 1
Double Exposure, Book 2
Frozen in Motion, Book 3
Photo Finished, Book 4
Negative Reaction, Book 5

Subscribe at www.lorirobertsherbst.com for fun stuff
(including FREE Callie Cassidy Prequel stories)

1

Sheer organza cloth hung in silver waves from the ceiling of the Creekside Event Center. Twinkle lights dangled from above, glittering like fireflies. Outside the floor-to-ceiling picture window, the sun was just setting over the western mountain range, painting the clouds a muted orange. Snow began to fall, delicate flakes that drifted down like a wedding gift, giving the scene inside the aura of a warm, romantic oasis.

Candles flickered around the raised platform on which I stood, wearing a satin, pearl gray, off-the-shoulder gown and two-inch heels, at least an inch too high for my comfort zone. My hair, brown with auburn highlights, was twisted into an elegant chignon. A look in the mirror before the wedding had assured me that my forty-five-year-old self looked decent. Better than decent, even. My ex-colleagues, who'd been used to seeing Callie Cassidy, former investigative photojournalist, ponytailed and makeup-free in the requisite jeans and jackets, probably wouldn't even recognize me.

Still, here I stood, maid of honor—or rather, Grande Dame—at my best friend Tonya Stephens' wedding, clutching my chic spray of white lilies. As I tottered on the heels, I took a moment to consider the delight and anxiety competing in my brain. Delight said, *Your best friend is marrying the man of her dreams.* Anxiety responded, *What if you wobble off those heels, knock over the candles, and set the whole place on fire?*

I pushed the dramatic thoughts away and turned to look at my two cohorts on the platform that served as altar. David Parisi, Tonya's handsome Italian groom, appeared remarkably at ease in his gray dinner jacket and matching bow tie. Next to him stood his similarly attired best man, my boyfriend, Sam Petrie, who was even more handsome than when we'd dated in high school some thirty years ago. His blond hair still swept back from his forehead, except for one stubborn curl that tickled his eyebrows. These days, he carried himself with a self-assurance he hadn't possessed back then, and it boosted his sexy-factor over the top. He caught me staring and gave me that smile of his, the one that made me weak in the knees. Just what I didn't need in these heels.

I sighed happily. The scene couldn't get more perfect. Except then it did.

The song, "What a Wonderful World" began playing through the speakers. Show time. The guests rose. David glanced from Sam to me, then rested his eyes on the aisle stretching before us.

The bride appeared, carrying a bouquet of white roses and lilies in one hand, while the other held tight to the arm of my father, Butch Cassidy.

I gasped at the sight of her. I'd been in the room while she was getting ready—keeping her company as the makeup artist buffed and powdered and painted and the hairstylist smoothed and brushed and sprayed. I'd helped her zip into her white crepe halter dress, its full-length skirt slit to the thigh, then watched as she applied a final coat of her signature red lipstick and topped it off with shiny gloss.

I'd seen the entire product at the end of the preparations—but not like this. Her radiance. Her joy. Her love. Tonya was perpetually gorgeous, but tonight, she was ethereal. She took my breath away, and it was obvious she had the same effect on her husband-to-be. The tenderness of his expression displayed the depth of his love. I chided myself for ever doubting his intentions.

As Tonya glided down the aisle on my father's arm, she

seemed so calm she might have been a guest rather than the bride. Her glossy, dark hair fell in waves across her bare shoulders, and her brown eyes gleamed in the candlelight. She smiled at the guests as she passed them. When she arrived at the front row, she paused, bending to pat Woody, my lovable golden retriever, and Carl, my not-so-lovable-but-with-other-redeeming-qualities orange tabby cat. I'd balked at the idea of Woody and Carl attending the wedding, but Tonya had insisted, saying they were as much family as the rest of us. To their credit, the animals I affectionately referred to as my creatures now sat obediently at my mother's feet, behaving with dignity and manners. I had to concede, they were adorable in the tuxes Mom had made them.

Then Tonya embraced my mom, Maggie, who'd been like a surrogate mother to her over the years. With her chin-length silver hair and floral jacquard gown, Mom looked regal. She cupped Tonya's chin in her hand and kissed her cheek.

Tonya turned to hug her own mother next. Regal wasn't the word I'd use to describe Lydia Fredericks. Wearing a knee-length crimson lace dress and zebra-print stilettos, Lydia stood beside her current plus-one, a thirty-something Adonis with purported Vegas mob ties.

While all the hugging was taking place, my eyes sought out the official wedding photographer. Braden Ratliff, a tall, broad-shouldered boy—*man*, I reminded myself— with a mop of thick blond hair, served as my apprentice at the photo gallery, and he'd been both thrilled and terrified when Tonya hired him for his first professional gig. I spotted him snapping pictures at the foot of the platform and felt a rush of pride. When I'd first met Braden and his identical twin brother, Banner, who hovered nearby holding equipment bags, I'd considered them hooligans—possibly irredeemable ones. But now, not even two years later, they were my employees and, dare I say it, family.

Leaving Dad to sit beside Mom, Tonya continued toward the platform, taking the last few steps on her own. But she wasn't alone for long. David descended to the bottom step and waited for his bride with a loving smile and glistening eyes. He took her hand in his, and together they climbed the steps.

The ceremony began with the minister speaking about commitment, loyalty, and love. She talked of turning toward one another, honoring each other's individuality, and nurturing not only passion, but friendship. Then it was time for the vows. David spoke first, clutching Tonya's hands in his. Only a few words in, tears began leaking from his eyes. He turned to Sam, who handed him a handkerchief. They'd anticipated this. David's Italian heritage meant he was no stranger to public displays of emotion. I glanced at his parents, who'd flown in from Siena, Italy last week. Their shoulders shook as they sobbed with joy. Emotion was definitely embedded in David's genes.

When David finished, everyone looked to Tonya. A second ticked by. Then another. And another. "Tonya?" the minister whispered. David shifted from one foot to the other. *"Mi amore?"*

Still, Tonya said nothing. Had she gotten cold feet? Descended into a catatonic state?

But her eyes were fixed on her groom, and she wore a soft smile. That, at least, boded well.

I stepped toward her, swaying on my heels, and nudged her shoulder. "That's your cue, girlfriend. I know you're big on a dramatic pause, but enough is enough."

She looked at me over one bare shoulder and sighed. "Isn't he amazing? I can't stop wondering how I got so lucky."

David's face relaxed, and a titter of relief burbled through the gathering of friends and family. Finally, Tonya turned her shining eyes to David and began speaking—in gibberish.

At first, I couldn't comprehend what was happening. Was Tonya playing some sort of practical joke? If so, her timing was totally inappropriate. Then I saw Sam grinning, and I focused on the gibberish. I started to comprehend a few of the phrases: *Mi amore. Felice. La mia vita.* My mouth dropped open. Tonya was reciting her vows in fluent Italian. I had no clue my best friend, my confidante, the keeper of all my secrets, had learned the language. David's expression conveyed his surprise, too, as well as his delight. Though I didn't understand what Tonya was saying, it started David crying all over again.

The rest of the ceremony flew by. Tonya handed me her bouquet, the happy couple said their I dos—in English—and exchanged rings. The minister pronounced them husband and wife, and before she could say, "You may kiss the bride," David had swept Tonya into his arms, twirling her as they shared their first embrace as a married couple.

When my friend's feet were back on the ground, she hugged me tight and kissed my cheek. I knew she'd left a red lipstick mark, but I didn't care. "I love him so much, Callie," Tonya said into my ear. "And I love you. Thank you for being here for me. My best friend. My Grande Dame."

She took her bouquet from my hand, and she and David practically danced down the steps. Sam offered me his arm, and we followed the bride and groom off the platform. With my free hand, I dabbed at my eyes with my own hankie. Sam grinned.

"Look at you, Ms. Emotional," he whispered. "If you're crying this much at Tonya's wedding, I can only imagine what you'll be like at your own."

My fingers tightened on his sleeve. *My own wedding? Was Sam hinting at something?*

"Relax." He patted my hand. "I'm not proposing."

As I eased my grip, he leaned in close. "Not yet, anyway," he said.

***

As the rest of the guests mingled in the bar area, the wedding party and family members arranged themselves in different groupings so Braden could take portraits. Woody and Carl posed for a shot with the bride and groom before my parents shuffled them off to the office for treats and a nap. Lydia insisted on a picture with her newest beau, posing with a hand on her hip and one knee bent and contorted her mouth into fish lips.

When the photographs were complete, we began making our way toward the dining area, where the rest of the guests had already gathered. The sight of the white china and sterling silver place settings generated a pang of anxiety. I still hadn't quite mastered the etiquette of which fork to use when.

Tonya and I walked arm-in-arm, laughing over a shared memory of us dressed up for prom so many moons ago. Behind us, David entertained Sam with stories of his upbringing in Italy. Everything was proceeding according to plan—until the Event Center door burst open.

All heads turned as a flurry of snow swooshed across the threshold, followed by a stocky man who stood in silhouette in the doorway. Beside him, a slender woman grasped his hand.

When the man moved into the light, I recognized him. My stomach clenched.

Tonya hand squeezed my arm. "Is that…?"

I nodded. "Brian Ratliff. What on earth is that creep doing at your wedding?"

2

Well, I didn't invite him," Tonya muttered. "He's a crasher."

I frowned. Brian's presence could put a terrible damper on the party. My eyes searched the small crowd for Braden and Banner, Brian's sons. I wondered why neither had mentioned their father's return to town. Embarrassment, I surmised. Brian wasn't exactly a father to be proud of.

I'd moved back to my hometown of Rock Creek Village two years ago, resigning from the *Washington Sentinel* after one of my stories helped send an innocent man to jail. Soon after my return, Brian's wife—the twins' mother—had been murdered, and Brian had been a prime suspect. The minute he was cleared, he slunk out of town, leaving his then-seventeen-year-old sons to fend for themselves. I doubted his homecoming elicited cheers of joy from them.

And there was another twist to the drama, one that had me reaching for my boyfriend's hand. Sam wouldn't be happy to see the guy again. Brian was the biological father of the twins' half-sister Elyse—Sam's adopted daughter from his prior marriage.

"Hellloooo to my village peeps," Brian bellowed, slurring his words and staggering. Was the woman holding his arm out of affection, or to steady him? The man was clearly blitzed.

"The prod…prod…" He shook his head. The woman whispered in his ear, and Brian raised a finger. "The prodigal son returns."

The prodigal son. Did Brian understand the parable at

all? Unless he was here to beg forgiveness, which didn't seem to be the case, he'd totally missed the point.

Then Brian spotted Tonya and me, and his eyes lit up. He started toward us, pulling his companion in his wake. That prompted Braden to jump into action. He stepped in his father's path and placed a hand on the man's chest. Without a word, Brian stared at his son's fingers as if they were cockroaches. Humiliated, Braden dropped his hand.

Two instinctive reactions warred within me: comfort the boy, or slap the snot out of his father. But realistically, all I could do was wait and watch.

Pushing past his son, Brian continued a wobbly trek, his bleary eyes honed in on Tonya. She rolled back her shoulders and lifted her chin—a queen who would tolerate no nonsense from the peasants. David moved close to his new wife and put an arm around her waist.

Across the room, none of the wedding guests seemed prepared to interfere at this point, but I knew they'd all come running if things went south. Detective Raul Sanchez and his partner, Detective Lynn Clarke, edged our direction, with Frank Laramie, current chief of police, a step behind them. Pamela Ashton, owner of the Fudge Factory, stared at the wedding crashers with unmitigated fury. Beside her, my good friend Mrs. Finney, her stocky septuagenarian body draped in lavender silk, seethed. If anyone was primed to barge in, it was the retired CIA agent, now owner of the Rocky Mountain High coffee shop. Her new paramour, Mr. Purdy, placed a comforting hand—or perhaps a restraining one—on her shoulder.

Brian Ratliff didn't have many fans in Rock Creek Village.

He halted in front of us. Short and stocky, his hockey player muscles had long since turned to flab. His salt-and-pepper stubble and tanned skin imbued him with a rugged, mountain man vibe. An objective observer might say he wasn't all that bad looking, but I wasn't anywhere close to objective. From my perspective, the man was less appealing than a train wreck.

Brian leered at the bride. "Tonya Stephens, you look delicious." I had to restrain myself from scratching that lascivious look off his face. David took a step forward, but Tonya clutched his arm and shook her head.

Brian's companion cleared her throat, as if to draw his attention back to her, and he responded with a little slap to her rear end. "Never mind, baby. She's pretty enough, but she don't hold a candle to you."

The woman pushed Brian's hand off her backside and turned to Tonya with a conspiratorial smile. "Men! Am I right? I apologize for Brian's uncouth behavior." She thrust out a manicured hand. "I'm Desiree Bouton. Congrats on your marriage."

Tonya hesitated, but politeness prevailed, and she shook the woman's hand.

"I know showing up uninvited may be rude, but I couldn't resist. I'm new in town and excited to make friends. What better place to start than a wedding? I insisted Brian escort me. Since his sons were on the guest list, I assumed we'd be welcome." She glanced toward the guests assembled in the dining area. "Don't worry, we won't eat anything."

With her skin tight, low-cut pink dress, I figured one teensy bite might cause a wardrobe malfunction anyway. Liposuction, I thought uncharitably. The woman's long, blond hair had been expensively styled. Pink lipstick lined a mouth that had danced with more than one Botox injection. Thick, tarantula-like lashes framed eyes so violet I suspected tinted contacts. Her appearance shouted floozy, but those eyes spoke of cold intelligence. I caught a whiff of her heavy perfume—Poison, by Dior, if I wasn't mistaken.

Braden and Banner hovered a few steps away. Their father's beady green eyes slid to them, then to me. I flashed back to the moment a couple of years ago when

I'd sent the heel of my hand cracking into the bridge of his nose. Oh, how I longed to recreate that moment.

Brian must have remembered it, too, because he took a halting step back. Then he gave me a smug smile. "Surprised I'm here, Callie Cassidy? You musta thought you'd run me outta town for good. Got your hooks into my boys, didn't ya? Especially this one." He pointed to Braden. "Trying to make my son into your mini-me? Ain't happening, darlin'. No son of mine is going to turn into some sissy photographer."

Braden's face bloomed scarlet, and he pressed his lips tight. If he'd been a cartoon character, steam would have spewed from his ears.

Brian snickered. "Whatsa matter, boy? Cat got your tongue?"

Woody and Carl must have sensed the drama in the ballroom, because they chose that moment to make an appearance. In response to the cat comment, Carl arched his back and hissed. Woody chimed in with a growl of disapproval.

I snapped my fingers, and Woody fell into position at my feet. Carl, never big on obedience, sashayed forward and sniffed Desiree's sparkly, high-heeled sandals.

She squealed and kicked out a foot, which Carl nimbly dodged. "Get that thing away from me! I'm allergic!"

I took my time scooping Carl from the floor. Desiree ran her hands down her dress, as if checking for wounds. "Why would anyone invite *animals* to a wedding?" she grumbled.

Quite a departure from her can't-wait-to-be-besties introduction a minute ago.

Sam finally had enough. He stepped around me, his hands clenched at his sides as he addressed Brian. "All right, we're done here. You need to leave. Now." Though my boyfriend was usually even-tempered, I could tell he was itching to take a swing at the man.

Banner moved to his father's side. "Hey, Dad, how

about we head home? The Avalanche are playing tonight. We could catch the third period…"

But Brian's attention had drifted elsewhere. I followed his gaze to Elyse, who stood a few yards away with her mother, Kimberly, and stepfather, Parker.

Uh oh, I thought. Things were about to get messy.

"Ah, there's my girl, pretty as a picture." Brian looked directly at Sam. "Takes after me, don't you think?"

Sam sprang forward, and I wasn't quick enough to stop him. He shoved Brian hard, sending him crashing to the floor. Desiree screamed. Elyse rushed over and put her hands on Sam's chest. "Dad, stop!"

Brian tried to get to his feet but couldn't manage it. *Just how drunk was he?* Then a tall, well-built man stooped over him, grabbed his armpits, and lugged him to his feet. It was Trent Wallace, the Rock Creek Village High School hockey coach.

I felt a surge of relief. Though I didn't know Trent well, I'd always liked him. He was a quiet, kind man, and from everything I'd heard, an outstanding leader. My friend Renata Sanchez, the school's assistant hockey coach, spoke highly of Trent, as did Braden and Banner, who'd spent four years on his team. He was the perfect choice for the role of peacekeeper.

But Brian didn't seem to hold the man in the same esteem. "Get your hands off me," he growled, shrugging out of Trent's grasp.

Trent held up his hands. "Listen, friend, let's not mess up this celebration. Why don't we just step outside—?"

"Step outside?" Brian yanked up his sleeves. "I don't think you want to step outside with me, *friend.* I'd mop up the snow with your face."

"Dad!" Braden sounded horrified. Beside him, Banner turned pale.

Brian stared at his sons and barked a bitter laugh. "You two always had a soft spot for dear old Coach Wallace, didn't you? Let me tell you a few things about your hero."

He slapped Trent on the back. "Did you know my old buddy here dated your mom in college? Soon as she met me, she dumped him. Why wouldn't she? I was starting goalie, and he was a second stringer. I made it to the pros, and he settled for coaching a bunch of snot-nosed teenagers."

Trent's face clenched. Lauryn, a cute, petite woman with a thick mass of curly brown hair and Trent's wife for less than a year, edged in beside him and took his hand. As she stroked his fingers, he visibly calmed.

But Brian wasn't ready for a de-escalation. He widened his stance and poked a finger in Trent's direction. "Anything you have, *friend*, I can take. So back off before I decide I want your job." He lifted his chin toward Lauryn. "Or your woman."

Trent's tenuous hold on a calm demeanor evaporated. He moved forward, even as Lauryn tightened her grip on his hand. In a coordinated move, Raul, Dad, and Frank inserted themselves between Brian and Trent, forming a buffer of law officers, past and present.

The room seemed to freeze. Then Desiree smiled and wrapped her arms around Brian. "Such a joker," she said. "One of the many things I love about this guy."

Dad looked Desiree in the eye and managed a smile. "I'm afraid I didn't catch your name, ma'am."

"Desiree Bouton," she said. "Pleased to meet you."

Dad nodded. "Ms. Bouton, as you can see, we're trying to celebrate a wedding here, and this man's presence is putting a bit of a pall on the festivities. We'd be grateful if the two of you left now. We'll get to know each other at a more appropriate time."

I snorted softly. My father, ever the diplomat. It was part of what had made him such an effective and beloved police chief.

Brian, however, didn't seem to be a member of the retired chief's fan club. He puffed out his chest. "Whatcha gonna do, old man? Throw us out?"

Raul put a firm hand on Brian's shoulder. Brian tried to shrug it off, but Raul squeezed hard enough that Brian flinched under the pressure. Finally, Brian took a step back. "Okay, okay. I can take a hint."

Raul released his grip. Brian took Desiree's elbow and headed toward the door, stumbling as he glanced back over his shoulder. "Just so you all know, I'm here in Rock Creek Village to stay. I'll be seeing you soon. Bet on it."

He snapped his fingers at the twins—or tried to, anyway. His couldn't seem to get his finger and thumb to make contact. "Come on, boys, let's get outta here."

Banner shot me an apologetic look and shuffled to his father's side. Braden stayed put, his expression defiant.

"Braden!" his father barked. "Get a move on, son."

"I'm not going anywhere with you." Braden's eyes blazed. "I wish it hadn't been Mom who died," he blurted. "I wish it had been you."

His words sucked the air out of the room. I tensed. Brian was staring at his son with such rage I feared he might strike him. Instead, he turned and stomped toward the exit, kicking over a chair on his way. He slammed through the door and disappeared into the darkness, with Desiree and Banner right behind him.

3

As soon as the door closed, the hush that had settled over the ballroom turned into an electric buzz. In response, David clapped his hands and smiled. "Well, *cara famiglia e amici*, dear family and friends, Tonya and I hope you enjoyed that dramatic interlude. Of course, we didn't plan for…how do you say it?…wedding crashers, but what a story we'll have to tell our grandchildren. Now, let's put all that nonsense behind us and return to our celebration. Who's hungry?"

Tonya gazed at her new husband with pride and affection as they headed toward the bride and groom's table. I excused myself to reinstall Woody and Carl in the office. This time, I'd make sure to securely latch the door.

I'd started back toward the ballroom when Braden rounded the corner, heading toward the men's room. I hurried over to him. "That must have been uncomfortable," I said. "Are you okay?"

"All good," he said, but I could tell he was putting on a brave front. "I'm used to my dad's idiot behavior. I only wish he hadn't ruined the wedding."

"It's not ruined. But I get it if you'd rather not stay. My duties as Grande Dame have been executed. I'll take over as photographer if you'd like to go home."

He scoffed. "Home? As if. Thanks for the offer, but I just want to get back to work. Photography is the only thing that makes sense in my life right now."

I understood, having experienced that feeling myself more than once. "All right. But if you change your mind…"

"I'll come find you," he said with a grateful smile.

I returned to the main room and found my seat next to

my boyfriend, where we enjoyed a delicious Italian meal prepared by Jamal and Rodger, Sam's chefs at Snow Plow Chow. First up was a mixed green salad with lemon pepper vinaigrette, followed by a choice of three entrees: grilled steak with Cabernet whipped potatoes, chicken breast with pesto risotto, and for the vegetarians, butternut squash ravioli with sage sauce. I'd chosen the steak, but I sneaked a few bites of Sam's chicken, too. As expected, the food was exquisite.

Between courses, I tried to gauge Sam's state of mind. Like Braden, he said he wanted to let it go, but I caught his eyes darting frequently toward his daughter.

After dinner, guests gave speeches and made toasts. There were jokes and plenty of laughter. Afterward, we all sauntered over to the dance floor to watch Tonya and David share their first dance as husband and wife. Braden scurried around the periphery with his camera, distant enough to be discreet but close enough to capture the important moments. Then the music ramped up, and guests joined the bride and groom on the dance floor.

I forgot the evening's conflicts, shucked off my heels, and made merry. I danced with Sam, then Dad, then Ethan MacGregor, my partner at the Sundance Studio photography gallery. I joined my friends Jessica Fannon and Summer Simmons for our own unique rendition of the Hustle. I even took part in a raucous version of the Macarena with Mrs. Finney and Mr. Purdy.

When Sam went to the kitchen to check on Jamal and Rodger, I spotted Raul leaning against a wall and crooked a finger at him. He obliged, and the two of us made our way to the center of the dance floor. He wrapped an arm chastely around my waist, and I rested a hand on his shoulder, certain we looked like two tweens attending a middle school dance. I thought of Raul like a younger brother I couldn't quite tame into submission, but there'd always been a tiny undercurrent of attraction between us. We were both careful to avoid fanning that flame.

"Well, that was interesting," I said. "I'm surprised you didn't punch Brian in the nose."

"And I'm surprised you didn't knee him in the groin, like you've always wanted," Raul said with a grin. "Did you know he was back in town?"

"Nope. Not a clue. Neither of the boys mentioned it to me."

"I'm sure they're embarrassed," Raul said. "I can't imagine having Brian for a dad."

"Agreed. Their mother was no great prize, but at least she loved them."

He spun me expertly, and when we were back in vocal range, I said, "What will happen now?"

He shrugged. "Probably nothing. We'll keep an eye on him, though."

I grinned. "Speaking of *we'll*…how are things going with Lynn?"

"Fine, as long as she remembers I'm the senior detective and obeys my every command."

I smacked his arm. "I don't mean work-wise." I pulled my hands away and made a little heart with my fingers.

Raul rolled his brown eyes. "We're strictly professional, Callie. I've already told you that."

His lips said professional, but his face said there was more to the story. Raul and Lynn's burgeoning romance was common knowledge in the village. Everyone assumed they'd end up together eventually.

"Uh-huh," I said. "We'll see about that."

When the song ended, I went to the bar for a drink, while Raul took his *partner* for a *professional* spin. As I sipped, Tonya sidled up beside me, resplendent in white. I put an arm around her, careful not to dribble red wine on her dress. "You look happy, girlfriend," I said. "Ready to journey to the Italian countryside with your husband?"

"Husband," she said in wonder. "It sounds strange, but at the same time, so right. I can't wait for you to experience it yourself. I predict I'll be dancing at your wedding before another year passes. When I throw my bouquet later, I'm aiming right at you, sweet potato. You'd better not fumble the pass."

Yet another reference to the potential of my impending nuptials. It made my head spin. "Tonya, you know I'm not ready—"

"Uh-huh. We'll see about that."

She echoed the very words I'd spoken to Raul. Was I as clueless as he claimed to be?

Sam had not-so-subtly hinted at his desire to be married. I loved him with my whole heart, and he loved me. But a lifetime commitment? The idea once scared the wits out of me, but as time passed, I wondered if my fear was more of a habit than a truth. Was I getting closer to yes?

Thoughts to chase another time. Tonight, I just wanted to be present in this moment.

"You seem to be doing all right," I said, "especially considering…earlier events."

She snorted. "I don't waste time ruminating over people like that. Besides, Lydia mentioned that she'd be happy to have her latest boyfriend use his mob connection to take care of Brian. So, there's that option."

We laughed. Then Tonya waved her hands over her head, attempting to get the attention of a young red-haired woman across the room. Girl, really—she couldn't have been much older than Elyse. Though we hadn't yet been introduced, I already knew who she was: Monika Schiff, Tonya's cub reporter, hired less than a week ago fresh out of college.

Monika dashed over as if the head honcho had summoned her—which I supposed she had. A head honcho wearing white satin and sporting a huge sparkling diamond on her finger.

"Yes, Ms.…um…" Monika stumbled over the title, not sure what to call her new boss. Ms. Stephens? Mrs. Parisi?

"Oh, I'm keeping my name," Tonya said. "Over the

years, my mother has gone by Silverton, Stephens, Haskins, Fredericks, and probably soon whatever Mr. Mob Guy's last name is. No thank you. My name will remain intact, regardless of marital status."

Monika looked like a deer in the headlights. She'd gotten a lot more information than she'd bargained for. Tonya chuckled. "Just call me Tonya, okay?"

Monika nodded, and Tonya threw an arm around my shoulder. "I wanted to introduce you to Callahan Cassidy, the heart of my heart, the soul of my soul."

Now Monika turned to me, wearing an expression I recognized as starstruck. I used to get that a lot from fledgling journalists, but not so much since I'd moved back to my hometown. Her reaction stirred a buried reserve of ego I hadn't dipped into for a while. "Hi, Monika. I'm Callie." I stuck out my hand.

She shook it with vigor. "I know who you are. You're legendary."

"Well, that's a bit of an exaggeration," I said modestly.

"I've followed your career since I decided to become a journalist," she said. "We learned about you in my high school journalism class. And in college. You were a case study in our ethics class. You know, that story about…"

She trailed off, her face flushing as she realized she'd referred to the last story of my career—the one that ended it. My burst of ego drained away as quickly as it had risen.

Monika studied her shoes. "I'm sorry. I didn't mean to…"

"No worries," I said, flapping a hand. "It's been a couple of years. I'd practically forgotten about it."

"Well, regardless of how it ended," Tonya said, inserting herself into the writhing pit of awkwardness, "Callie carved out a long and stellar career and possesses a wealth of knowledge and experience. If you have questions while I'm away, I'm sure she'd be happy to help."

"At your service." I bowed my head.

"That'd be great! Thank you." She shifted her eyes around the room and leaned toward us, keeping her voice low. "What was going on with that Brian Ratliff guy? Seems like there's something there that would make a good story."

Tonya sucked in a breath. I shook my head. "This isn't really the time or place," I said.

Monika's face colored, and she looked down at her feet again. "Of course. Stupid of me. I'm sorry."

"No worries," Tonya said, patting her arm. "I'm glad to see you thinking like a reporter. That's why I hired you. It's just—"

From the raised platform at the back of the room, David called to Tonya, providing a welcome interruption. Tonya looked at me and raised an eyebrow. "The time has come. Are you ready?"

With a spring in her step, she marched toward the platform. Sam returned from the kitchen, and we all gathered around as the husband and wife cut the three-tiered cake. They had agreed to forgo what Tonya referred to as the "primitive tradition" of shoving cake in each other's faces, choosing instead to feed one another tenderly.

Then it was time for the bouquet toss. In what I considered another "primitive tradition," the single women gathered around, waiting for Tonya to heave her flowers into the crowd, where they would supposedly land in the arms of the next bride. As Tonya stepped onto the platform, her eyes sought me out. When I bit my lip and shook my head, she pouted, but gave me a resigned nod. She turned her back and tossed the flowers, aiming them away from me. That's what best friends did.

There was a commotion and a tussle as the bouquet hit its apex. Renata was in the mix, I noticed, as was Lydia. But edging them all out in the run for the roses—a husky, older woman, clad in purple.

Mrs. Finney jumped higher than I would have imagined possible, snatching the bouquet from mid-air and brandishing it to the wild applause of the guests.

Minutes later, we all lined up outside in the chilly night air. Snowflakes still floated from the dark sky, giving the scene a fairy-tale feel. As the newlyweds emerged, waving and blowing kisses, we held sparklers aloft. Specks of flashing light reflected in the falling snow. Braden's shutter snapped non-stop. Everyone cheered. Then the bride and groom climbed into a limo and were whisked away.

Sam put an arm around me and kissed my cheek. I smiled and sighed contentedly. But when I glanced at Braden again, a prickle of dread ran through me.

The wedding might be over, but I had a feeling the fallout was yet to come.

4

The next morning, Braden and I met in the Sundance Studio darkroom to begin work on wedding photos. I sniffed the air appreciatively. "Say what you will about pine or fresh-baked cookies, but in my book, nothing beats the smell of developer."

He laughed. "I'll buy that."

I handed him a jug, and he poured the liquid into his film tank. We stood side by side, agitating our tanks as I considered how far he and Banner had come since the *ubuntu* intervention my friends and I had staged a couple of years ago. The boys had turned a corner, so much so that I'd hired them to work at the studio while they put themselves through college. We'd forged a deep bond. But with their dad back in town, I worried their allegiance to me might feed into a family conflict. Should I distance myself until their caustic family dynamic settled? Or did they need me in their lives now more than ever?

I sneaked a glance at Braden. I was forty-five years old and had never been anyone's mother. Even my relationship with Woody and Carl was more of a triumvirate than a hierarchy. Was I equipped to provide whatever emotional support the twins needed in these new circumstances?

The timer beeped. As if we'd choreographed the move, Braden and I poured the developer from our tanks back into the jugs. We replaced it with blix, a bleach and fixer mixture, and gently rotated the tanks. This step would take six and a half minutes—plenty of time to address the elephant in the room.

"So, we had a bit of drama last night, huh?" I began.

Braden turned pink and dropped his eyes. "Yeah. Sorry about all that."

"No need to apologize. You did nothing wrong. In fact, staying on to finish the job took guts. I was impressed with how you handled the situation."

"Well, I couldn't duck out of a paid job. Besides, I enjoyed it. I got some great shots of the cake cutting. And those sparklers at the end…man."

"Don't forget the bouquet toss."

"Classic," he said. "The shock on Tonya's face when Mrs. Finney jumped up and snagged the flowers. She looked like a football player going up for an interception."

We both laughed. "Question," Braden said through his chuckles. "What ever happened to Mrs. Finney's husband? Mr. Finney, I mean."

I shrugged. "I'm not sure a Mr. Finney ever existed— or even that Mrs. Finney is our friend's real name. I mean, her British accent is manufactured. I'm guessing her so-called husband is, too. But if superstition plays out, she's likely to have one before long."

"You know," Braden said with a hint of mischief, "we all bet on you as odds-on favorite to catch the bouquet."

The heat rose in my cheeks. "All right, time to change the subject. Let's talk about your photos. I skimmed through the digital shots on your camera, and your work last night was exceptional. I'm proud of you."

Braden lit up at the compliment. "Photography seems so natural to me, like I was born to be it. When I'm taking pictures, everything else fades away. All the stress, the problems…Nothing else in my life has ever compared." Then his face darkened as his mood shifted. "I won't let my father take that away."

We stayed quiet for a moment as I pondered how to proceed.

"How, um…how did it go when you got home?" I finally asked.

Braden lifted a shoulder. "Dad was asleep—or passed out. Same when I left this morning. He was so wasted he probably won't remember any of it."

"Is that a regular thing? The drinking, I mean."

"Who knows? Banner and I haven't been around him much since Mom…" His voice trailed off.

"I don't mean to pry, Braden, but I'm guessing you and your brother must have felt a little abandoned by your father."

He frowned. "Mom was barely gone when our dad dumped us to chase women, first in Denver, then in Boulder. Told us he had to 'process' Mom's death. Said we were adults now, old enough to take care of ourselves. He actually expected us to be grateful he left us with a roof over our heads. We saw him every couple of months, and he spent most of that time telling us what disappointments we were. He didn't care about us then, and he doesn't care about us now."

"That must be painful," I said. "I wish you'd told me he'd come back to town."

He shrugged. "Some things people just don't want to talk about."

"Mm." After a few seconds ticked by, I said, "Why did he come back?"

"Well, not because he missed us, that's for sure." Braden twirled his tank with force. "You know he was working in Boulder as an assistant hockey coach, right?"

"I'd heard that, yes."

"Well, not anymore. He said he quit in protest over the head coach's mismanagement of the team. But Elyse told us he got fired for insubordination, at least, according to rumors. It's all so embarrassing."

Those poor boys. At not quite twenty, they were still trying to figure out the kind of men they wanted to be. I believed they were on a good path, but would their father's reappearance set them back? To me, Braden's defiance was a hopeful sign. I actually worried more about Banner. The way he'd trailed after his father like a puppy told me he still hungered for daddy's approval. I feared his hunger would never be sated.

"Tell me about Desiree," I said.

"The blond bimbo?"

"Now, Braden," I said. "Cheap shots are beneath you."

He looked chagrined—but only slightly. "Sorry. It just bugs me that Dad moved her into our house. My mother's house. Mom's clothes were still hanging in the closet, and Desiree put them all in bags like trash. It's like Mom never even existed."

I grimace at Desiree's insensitivity. Sure, the boys' mom had been gone for almost two years. On the surface, they appeared to have moved on. But grief didn't work that way. I wondered how often they'd sneaked into her room to touch her things, to inhale the scent lingering on her clothes. Another woman moving in and erasing those tangible memories must be like losing their mom all over again.

"Dad didn't even ask us," Braden said, his voice cracking. "Just showed up with her and that brother of hers…"

"Brother? I didn't know about a brother."

"Name's Weston. Couple years younger than her, I guess. One of those surfer dudes who never grows up. I think maybe Desiree supports him."

Interesting. I hadn't considered Brian and Desiree's financial situation. With Brian out of a job, it was a distinct possibility Desiree was supporting him as well. "What does Desiree do for a living?"

"She's a model. Used to be, anyway. She showed us her photos in a couple of magazines I had never heard of. She's pretty. Nice enough, too, I guess, but snobby. She wants us to like her, I think. It's just…"

"She's not your mother."

He nodded. "It's like Dad is erasing Mom and expecting us to do that, too. So now we've got the blond bim…I mean, the model and the surfer dude living in our house, partying and smoking weed and whatever else…"

He snapped his mouth shut, having revealed more than he'd intended. Despite his fury with his father, he didn't want to get him into trouble.

The timer beeped, and we poured the blix back into the jug and placed our tanks under running taps for a three-minute wash. "Don't tell Raul about the weed, okay?" Braden said.

I couldn't see any point in sharing that information with Raul, who hated Brian enough already. Besides, marijuana was legal in Colorado these days. What could he do about it anyway? "I won't, Braden. I promise."

After a moment's silence, Braden sighed. "I mostly worry about Elyse getting dragged into all this. She doesn't deserve our family drama."

Nor did Sam, I thought, but neither of them could avoid involvement. Victoria's death had unleashed a powder keg of dirty secrets. It turned out Elyse was the product of a vengeful affair between Kimberly and Brian Ratliff, the husband of her former "best friend." Luckily, Sam and Elyse's relationship had not only survived the seedy news but even strengthened. He was her legal father, and as she termed it, her "real" father.

Still, when Brian made the snide remark about Elyse resembling him, I'd seen all of Sam's submerged pain come bubbling to the surface. For the rest of the evening, he'd hovered over Elyse as if Brian might snatch her away.

"Elyse will be fine," I said. "She has a lot of good people who care for her. So do you and Banner. Lean on us when times are hard. We'll always be there for you, Braden. We're as much your family as Brian is."

A strand of hair fell across his eyes. He brushed it back and looked at me like a lost little boy. Impulsively, I hugged him, and his arms tightened around me. The pain and love I experienced in that moment united inside me with such force that I thought my heart might cleave in two. I knew I'd do anything to protect this kid. Was this what motherhood felt like? If so, how had my mom survived it?

The timer beeped. We turned off the faucets, dumped the water from our tanks, and busied ourselves with the stabilizer. That step took thirty seconds, and afterwards, we unraveled the spools of negatives and hung them from a clothesline to dry.

We bent toward the film and scanned the frames. First came Tonya and David gazing at each other as they recited their vows. Next, their kiss as the minister declared them husband and wife. Then, Tonya hugging me, our joy palpable.

"Wow," I said softly. "You nailed these, Braden. You have as much natural talent as I've ever seen."

He allowed himself a moment of pleasure before his face clouded. "Wish you could convince my father of that. Maybe then I wouldn't spend every waking moment wishing he'd disappear again." He sighed. "Life sure was easier before Dad came back into the picture."

5

Flames roared in the stone fireplace of the Knotty Pine, my parent's resort. A couple of hours after Braden and I had called it a day, I found myself curled into the corner of a soft leather couch with Sam beside me. Woody snoozed near the hearth with his head resting on his furry paws. On an adjacent couch sat my parents. Carl dozed in Mom's lap. I took a sip of warm mulled cider and popped a crab-stuffed mushroom into my mouth. "Not bad," I said. "Mr. Farmington has filled the void nicely since Sam stole Jamal away from you."

I was referring to Sam's talented young chef at the Snow Plow Chow, who had once done double duty manning my parents' front desk and creating succulent delights for their evening buffet.

"I did not steal him," Sam responded. "Jamal needed a full-time chef position to complete his culinary program. Anyway, I doubt he'll be at the Chow much longer. Some upscale restaurant in Denver will snatch him up any day. I foresee him opening a place of his own soon after."

"Well, there's no one more deserving," Mom said. "Jamal is talented, and a kind, intelligent person to boot."

"Speaking of young talents," Dad said, "what do you think of the village's new reporter?"

"Monika Schiff? Tonya has nothing but praise for her," I said. "But in my opinion, the girl has a lot to learn. Did you see her during the fiasco at the wedding reception? Her eyes lit up like it was Christmas morning. She even asked Tonya about the possibility of a story. She's a little aggressive, if you ask me."

Dad looked at Mom, then Mom looked at Sam. The

three of them burst out laughing.

"What?" I asked.

"I'm not going to break it to her," Sam said to my parents.

Mom nudged an elbow into Dad's ribs. "Tag. You're it."

Dad grinned. "I guess you don't see it, Sundance," he said, using the nickname I'd carried since childhood—always Sundance to my father's Butch.

In this instance, the sweet moniker didn't placate me. Whatever the joke was, I wasn't getting it. "See what?"

"That young woman is the spitting image of you at that stage of your career. Not physically, of course, but in every other sense. Focused and assertive, scrutinizing situations with an eye toward how to get the story. She could be your doppelgänger."

My brow furrowed. "You're kidding, right? I mean, I admit I've always been…well, motivated, but I was never aggressive…" I trailed off, flashing back to my early days as an investigative photojournalist. I'd chased every lead with both passion and dispassion. Staring into a mental mirror, I realized Dad was right. Slap some red hair on me and whisk me back twenty-some years, and Monika and I could be twins.

Dad noticed my uneasiness and gave me a sympathetic smile. "Nothing to be embarrassed about. You are who you are, and as far as I'm concerned, you're pretty fantastic."

"We wouldn't want you any other way, Angelface," Mom said.

Sam leaned over and kissed my cheek. "As always, your parents are a hundred percent correct."

Dad's gaze flicked back and forth between me and Sam. "Let's change the subject," he said, with a hint of mischief in his voice. "Lovely wedding last night, wasn't it?"

"If you don't count the crashers," I said.

"I'm not talking about the drama. I'm wondering if the wedding gave the two of you any ideas."

"Butch!" Mom scolded. "I told you not to bring that up. Callie and Sam's relationship is none of your business."

"Of course it's our business." Dad leaned his elbows on his knees. "I need to know whether I should have my suit cleaned."

Sam appeared perfectly at ease during the exchange. I shifted in my seat. As I opened my mouth and closed it, raised voices from four people seated across the room provided a welcome distraction.

The group of three men and a woman noticed us looking and lowered their voices. One of the men raised a hand in apology. "Sorry. We're just debating and got carried away."

"No problem," Dad said.

"Debating?" I said in a low voice. "What are they, a bunch of politicians planning their campaigns?"

Mom's lips curved. "Philosophers. They call themselves Bentham's Progeny. They're professors from different colleges around the country who meet a few times a year to discuss moral and ethical conundrums."

Dad scoffed. "If you ask me, they just want to show off their so-called intelligence and dicker about issues of no importance."

"Now, Butch. Without ideas and philosophies, where would we be? Stuck in the Dark Ages, that's where." Mom turned to Sam and me. "From what I gather, utilitarianism is their doctrine of choice. They profess that an action is morally right if it promotes happiness and pleasure."

"They'd promote my happiness and pleasure if they'd quit flapping their gums and take some action," Dad said. "Go cure cancer. Do something about climate change." He sat back and sighed. "But they're renting two rooms in the lodge and two of the cabins. I suppose taking their money results in my happiness and pleasure."

Sam snickered. "They've been in the Chow and racked up a decent bill. I can get on board with taking their money."

I thought back to my college days. "I vaguely remember studying Jeremy Bentham and utilitarianism in my philosophy course. But I just couldn't get interested. Philosophy seemed too, I don't know, cerebral. I was more interested in practical pursuits."

Dad nodded in agreement. Mom started to respond, but my phone rang. I frowned when I pulled it from my pocket and saw Banner's name. Why would he be calling? The boys always communicated with me via text. Something serious must be going on.

I held the phone to my ear. "Banner? What's—"

"Is Braden with you?" His obvious stress shot through the phone. I tensed and perched on the edge of the couch.

"Not since early this afternoon. Why?"

"I need to find him. Fast."

"Banner, take a breath. Tell me what's happening."

"I'm at the hospital in Pine Haven. Tonight, when I got home, I found Dad on his bedroom floor. He had this white foamy stuff on his lips. I couldn't wake him up. I called an ambulance, and..." He paused, and I heard the beeps and whirs of hospital sounds behind him.

"Banner? Is your dad...?"

"He's alive. For now. But the doctor says Dad's in a coma. She...she won't say if he's going to make it. And I can't reach my brother!"

6

I promised Banner I'd locate his twin and get him to the hospital. I hung up and dialed Braden's number, hoping he'd just been dodging his brother's calls. No such luck. The phone rang four times and went to voicemail.

As I got to my feet, I told Mom, Dad, and Sam what was going on. "I'm going to find Braden," I said, my voice tight.

"Of course you are, sweetheart," Mom said. "But first, you need to calm down. You'll be of no use to anyone in a state of panic."

I could feel her transmitting some of her inner Zen my direction. I took a couple of deep breaths—four counts in, eight counts out, as Summer taught in meditation class. I immediately felt more grounded, and I gave Mom a quick hug. "Thanks. Will you look after the creatures?"

"Do you even need to ask?" She lifted Carl into her arms and put a hand on Woody's head before addressing Sam. "You're going too, I assume?"

"You assume correctly," Sam said. My old predisposition toward self-sufficiency reared up, and I considered objecting, but I tamped down the knee-jerk reaction. Truth was, I felt grateful to have him by my side. Until I'd moved back to the village, I hadn't understood that managing adversity was easier alongside someone who cared about you.

As we headed toward the door, Dad called out, "Keep us posted."

I waved over my shoulder. Sam and I pulled on our coats, stepped through the doors, and hurried outside.

Though it was late March and officially spring, Rock Creek Village hadn't gotten the memo. We were in that roller coaster time of year when it might be warm and bright one day and below freezing the next. Over the weekend, an inch of snow had fallen, and now temperatures hovered in the low thirties. As soon as we climbed inside Sam's SUV, he jacked up the heater. Then he pulled out of the parking lot and turned left on Evergreen Way, driving more slowly than I would have preferred.

He saw me jiggling a knee and placed a hand on it. "We'll find him, Callie."

"Shouldn't we be heading to their house?"

"If Braden was home, Banner wouldn't need us to find him," Sam said softly.

Duh. I wondered if my investigative instincts had begun to atrophy from lack of use.

I scanned the street. Except for Pearly's Steakhouse and Quicker Liquor, businesses were closed at this hour, meaning traffic was light. A few cars lined the curbs, but Braden's blue Kia wasn't among them. I realized I didn't know where the twins' friends lived—or even who they were.

Suddenly, an idea popped into my head. "Drive down the back way," I told Sam.

He instantly understood and maneuvered the car into the alley that ran behind the shops on the north side of the street. "There," I said, pointing at Braden's car, parked near the back entrance of Sundance Studio. "I bet he's working on wedding photos."

Before Sam even pulled to a complete stop, I was out of the car. I snatched my keys from my pocket and fumbled them. When I reached down to pluck them from the cement, I felt Sam's hand on my back. "Best to go in calm," he said. "You're giving off a world-is-ending vibe."

I nodded, breathed, and forced my shoulders to relax.

Then I successfully inserted my key into the lock and opened the back door.

The gallery lay cloaked in darkness, but the muted sounds of music drifted from the darkroom. I headed down the hall and paused at the revolving metal door. "Braden?" I called. "I'm hoping that's you in there and not some camera-wielding lunatic."

The music clicked off. "Callie? Don't come in!"

I cocked my head. Why wouldn't Braden want me in the darkroom?

Seconds later, the wooden safety entrance next to the revolving door groaned open and Braden appeared, gripping a set of tongs. Behind him, the red safety lights glowed. I tried to peer inside, but he moved to block me.

"What are you doing here?" he asked.

I lifted an eyebrow. "I was going to ask you the same question."

"You gave me a key, remember? Told me I could use the darkroom whenever I wanted."

"Are you working on Tonya's wedding photos?" I asked, craning my neck.

He took a sideways step. Yup, he definitely didn't want me seeing inside. But his eyes sparkled, and he grinned. "Stop being so nosy. Go away, would you?"

Ah. Now I got it. Braden was working on a surprise. For me. My heart swelled, and I smiled back. Then Sam cleared his throat, and I remembered why we were here. "Banner's been trying to reach you," I said.

Braden patted his back pocket. "Must have left my phone at home." He frowned. "Wait, why does Banner need to talk to me?"

I laid a hand on his shoulder. "We don't know all the details, but he said he found your dad unconscious at home. He called an ambulance, and they're at the hospital in Pine Haven."

Braden's face paled. The tongs clattered to the floor. "Dad? Is he...?"

"He's alive. Sam and I are going to drive you to the hospital. We'll get answers there."

Braden appeared shell-shocked. In a daze, he reached down to retrieve the tongs. "Okay. Just let me clean up."

"Don't worry about that," I said. "I'll call Ethan. He'll take care of the darkroom. Get your coat and let's go."

"But my car…"

"We'll get it later, when all this is figured out."

For a moment, Braden didn't move, his mind obviously reeling. Then he disappeared into the darkroom. We heard the water faucet turn off and saw the red lights go dark.

A couple of minutes later, we were on the road to Pine Haven. Braden stared out the window, silent and barely breathing. Tiny snowflakes glinted in the car's headlights. The drive would take about thirty minutes on a route that wound through the craggy mountains. Cell service was hit or miss, but I offered Braden my phone. "You should try calling your brother."

He looked at the phone for a moment, as if he didn't remember how to use it. Then he tapped a button and pressed the cell to his ear. Sam and I heard Banner answer, but we couldn't make out what he was saying. "No, it's me," Braden said. "I'm using Callie's phone. We're on our way to the hospital."

A muffled barrage of angry words issued from the other end of the line. Braden cut his brother off. "Shut up, moron. I was at the studio. Forgot my phone at home. But I'm on my way." He hesitated. "How's Dad?"

He listened, then pulled the phone away from his ear and frowned at the screen. "Lost him."

I knew he meant he and his brother had been disconnected, but I felt a shiver of foreboding. I hoped the call was all the two of them lost tonight.

7

As soon as Sam pulled up in front of the hospital, Braden and I hopped out of the car. "I'll be in as quick as I can," Sam called as I shut the door. Braden and I hurried toward the entrance. Before we made it to the door, Banner stepped from the shadows, wearing a heavy coat, a thick cap, and an angry scowl. "Nice of you to show up."

Braden glared back. "I don't need your crap, Banner. Just tell me what's going on with Dad."

"What do you care? You probably wish he was dead."

I stepped between them and put a hand on each of their chests. "Stop it, guys. You need each other right now. Your dad needs you."

In identical moves, they dropped their eyes, and their angry expressions melted into shame. After a moment, Braden spoke in a halting voice. "What happened?"

Banner put an arm around his brother, and the two of them leaned on each other. Sam approached from the parking lot. "Let's get inside where it's warm," he said.

We entered through the sliding doors and found seats in the corner, away from the half dozen other occupants in the waiting room. Sam and I sat facing the boys. Banner started talking, his words erupting in a flurry.

"I got home from Jordan's house…a bunch of us were playing video games…then his mom made us leave…"

Braden nodded patiently.

"The house was dark," Banner went on. "I figured everyone was out to dinner. But when I headed upstairs, I saw a light in Dad's room. I popped my head in to say hey. That's when I saw him. He was on the floor…lying on his back."

I reached out to put a hand on Banner's knee. "That must have been scary."

"Not really. Not at first. I figured he'd had too much to drink again and passed out." He glanced at Braden, whose pressed his lips tight. "I just wanted to get him into bed so he could sleep it off. I put my hands under his arms to lift him, and his head flopped sideways. That's when I saw the foamy junk around his mouth…" He sucked in a breath and put his face in his hands.

Braden scooted his chair closer. "I'm sorry I wasn't there, bro. I shoulda been. But we'll get through this. He'll be okay."

I turned my head away and blinked back tears. After giving the boys a moment to comfort each other, I leaned in again. "What did the doctor say?"

Banner sat up and swiped a hand under his nose. "Not much. She only came out once, to say Dad was in a coma."

Braden's eyes shot to me. "A *coma?* You didn't tell me that. Oh, no!"

I grimaced, then tried to look reassuring. "Hey, I know that word is frightening, but a coma isn't always as serious as it sounds. When I was a journalist, I covered a couple of stories involving accident victims who'd gone into comas. From what I learned, it can be the body's way of conserving resources. I remember one comatose patient who woke up the next day, good as new."

The twins listened hopefully. I didn't mention the other victim—the one whose coma lasted four years and ended with his death.

"What did the doctor say caused the coma?" I asked. Based on Banner's speculation that his father was drunk, along with his observation of foam around the mouth, I was guessing alcohol poisoning.

Banner shook his head. "They're running tests. They won't know more until they get the results."

I sat back in my chair. "All right. We wait."

We sat in silence for a while. Then the hospital's front doors slid open and Desiree burst into the waiting room, accompanied by a man I assumed to be the brother Braden had mentioned. A muscular man in his late twenties, he had shaggy, wheat blond hair that fell to the nape of his neck. His unzipped coat revealed a faded T-shirt stretched taut across his chest, suggesting significant upper body strength. His face was tan and creased—a guy who spent time in the sun.

Desiree scanned the waiting room. When she spotted the twins, she bustled over, pulled them to their feet, and wrapped them both in a tight embrace. The boys stood, not fighting the hug, but not returning it either.

Once she released them, she wrung her hands. "Dear Banner, dear Braden. Your father will appreciate knowing his sons are here for him."

She slid her eyes to me, then to Sam. "Callie, isn't it? And Sam? I can't thank you both enough for looking after the boys until I arrived. I'm so grateful, and Brian will be, too. I mean, when he…"

She held her knuckles to her mouth, and I was certain she was putting on a show. She reached for her brother and clutched his arm as she sobbed. Amidst all the boo-hooing, I didn't glimpse a single actual tear.

Her brother didn't seem especially overwrought. In fact, he looked a little bored—and his eyes were very red. I took a step closer and immediately recognized the telltale aroma. The surfer dude had been smoking a little pot, and not too long ago.

"Are you Desiree's brother?" I asked him.

He gazed at me in a mellow stupor. Desiree made a show of composing herself and said, "Please excuse my manners. This is my brother, Weston."

He lifted his chin by way of greeting, then walked away and slumped into a nearby chair.

Desiree fixed me with a weak smile. "I hope you can forgive my display of emotion. The news about Brian rattled me. But I assure you, I've pulled myself together now. Again, thank you for keeping the boys company. I'll see that they call you when we get an update."

I tilted my head. Was she dismissing me and Sam? From the corner of my eye, I caught a fleeting smirk on my boyfriend's face. He knew what was coming.

"They won't need to call," I said. "Sam and I will wait right here."

"That's very kind, but completely unnecessary. This is best left to family."

"Callie's the closest thing we've got to family," Banner said. "Sam, too."

"They stay," Braden added.

Irritation flashed across Desiree's face, but she quickly replaced it with a smile. "Well, that's nice of you both."

She slid off her coat, revealing a tight, coral-colored sweater dress with a hem that fell several inches above her knees. I wondered where she'd been when Brian was busy falling into a coma, but now didn't seem the time to ask.

Draping her coat over a chair, she looked around the room until she spotted a sign pointing to the cafeteria. "I'm off to find some coffee." She flipped her hair and flounced away, snapping her fingers at her brother. "Let's go, Weston."

He sighed, dragged himself out of his chair, and sauntered after her.

The rest of us looked at each other. Banner just shrugged. Braden rolled his eyes. Then Sam stepped away to call Elyse and tell her what was going on, while I made a quick call to Dad to update him. Next, I texted Ethan, who said he'd clean up the darkroom and head straight to the hospital. I told him it'd be best to wait until we had some definitive information, and he reluctantly agreed.

Sam returned and slid into the chair beside me. "Elyse wanted to come by—"

"No," Braden cut in. "This is not her problem. She

shouldn't have to deal with any of this."

"She said she wanted to be here for her brothers," Sam said. "I told her it'd only cause the two of you more stress if you had to worry about her, too. She finally agreed to stay put, on the condition that you contact her if there's anything you need."

Braden and Banner's lips quivered identically. I recalled a time not so long ago that I'd come across the boys taunting Elyse in the hallway of the high school. Now, the three of them had formed a bond I would never have predicted.

Desiree and Weston reappeared, carrying cardboard cups of coffee. "Any news?" she asked.

We shook our heads, and she took a seat. Weston plopped down beside her, and his chin fell to his chest. A moment later, he began to snore.

Time ticked by. Desiree pulled out her phone and began scrolling. After another twenty minutes, I rose, stretched, and said it was my turn to go for coffee. Sam offered to join me. As we turned toward the cafeteria, Monika Schiff entered through the hospital's front doors and headed straight for the twins.

I intercepted her before she reached them. "What are you doing here, Monika?"

"I heard they rushed Brian Ratliff to the hospital in serious condition. I'm here to report the news."

The twins were watching intently, so I kept my voice low and even. "It's nothing that merits the presence of a reporter. Probably just a case of food poisoning."

"My source said Mr. Ratliff was the victim of a poisoning and had fallen into a coma," she said. "Now, if you don't mind, I'd like to speak to his family."

I gave a start. *Victim?* My assumption had been alcohol poisoning. But Monika clearly believed there was something more nefarious at play.

"Who's your source?" I asked.

"You know better than to ask me that, Callie." She

tried again to move past me.

I again blocked her path. "Monika, those boys are scared to death right now. They don't need a reporter making things worse. It's inappropriate. Unethical."

"It's *news*. I'm a *reporter*. I have a responsibility. You, of all people, should understand that." She folded her arms. "What would you have done in my position? Back when you were doing the work?"

I realized I would have chased the lead, too. I glanced over my shoulder at the twins. Funny how perspective changed when you knew the people involved.

Weakly, I repeated that there wasn't any story. *Not yet.* "I'll call you if we get any information otherwise. You'll get the scoop, Monika, I promise. Until then, I have to insist you leave the Ratliff boys alone."

She shook her head, red tresses flying. "They're not minors, Callie, and even if they were, you're not their guardian. If they don't want to comment, they can say so themselves."

I opened my mouth to tell her I'd wrestle her to the ground to keep her away from the twins. But before I had to render a chokehold on the rookie reporter, the hospital doors slid open again. This time, Raul and Lynn entered.

My face crumpled at the sight of them, but Monika's eyes immediately lit up. Two Rock Creek Village detectives wouldn't have appeared on the scene unless they suspected a crime had been committed. It looked like Monika would have a story after all.

8

onika and I raced toward the detectives. I won. The old girl still had it in her when circumstances demanded.

"What are you guys doing here?" I asked Raul and Lynn in a low voice. Behind me, Banner had risen to his feet, while Braden perched on the edge of his chair. Desiree looked at us inquisitively.

"Police business," Raul said. "That's all I'm prepared to say."

I folded my arms. "Raul, you have to tell me why you're here."

He scowled. "The only person who can insist on any information from me is Chief Laramie. You're not him."

Lynn and Sam exchanged weary sighs at the all-too familiar exchange.

Before I could formulate a retort, a woman wearing a white coat and a stethoscope approached. "Are you the detectives?" She directed her gaze to Lynn and me.

Raul bristled. "I'm Detective Sanchez, and this is Detective Clarke." He jerked his head to me. "She is not a detective, though I'm not sure she understands that."

The doctor looked confused, but shook it off. "I'm Dr. Johannes," she said. "I'm the one who called you. May I speak to you privately?"

The three of them stepped aside and conferred quietly. Then Raul accompanied the doctor down the hall while Lynn, clearly tasked with the inquisition, stayed behind.

She took me by the elbow. "I need to ask some questions. You won't give me any flack, right?"

"Of course not. I don't think you need to talk to Banner and Braden right now, though."

Her jaw clenched, just as Raul's always did. Soon, she'd be closing her eyes and counting to ten. "You know we have to speak to them, Callie. It's our job."

She had a point. "Okay, but just one question. Are you thinking someone purposely poisoned Brian?"

"I can't go into that," she said. "I just telling you I need to talk to the people who live in that house. And I need to do it now."

"I'd like to sit in on the conversation," I said. I felt tears in my eyes and blinked them away.

"Callie, that's not—"

"Please, Lynn."

Her gaze was sympathetic as she considered my request. After a moment, she shrugged. "This isn't an interrogation. As long as Banner and Braden give permission, I'll allow you to be present. But not a word out of you. Promise?"

"I swear," I said.

Her eyes flicked to Monika, who brandished her phone as she moved toward us. "As for you, all you're going to hear from me is 'no comment.' So, don't even bother turning on your recorder. Got it?"

Monika nodded, but I noticed she didn't put her phone away.

Lynn strode across the room and introduced herself to Desiree and Weston, who was now semi-awake. "I need to ask you all a few questions," Lynn said. "Dr. Johannes has arranged for us to use the chapel so I can talk with each of you individually."

Desiree twisted her hands in her lap. "Why are the police involved? I thought Brian simply swallowed something he shouldn't have."

"We're required to check into the situation, that's all."

Desiree clutched Weston's arm. Lynn gave the twins a kind smile, then indicated she'd talk to Banner first. "Callie has asked to join us," she told him. "I've agreed to that, but only if you consent." He nodded, and I followed the two of them across the waiting room and into the vacant chapel. Lynn closed the door behind us.

At the front of the room, a small altar stood beneath a stained-glass window. Votive candles flickered from a narrow table to the side. Two rows of pews stretched the width of the space, and wooden chairs lined the walls. Lynn gestured Banner into a front pew and positioned a chair to face him. I stood to the side—unobtrusive, but close enough to hear and see everything.

Lynn's expression was kind and her voice gentle. "I realize this is a stressful time, Banner. I'll keep this as brief as possible. Okay?"

He nodded and clasped his hands between his knees.

"Why don't you start by telling me about your activities this evening?"

"I've been here." He looked at her like she was clueless.

"No, I mean, before you got home and found your father."

"Oh. I was at my friend Jordan's house with a few friends playing video games. After a while, Jordan's mom said we had to go because it was time for dinner. I headed straight home after that."

She jotted a few words in a small notebook she'd taken from her bag. "What happened when you got home?"

Banner inhaled, then repeated what he'd told Sam and Braden and me an hour earlier. No details of his story changed, leading me to the obvious conclusion: He was telling the truth.

When he finished, Lynn sat back and crossed her legs. "Where was everyone else?"

"They all went home, too. I told you, Jordan's mom kicked us out."

"The residents of your house, I mean. Where was Ms. Bouton? Her brother? Where was Braden?"

"No one else was home. Just me and my dad. But I didn't know he was there. Not until I went upstairs." His voice turned husky. I twitched, and Lynn shot me a warning glance.

"I understand," Lynn said. "I'm asking if you have any knowledge of their whereabouts at the time."

He shook his head. "Nah. No one talks to each other much in our house, except me and my brother."

"When you found your father, did you try to get in touch with the others?"

A flash of something that might have been fear crossed his face. "I…uh…I called 9-1-1. I wanted to get an ambulance there fast."

"Yes, but after that? Did you call Ms. Bouton?"

"I don't have her number."

"What about Braden?"

He shrugged. "I tried, I think. It's all a blur."

"So, you were unable to reach your brother?" Lynn persisted.

Banner glanced at me, then back at Lynn. "He left his phone at home, and I didn't know where he was."

Lynn nodded and scribbled. "Anything else we should know?"

He shook his head. "All right," Lynn said. "I think we're done for now. Please send Braden in."

As Banner passed me, I gave him an encouraging smile. Lynn and I didn't speak while we waited for Braden. When he came in and took a seat across from the detective, his feet bounced on the floor, sending his knees rising and falling like pistons. Lynn studied him for a moment, and I didn't like what I saw on her face. Again, a sense of dread rippled through me.

"Braden, where were you tonight?" she began.

He glanced at me, and I gave him a small nod. "At the studio. Working in the darkroom."

"What time did you get there?"

"About five. I'd been there earlier and went home to eat. Then I went back."

"Is there anyone who can vouch for you?"

I raised my hand. "I can. When Banner told us what

was going on, Sam and I found Braden at the studio and brought him straight to the hospital."

"Callie," Lynn said, her voice taut, "remember our agreement."

I frowned, but stopped talking.

"Braden, did you tell Callie, or anyone else, where you were going to be?"

He winced. "No."

"Why didn't you answer when Banner called you?"

He looked worried. "Why are you asking me all these questions?"

"I'm gathering the facts, Braden. Please just answer my questions." Lynn's voice was sharp.

I pressed my lips together. It was taking every ounce of willpower I possessed not to grab Braden and hustle him out of the room.

"Braden," Lynn said more gently, "I know there's been some rancor between you and your father. It must have been difficult for you when he returned to town—especially since he brought his new girlfriend. That can't have been easy."

Braden's eyes glistened. I saw where Lynn was heading, and I wasn't having it. To heck with staying quiet.

"Listen, it's been a long day," I said, keeping my voice cordial. "I suggest we table this conversation for now and resume tomorrow."

Now it was Lynn using every ounce of willpower. She kept her eyes locked on Braden. "Is that what you want, Braden? Or should we finish this tonight? It'd be best to get it over with."

He looked at me, and I kept my expression neutral. Finally, he heaved a sigh. "I'm pretty beat right now. We can talk tomorrow."

Lynn slapped her hands on her knees and stood. "So be it. We'll contact you first thing tomorrow to schedule a formal questioning. I'll go get Ms. Bouton and see if she's more willing to cooperate."

9

Back in the waiting room, Detective Clarke asked Desiree to join her in the chapel. Brian's girlfriend crossed her long legs and swung a high-heeled foot. "Can't we just talk here? Weston and I have no secrets."

She looked pointedly from Braden to Banner, as if to imply they did. I seethed. None of this was progressing as I would have liked.

"Up to you." Lynn took a seat across from them and opened her notebook.

Braden sat next to his twin, and I positioned myself in a prime eavesdropping spot behind Sam's chair. I noticed Monika hovering well within earshot as well.

Weston was snoring again, and Lynn stared at him. Desiree took the hint and shook her brother by the shoulder. He roused and wiped the drool from the corner of his mouth.

"Wake up, sleepyhead," Desiree said. "Detective Clarke needs our help." She smiled at Lynn. "Men. They can sleep through anything."

Lynn gave her a tolerant smile. "Ms. Bouton, I know you must be worried, so I won't take much of your time. Just a couple of questions."

"Whatever you need."

"Where were you when Banner found his father?"

"Weston and I were eating dinner at Pearly's Steak and Chop House. It's the only decent restaurant in town." She fluttered her thick false eyelashes at Sam. "No offense. I've heard Snow Plow Chow is a sweet little diner. But we're used to something more...upscale."

I glanced at Weston, with his uncombed hair and the sleepies gathered in the corners of his eyes. *Upscale?*

"No offense taken." Sam's tone was unperturbed. I envied him that even disposition—though I remembered how it had evaporated in Brian's presence.

"Mr. Ratliff didn't accompany you," Lynn continued.

Desiree gave a tiny frown.

"Well?" Lynn asked.

"Oh, was that a question? It sounded like a statement."

Lynn's eyes narrowed. "Let me rephrase. Why didn't Mr. Ratliff accompany you?"

"Brian wasn't feeling well. Stomachache, he said. He hasn't been himself for a couple of days. I told him if he wasn't better by tomorrow morning, I was taking him to the doctor, no argument. And now, he's in the hospital. In a coma, no less. If only I'd insisted sooner."

I half-expected her to swoon, such was the apparent depth of her despair.

Lynn flipped a page in her notebook. "Did everyone in the household share the food? Did you all drink the same beverages?"

Desiree tapped her chin with a long fingernail as her brother struggled to keep his eyes open. "Well, I'm a vegetarian, of course, so I wouldn't have eaten any of the meat products."

Vegetarian? I hoped she'd gotten her money's worth at Pearly's Steak and Chop House.

"My brother is a total carnivore, though. The boys, too. We didn't really eat meals together, but we all had equal access to everything in the fridge and pantry."

As Lynn jotted notes, Raul and the doctor returned to the waiting room. Raul lifted his chin to his partner, and she walked over to them. After some quiet discussion, Lynn put on her coat and hurried out the door.

When Raul and Dr. Johannes approached, the rest of us stood—except Weston. "Which of you is Brian Ratliff's next of kin?" the doctor asked.

Braden and Banner pointed at themselves and then each other. "We're his sons," Banner said.

Desiree delicately cleared her throat. "Actually, Brian and I weren't going to announce this just yet…"

Monika drew an anticipatory breath. I glanced at Raul, whose eyes bore into the woman.

"Brian and I are married." She beamed at the boys. "I'm your new stepmom."

We all looked at her ring finger. She followed our mutual gaze and held up her hand. "My ring is at home. We decided to keep the marriage secret for a while. Brian wanted the boys to get to know me before we broke the news." She smiled at the doctor. "Anyway, I assume that makes me next of kin."

"No way," Banner said gruffly.

"I don't believe this," Braden muttered.

"Do you have a marriage license?" Raul asked.

Desiree ran her hands down her tight dress. "Not on me. I didn't realize I'd need paperwork to validate my word. But I can supply it if need be."

Dr. Johannes looked impatient. "Okay, let me ask this: will all family members give permission for me to share information on Brian Ratliff's status with everyone present here?"

"Yes," Banner said. Braden nodded.

Desiree hesitated. "I'm okay with Callie and Sam, I guess," she said, "but not *her*." She pointed at Monika. "There's no reason for a reporter to hear private info."

The doctor looked at Monika, who put up her hands and backed away to a far corner of the waiting room.

Dr. Johannes consulted her clipboard, then lowered it to her side. "Mr. Ratliff is stable but remains in critical condition. He is in a comatose state, unresponsive, but an EEG shows a level of brain activity. Testing indicates the presence of a poison is his system—something caustic in nature. It will take time to narrow down the exact toxin, if we're even able to do so."

"Poison? Are you sure?" Desiree asked. "Couldn't he have just had a negative reaction to something he ate? He's been obsessed with sweets, hasn't been eating healthy at all..."

The doctor shook her head. "Poor eating habits, even food poisoning, wouldn't lead to this outcome. I'm certain his condition is the result of a toxin." She glanced at her clipboard again. "There's some minor damage to the lining of his stomach and intestines. His neurological status remains unclear. We're doing everything we can for him, and we maintain optimism. But I want you all to understand that we're playing a waiting game right now."

A troubled hush fell over the group. Despite the doctor's claim of optimism, the prognosis seemed dire.

Raul broke the silence. "Doctor, can you tell us how long the poison may have been present in Brian Ratliff's system?"

The boys looked confused at the question, but I understood what Raul was getting at. He wanted to know if Brian's condition resulted from a one-time ingestion of poison or if someone had been dosing the man over time.

"We can't determine an exact time frame," the doctor said, "but the toxin has likely been building up in his system for a couple of days." She turned to the boys and Desiree. "Have you noticed any differences in his behavior? His speech, perhaps? Sleep patterns?"

"Hard to tell," Braden said. "He's mostly been drunk."

I remembered Brian at the wedding—the stumbling, the slurred speech. I'd been irritated that he'd shown up inebriated. But what if he wasn't?

Desiree drew in a breath. "Honestly, I thought he'd been drinking, too. I even confronted him about it this morning. He told me he hadn't had a drop in weeks." Her lips quivered. "I didn't believe him. I feel so guilty."

The doctor looked at Desiree with sympathy, but I wasn't buying her act. If someone poisoned Brian, the new wife topped my list of suspects.

10

Dr. Johannes told us she'd keep everyone apprised and left the waiting room. Raul asked us to stay put and followed her down the hall.

The second he was out of sight, Desiree whispered something in her brother's ear and gave him a set of keys. Weston looked slightly dazed, but he took the keys and turned toward the front door.

"Hey, Detective Sanchez said we shouldn't leave," I called after him.

Weston halted, but Desiree gave him a little shove, and he walked out the door.

Desiree turned back to me and gave me the stink eye. "Not that it's any of your business, Callie, but I take medication for my thyroid." She touched her neck, as if to demonstrate her need. "If I'm late with a dose, it wreaks havoc on my system. Weston is going to get my meds. He'll be back in a flash."

A flash? Rock Creek Village was a half hour's drive. I didn't believe her story, anyway. I didn't know what Desiree was up to, but I made a mental note to get to the bottom of it. Fast.

She flounced over to the seating area. Across the room, Monika looked on with unbridled interest. The rest of us waited in silence. When Raul returned, he walked toward Desiree and gestured for the rest of us to gather around. He scanned the waiting room. "Where's your brother?" he asked Desiree.

She repeated her farfetched story, and I could tell Raul wasn't buying it either. Nothing he could do about it, though—for now.

"Okay, here's the deal," he said, swallowing his frustration. "Chief Laramie wrote up a request for a warrant, and Detective Clarke went to secure a judge's signature. We will be searching your home for possible toxins Mr. Ratliff might have ingested. The search will take a day or two. Everyone will need to find somewhere else to stay during that time."

The twins sprang to their feet. Desiree lodged a vehement objection. Raul shook his head. "It's not up for debate. If you need help securing accommodations, the department will assist you."

I turned to the twins. "You two can stay with me. I have a spare room. Woody and Carl will be thrilled."

They nodded, looking relieved. Desiree crossed her arms. "What are Weston and I supposed to do?"

I considered her predicament. What was it Dad always said? *Keep your friends close and your enemies closer.* Desiree wasn't exactly my enemy, and I wasn't about to offer her lodging in my home, but it wouldn't hurt to have her in familiar territory.

"My parents own the Knotty Pine Resort," I said. "With spring break and all, they've been pretty busy, but I don't think they're booked. I'd be happy to call and ask."

A quick flash of suspicion crossed Desiree's face before she arranged her expression into one of friendly gratitude. "That'd be lovely. I appreciate your kindness in this difficult time."

She looked at Raul. "If we're to be put out of our home, we'll need some of our things—clothing and toiletries and such. Unless the department intends to reimburse us for the purchase of such essentials."

"That's fine," Raul said. "We'll have officers accompany you while you pack your bags. They'll need to examine whatever you remove from the premises."

I suddenly realized Desiree had likely seen this coming, and that's why she'd sent Weston off on his mission. The woman was savvy, I'd give her that. What did she want retrieved from the house before they sealed it off? Obviously, it wasn't thyroid meds.

I stepped aside to call Dad, who confirmed that Cabin One—where I'd lived in for several months following my return to Rock Creek Village—was vacant. "Only one bed," he reminded me, "but the couch is a futon."

I put him on hold and gave Desiree the information. "A one-room cabin? Are you sure there's nothing more suitable?"

I remembered the comment she'd made about Sam's café not being upscale, and I bristled. Sam sensed I was about to pounce and took my hand. I closed my eyes, counting to five instead of ten. "Nothing else available," I said. "I doubt you'll find any nicer accommodations in the village right now. We have spring breakers in town for the next month. Take it or leave it."

She sighed. "I suppose we can make do."

The twins shifted on their feet, and I figured, like me, they were probably resisting the urge to smack her. I turned away, took Dad off hold, and told him to reserve the cabin for Desiree and her brother.

As I disconnected, I suddenly remembered Monika. I glanced around the waiting room, surprised not to see her there. When had she left? I'd been so entrenched in conversations and plans that I hadn't noticed. I felt a flicker of disappointment. She'd seemed so eager and tenacious. Maybe I'd misjudged her doggedness.

Or maybe she'd decided to chase the story from a different direction.

***

An hour later, Sam and I sat in his car at the curb of the Ratliff house. Heat blasted from the vents, but I couldn't seem to get warm. The boys had gone inside to pack whatever boys needed to see them through a couple of nights. It would be a while before Desiree made it to the premises, since she had to wait for her brother to return to the hospital. We should have offered her a ride back to Rock Creek Village, I supposed, but I'd been too petty. Besides, I couldn't imagine cramming her into the backseat with the twins for the half-hour drive. Talk about uncomfortable—and not just physically.

The house had been dark when we arrived. Raul had cautioned us not to enter until Officers Tollison and Hardesty arrived, but we didn't have to wait long. Five minutes after we pulled up, their squad car rolled in behind us. I had a good relationship with both officers, but when I rolled down the window and called out a greeting, they responded with a professional nod and escorted the boys inside. So that's how it was going to be.

"I can't believe this is happening," I said to Sam. "Leave it to Brian Ratliff to cause trouble just by returning to town."

Sam took my gloved hand. "I know you're upset, Callie. But you need to be careful what you say in front of the boys. No matter how vile the man was, he's still their father."

"Was?" I said.

"What?"

"You said *was*. You just referred to Brian in the past tense. Do you think he's going to…?"

Sam sighed. "It wasn't intentional. I hope for Braden and Banner's sake he pulls through. For Elyse's sake, too, I guess. But…" He gazed out the window, searching for words. "I won't say this to anyone except you, but I wouldn't mourn his passing. He's been a menace in my life."

I leaned across the console and kissed him. Then I stroked his cheek, feeling the stubble like sandpaper beneath my fingertips. "I know your heart, Sam. You're a good man. The best I've ever known. And Brian has been a thorn in your side. But you'll need to tread lightly when you speak to Elyse about this."

He nodded. "Her feelings are complicated, more than she's been able to communicate to me. Counseling has been beneficial, but she still has a lot to sort out. This won't help."

"Just stay in the present tense, and you'll be fine."

He smiled wryly.

"What's so funny?" I asked.

"How the tables have turned. Usually, it's me cautioning you to tread lightly."

I nodded. "It's called relationship balance. I give advice when you need it, and vice versa."

Headlights pierced the darkness then. I peered into the side mirror and recognized Raul's department-issued SUV pulling in behind us. He and Lynn exited the vehicle and headed toward the house.

As they walked up the porch stairs, the door of the house opened, and Banner and Braden came out, carrying duffel bags. When they passed the detectives, neither boy said a word. The twins got in the car, and we pulled away. In the mirror, I saw Raul and Lynn heading into the house.

It was going to be a long night.

11

We made a quick stop at the Knotty Pine to pick up Woody and Carl. The boys were in no mood for further conversation, so they stayed in the car with Sam. I took five minutes to summarize events for Mom and Dad. Then I carried Carl down the stairs with Woody following, his nose nuzzling my calf at every step.

My golden retriever leapt into the backseat with the boys, wagging as he hopped from one lap to the other. The sound of the twins' laughter at his exuberant greeting warmed my heart. Even Carl joined the party, jumping from my arms into the backseat and allowing the boys to stroke his back.

When we arrived at my townhouse, I led the twins upstairs to the guest room, showed them where I kept the soap and shampoo and towels, and told them to help themselves to anything in the refrigerator or pantry. *"Mi casa es su casa,"* I said.

"Your accent is terrible," Banner quipped.

"We took three years of Spanish in high school," Braden said. "We can give you lessons."

"No need," I said. "I get tongue-tied enough with English. The point is, I'm not the hostess with the mostest, so I might forget to offer snacks. Just take whatever you want."

"What if what I want is one of your expensive cameras?" Braden asked.

I swatted his arm. "Keep your grubby hands off my equipment."

Banner yawned. "Well, thanks for taking us in, Callie. But I'm beat. I'm gonna get ready for bed, if that's okay."

"For once, I agree with my brother," Braden said.

I checked my watch. It was just past nine o'clock. "Party animals, huh? I get it, though. This has been a grueling day. But if you wake up and want a midnight snack, help yourselves. I'll inform my ferocious watchdog and his sidekick that you have free rein."

They smiled their identical smiles, and I left the room and headed down the stairs. Behind me, I heard bickering over who got the bathroom first, followed by a round of Rock-Paper-Scissors. I didn't stick around to find out who won.

***

Sam and I curled up on the couch, sipped wine, and talked of inconsequential things. His newest recipe. My latest photo display. He told me his parents were planning a visit this fall. That meant I needed to schedule a therapy session.

By ten o'clock, the two of us were yawning. We said our goodnights at the front door, and by the time I'd rinsed the wineglasses and popped them into the dishwasher, the creatures had completed their nightly business. I locked the doors, turned out the lights, and plodded upstairs, looking forward to my comfy bed.

When I crested the stairs, I hesitated at the sound of quiet but angry voices. Were the boys arguing? They'd seemed fine an hour ago. I bit my lip, considering whether eavesdropping in my own home constituted an invasion of privacy. The journalist in me won the ethical battle. I tiptoed toward the closed door and leaned in.

I still couldn't make out everything the boys said, or even which voice belonged to which twin. But it was clear one of them was defending his father, and I surmised it was Banner.

"You don't even…a flying…happy if he never…"

"Shut up!" Those two words rang loud and clear. Then

the voice dropped. "…kiss up…like he cares…"

A thud came from inside the room, as if someone had stumbled into the dresser. Beside me, Woody's ears perked and Carl's back arched. I looked down at them, asking a silent question: should I intervene?

Just as I raised my hand to knock, I heard voices again. I leaned closer and put my ear near the door.

"Braden, I'm not clueless. Dad's a jerk. But he's the only parent we've got left. And I'm scared."

A long pause. Then Braden's voice. "I get it, Ban. I don't want to lose him, either. But whatever happens, we've gotta stick together."

There was some muffled movement. Were they hugging? More likely, they were engaging in a manly fist-bump.

"Now, can you please shut up so I can get some sleep?"

"Night, bro."

I put a hand on my chest and felt my eyes tear up. Then I herded Woody and Carl into my room and quietly closed the door.

***

The next morning, I was awake by seven. I grabbed my phone. No news about Brian, but I'd received a text from Tonya with a few photos of the happy couple in sunny Florence, Italy. I smiled and texted back, refraining from any mention of the drama in Rock Creek Village. Let her enjoy her honeymoon.

I showered and dressed. The creatures and I headed into the kitchen, and I opened the back door to be greeted by one of those clear blue skies you only seem to find in the mountains. Rays of early sunshine slanted across the thin layer of snow. If the sun stayed this bright all day, that snow would be nothing but a memory by evening.

Woody scampered across the yard. Behind me, Carl

stretched, his tail rising straight into the air. I was dressed in yoga pants and a long-sleeved t-shirt, and I shivered in the chill. Despite the sunshine, the thermometer on my back porch still hovered near the freezing mark.

Back inside, I filled Woody and Carl's bowls and took a coffee filter out of the cupboard. Before I could put it in the machine, Woody scurried toward the front door, his nails clacking across the wooden floor. A second later came a knock.

I shuffled through the entry in my socks and opened the door to Sam and Elyse. "Pleasant surprise," I said as they entered.

"I can't stay," Sam said after planting a kiss on my cheek. "Rodger has a doctor's appointment this morning, so my presence is required at the Chow. Elyse insisted I drop her off. Hope that's okay."

Elyse smiled at me, but the smile didn't reach her worried eyes. A visit with the twins would be good for all three of them. "Of course," I said. "The boys went to bed early last night, so I'm guessing they'll be up and around soon."

Sam said a quick goodbye and jogged to his car. As he pulled away from the curb, another car took his spot: the silver Pathfinder belonging to my partner at Sundance Studio.

Ethan and Renata exited the car and trotted up the walk. Renata carried her little shih tzu, Terror, who wriggled in excitement. Woody nudged his way around me, his entire back end waggling at the impromptu playdate.

But it was what Ethan carried that made me wriggle in excitement. In one hand, he grasped a cardboard beverage holder, each of the six slots filled with coffee cups from Rocky Mountain High. In the other, he clutched a plump bag bearing the same logo. My mouth watered in anticipation of Mrs. Finney's pastries.

Renata stepped into the house and released her little

dog, who tore off into the living room with Woody hot on her tail. "Hope you don't mind us showing up so early, but at least we come bearing gifts. Before I forget, Mrs. Finney said she expects a full report, in person. Promptly."

I nodded. Since her arrival in the village a couple of years ago, Mrs. Finney had served as an integral part of solving several mysteries. She'd earned the right to the details of any local intrigues.

I moved aside so Ethan and his cargo could squeeze through the door. He paused in the entry, nodded to Elyse, and glanced up the stairs. "I can't believe this is happening," he said quietly. "How are they doing?"

"They're okay. Worried, of course. Still sleeping, which is good…"

"Nah, we're awake, so don't be talking smack about us," a voice called from above. Footsteps pounded on the stairs, and the twins appeared, wearing only their boxers—Banner's sporting a collage of Tweety Birds and Braden's covered in Bugs Bunnies.

"This is not a sight I need to see," Elyse said, putting a hand over her eyes. "Get back upstairs and put some clothes on, would you?"

They grinned at her and hopped back up the stairs. The rest of us went into the kitchen. I grabbed paper plates and napkins while Ethan doled out the coffee cups. Woody and Terror raced circles around the couch. "Outside," I commanded, and the two of them dashed through the doggie door and into the backyard.

Once the two pups were out of sight, Carl appeared, first jumping into my lap, then climbing onto my shoulder. The boys stumbled into the room, wearing sweat pants, sweat shirts, and thick socks, each using his left fist to rub his eyes. It amazed me how similar they were—looks, voices, mannerisms. I'd gotten better at telling them apart, but I still sometimes had to fall back on the tiny scar above Braden's lip for a positive ID.

Banner grabbed a flaky pastry and sunk his teeth into it. "I'm starving," he said, crumbs flying from his lips.

"Were you raised in a barn?" Elyse wiped the detritus from the table and onto a napkin. "Anyway, when aren't you starving?" Her face turned earnest then, and she looked from one twin to the other. "Seriously, though, are you guys okay?"

Banner swallowed hard and set his half-eaten pastry on a plate. "It's tough," he admitted.

"We called the hospital," Braden said. "No change. The nurse said Desiree's with Dad now. They only allow one visitor at a time in the ICU."

"Well, I'm sure she'll give you each a turn," I said. "Why don't I go with you? Maybe this afternoon?"

Braden nodded. "That'd be good. I'll work in the darkroom this morning. I could use the distraction."

Banner hung his head. "Wish there was something to distract me."

Ethan chimed in, "Renata and I are going on a hike this morning. Want to come with us?"

Banner's eyes lit up. "You wouldn't mind?"

"Not at all," Renata said. "You can keep me company. Ethan can't walk and talk at the same time, so I get a little bored." She turned to Elyse. "Why don't you join us? The more the merrier."

Elyse shook her head. "I promised Mom I'd help her with a project today. She's redecorating the guest bedroom. Callie, could you drop me off at her house on your way to the studio?"

I assured her we could. The twins ran upstairs to get ready, and Elyse followed along to keep them company. "You'll have to change in the bathroom," she said to them. "I'm not up for anymore Looney Tunes."

I sipped my coffee, letting the caffeine work its way into my bloodstream. "Thank you for showing up this morning. The twins may not say it, but it means a lot to have you two to lean on."

"They have more than us," Ethan said. "They have a village." He shook his head. "Not that long ago, I thought those boys were hopeless. Now they're a lesson in resilience, thanks to you. If it'd been up to me, they'd have been charged with vandalism for their antics back then. But you gave them a second chance."

I remembered those days. Wilted salad on the stoop of my gallery. Vulgar words scrawled across the window. The boys sneaking in through a hidden door and leaving undesirable substances on the floor. Hard to believe the two of them worked for me now and were even staying in my house. They were a testament to how, given the right circumstances and support, people truly could change.

"I only hope the whole situation with Brian doesn't set them back," I said. "Their father's return to the village was hard enough on them. And now this…"

The boys and their sister piled back into the kitchen. Woody and Terror barged in through the doggie door, skidded to a halt, and shook their entire bodies, spraying the room with droplets. I swear I saw Carl roll his eyes before he darted back upstairs. Banner and Braden snatched more pastries. Elyse pretended to scold them. The entire scene seemed so natural, so light and joyful.

I wished the little cocoon we'd created in this moment could keep the boys safe. But they wouldn't be able to stay in it forever.

12

Ethan, Renata, and Banner piled into Ethan's SUV, leaving Terror behind to spend the day with Woody. Braden and I dropped Elyse at her mom's and headed to the studio. He went straight to the darkroom, while I cut through the gallery and out the front door. Mrs. Finney had demanded my presence via Renata and Ethan, and I knew better than to defy her.

Shading my eyes against the sunlight, I looked toward Mt. O'Connell, rising in the cobalt sky like a monarch in a thick white robe. My parents' resort stood at the base of the mountain, as if curtsying at the monarch's feet.

Inhaling a deep breath of crisp mountain air, I made my way down the sidewalk, passing Tabitha's Treasures, shuttered as always for the winter months so Tabitha could lounge on a Florida beach. Next, I came to A Likely Story, the bookstore owned by Tonya's new husband, closed for the duration of their honeymoon.

As I approached the Fudge Factory, I reveled in the rich scent of chocolate but stopped short when I reached the front window. Inside, I saw Raul and Lynn at the counter, and they weren't making a purchase.

I ducked to the side and watched. Behind the counter, Pamela seemed harried, her hands flying as words I couldn't hear tumbled from her lips. A memory from the wedding flashed in my mind: Pamela in a sparkly gown, glaring at Brian and Desiree. I wondered…

Despite my clandestine efforts, Raul spotted me. I held up my hands in a *what's-going-on* gesture. He responded with a flick of his fingers that said, *None of your business. Move along.*

At least, that was my interpretation.

I stood my ground. He sighed, said something to Lynn,

and pointed at me. She swiveled to look past him. Pamela, too, followed his finger. I felt like a bit player who'd flubbed her entrance on stage. A moment later, Raul stepped outside, shutting the door behind him.

"What is it you need, Callie?"

"What's going on? Why are you and Lynn talking to Pamela?"

"We're detectives. There's been an attempted murder. We talk to people. It's called investigating."

"Attempted murder? So, you've ruled out accidental ingestion?"

He scrunched his face, realizing he'd given away more than he'd intended. "I guess there's no harm in confirming that. It'll be public knowledge soon, anyway. But that's all you're getting out of me."

I scowled. "Raul, you act like I'm some pesky tourist trying to pump you for gossip. I have a vested interest in this. Braden and Banner are my employees. My friends. And you know I can be useful in an investigation. Let me help."

"It's precisely because of your relationship with the twins that you need to keep your distance. You're too close to be impartial. You can't trust your own objectivity."

"Who says objectivity is always an asset in solving crimes? When we have something to gain or lose, doesn't it offer clarity?"

Lynn tapped her knuckles on the window. He nodded at her and turned back to me. "I don't have time to debate criminal investigation theories, Callie. When we have something definitive and can share it with you, we will."

"Okay, but what does Pamela—?"

He ignored me and went inside before I could finish my question. I stomped my foot in frustration. Then I trudged down the street, refusing to allow myself to pout. Instead of fixating on my exclusion from the investigation, I'd just have to find my own way in.

***

The bell above the door tinkled as I entered Rocky Mountain High. A current of warmth carried the earthy aroma that suggested another caffeine fix in my immediate future. Behind the counter, Mrs. Finney smiled, her cheeks as round as plums. She wore a loose smock dress accessorized by a strand of chunky beads, all in her signature shades of purple. Curls sprouted from her scalp like a lavender Brillo pad.

When I reached the counter, her smile faded into a frown. "Callahan, I've been so worried. Those dear, sweet boys. What can I do to help?"

"If you could get Raul to fill me in on the status of the investigation, that would be a start," I muttered.

Her eyes lit up, and I worried I'd unleashed the kraken on poor, unassuming Raul. "Never mind," I said quickly. "He'll tell me when he can. In the meantime…"

A customer loped up behind me. "Let me take care of this young man. Then I'll summon Mr. Purdy to take over while you and I visit."

I ambled toward one of the ceramic bistro tables. Once I'd shucked off my coat and draped it over a chair, I sat, fluffed my hair, and looked around. The crowd was mainly tourists, sprinkled with a few familiar faces. Trent Wallace, the hockey coach who'd made a gallant attempt at diplomacy at Tonya's wedding, sat nearby sipping coffee as he shuffled through a stack of papers.

A few tables away, I spotted the four visiting professors who'd been engaged in the passionate philosophical discussion at the lodge last night. What had Mom said they called themselves? The Scions of Socrates? The Acolytes of Aristotle? Bentham's Progeny, that was it. From the agitation in their voices, they were clearly gearing up for another hearty discourse.

By the time I returned my attention to the counter, Mrs. Finney had served the customer his drink and was making my coffee, dark roast with a squirt of vanilla and a pinch of cinnamon.

The silver kitchen door swung open, and Mr. Purdy took a spot behind the counter. He was a tall, slender man, with a bald, liver-spotted scalp. I guessed he was in his early seventies, about the same as Mrs. Finney. I knew little about him, only that he'd arrived in Rock Creek Village one day on a tourist bus and never left. From the little information I'd wrangled from Mrs. Finney, I surmised his appearance hadn't been a fortuitous twist of fate. The two of them had known each other in a previous life—one marked by subterfuge and spying—and Mr. Purdy had tracked her down to resume a relationship cut short by demands of the job.

And resume the relationship they had, with flair. As I looked on, he whispered something in her ear that caused the usually stoic woman to blush. Then he patted her on the behind and grinned with impish delight. She giggled and raised a finger to scold him before picking up two cups and heading my direction.

Once she'd arranged herself in an adjacent chair, she pointed to the cup in front of me. "My newest adage. What do you think?"

Mrs. Finney's quirky sayings, which she had printed on her paper coffee cups, provided one of the many allures of Rocky Mountain High coffee shop. I lifted my cup and read the words aloud. *"Love softens even the most cynical heart."*

My eyebrow quirked. I rarely understood Mrs. Finney's aphorisms, but this one was clear as a bell. "Why, Mrs. Finney," I said, "it's so…sentimental."

She smiled and glanced at Mr. Purdy. "I suppose so, dear. But one is entitled to a bit of sentimentality as one ages." She leaned her forearms on the table and clasped her hands. "Now, fill me in on everything."

"Not so fast," I responded. "I'm not going to spill my information until you offer me a titillating secret or two about Mr. Purdy. You've been far too close-lipped about the man who seems to have stolen your heart."

Her smile was predatory, like that of a purple-maned lion on the hunt. "I could tell you, dear, but then I'd have to…well, you know the rest."

I grinned. She fed me that line at least once a month, as if I needed any reminding about her CIA past. "All right," I said. "But someday I'm going to uncover the details of the man's past. Yours too, for that matter. I don't need you for everything."

"Humph. We'll see about that." Her expression turned grim. "Seriously, Callahan, you must tell me all about our boys' situation."

So I did, with the methodical attention to detail Mrs. Finney always demanded. At the first mention of Brian Ratliff, her face clouded. "That man is nothing but trouble," she said. "If it weren't for the potentially damaging effect on the twins, I'd consider ringing up a dear friend of mine and having Brian, shall we say, dealt with." She tapped the table and mused, glancing again in Mr. Purdy's direction. "It wouldn't be easy, with him in the hospital and all, but—"

I snapped my fingers in front of her face. "Enough fantasizing, Mrs. Finney."

She poofed her curls. "You're right, dear. No sense going down that rabbit hole. Do go on."

I spent the next few minutes telling her everything, and just as I finished, the bell over the door jingled again. A young woman in a puff coat, knit cap, and thick mittens entered the shop. When she pulled off her hat and shook out her red hair, I realized it was Monika. Mrs. Finney saw her, too, and in a move that surprised me, she sprang to her feet, yoo-hooing and waving. Monika smiled and made her way over to us. Mrs. Finney took her hand and air-kissed her cheeks. Somehow, these two had become fast friends. I experienced a twinge of irritation—and possibly a pang of jealousy.

"I'm delighted to see you, my dear," Mrs. Finney said. "Callahan, you've met Monika Schiff, Tonya's new reporter, haven't you?" I nodded, but Mrs. Finney's attention was focused on Monika. "Sit down, young lady. Let's get you something to warm you up. Your usual?"

Her *usual?* How much time had the two of them spent together?

"That'd be great, Mrs. Finney. Thank you."

As Mrs. Finney scurried to the counter, Monika removed her coat and laid it across mine. Rather presumptuously, in my opinion.

She sat facing me and folded her hands. Across the room, the Bentham's Progeny group let out a roar. The two of us looked over at them, then returned our gazes to the table in front of us. I sipped my coffee. Neither of us spoke until Mrs. Finney resumed her seat.

"So, you two are acquainted?" I asked, employing my brilliant deductive skills.

"Oh my, yes," Mrs. Finney responded. "Tonya brought Monika in weeks ago, when she first interviewed for the job. I can tell you, she impressed me right away. This young woman is going to make a top-notch reporter. I predict she'll win the Feldman Award for her journalistic achievements someday, just as you did, Callahan."

Monika blushed, and I nearly rolled my eyes. Mr. Purdy hustled over and placed a cup in front of Monika. He gave Mrs. Finney's shoulder a squeeze and headed back behind the counter. Monika cleared her throat. "I'm glad I ran into you, Ms. Cassidy."

"Oh, you can call her Callie," Mrs. Finney said.

"Sure," I said. "Callie."

Monika smiled. "Thank you, Callie. Anyway, as I'm sure you realize, I've been following the Brian Ratliff situation, and I was hoping…"

She paused, shifting in her seat. I waited.

"Well, I was hoping the two of us might join forces."

I raised my eyebrows. "What do you mean?"

"You know, work together. A dual investigation. Tonya mentioned you might be willing to help me while she was gone. I'd love to watch you in action—to learn whatever you can teach me."

I squirmed. "I'm not a detective, Monika—not even a journalist. Not anymore."

Mrs. Finney gave a delighted clap. "Oh, you mustn't be so modest, Callahan. Once an investigative photojournalist, always an investigative photojournalist, that's what I always say."

"I've never once heard you say that," I muttered.

"It's a fabulous idea," Mrs. Finney trilled. "You have contacts in town and insider knowledge of the people here. And Monika can easily access outside resources."

"Outside resources?" I asked.

"Didn't Tonya tell you? One of Monika's primary skills is computer research. The dear girl is a prodigy. She earned a bachelor's degree in journalism and master's in computer science, both by the age of twenty-three. From what I'm told, her fingers can tap a computer keyboard and make it sing with secrets. Why, the two of you as a team would be unstoppable."

Despite my misgivings, I studied the feisty young reporter across from me. My parents had said she was the image of me at that age in terms of drive, determination, and attitude. I envisioned myself as the crusty old-timer dispensing wisdom to the young pup. It could work…

"You'd have to agree to some ground rules," I ventured.

She leaned back and eyed me. "I'd have to hear them."

I liked that she hadn't simply fallen in line. Test number one passed. "Nothing gets printed unless I approve it."

Her bangs fluttered as she shook her head. "Sorry, but I can't agree to that. I'm a journalist, bound by autonomy and objectivity. I can't allow you to grant or withhold permission over my stories. But you already know that."

Test number two passed.

"Okay, then, how about this? Any conversations we have, any information that passes between the two of us, should be considered off the record unless otherwise stipulated. If we're going to join forces, as you call it, I can't be worrying that anything I say might end up in print."

She considered my terms and stuck out a hand. "Deal."

We shook. I wondered for a moment if I'd just made a deal with a red-haired devil. But since Tonya had vetted and hired her, and Mrs. Finney, who wasn't easily charmed, had vouched for her, I took a leap of faith.

"Let's get started," Monika said with enthusiasm. She pulled out her phone and swiped the screen.

"What are you doing?" I asked.

"Pulling up my notebook. I need to get you up to speed." She turned the phone to show me a list of typed notes. I suddenly felt ancient. In my day, we wrote everything in cardboard-covered reporters' notebooks. Crusty old-timer might not be far from the truth.

"I already have the relevant information," I said, a little defensively. "Brian was poisoned. Raul...Detective Sanchez...said they're treating it as attempted homicide."

Monika looked at me, hesitation on her face. "Is that all he told you?"

I raised my eyebrows. "Is there more?"

She glanced at Mrs. Finney, then back at me. "Callie, when the police searched the Ratliff home, they discovered a set of darkroom chemicals in Braden's room. They're having them tested to see if they match the toxin found in Brian Ratliff's system."

13

I felt the blood drain from my face. No wonder Raul hadn't wanted to discuss the case with me. My mind whirled. Why had Braden taken darkroom chemicals to his home? I knew the detectives would track him down for questioning soon, and I needed to talk to him before they did.

As I put on my coat, Monika and I quickly discussed a game plan. We agreed she would start by conducting some online research on Brian Ratliff. Why had he left his university coaching position? Without a job, where was he getting the cash he needed to pay his bills? Who had an axe to grind with him? We made a plan to meet up later that afternoon and formulate a list of suspects based on what she uncovered.

In the meantime, I'd figure out how to get Braden out of the crosshairs.

As I headed toward the studio, I glanced in the window of the Fudge Factory again and paused. The shop still hadn't opened for the day, but Pamela was inside stocking the shelves with fudge squares and truffles. I wanted to know why the detectives had been talking to her earlier, and since Raul wouldn't tell me, my next best bet was wresting the information from Pamela herself. No better time than now. Questioning Braden could wait a few more minutes.

I jiggled the door, finding it locked. Pamela saw me and shook her head. *Closed,* she mouthed.

"I don't want to buy anything," I called through the glass. "Just want to talk."

Her eyes darted around, and I worried she'd disappear

into the back room. But she reluctantly came to the door, unlocked it, and stood aside to let me in.

"Morning, Pamela," I began.

"Let's dispense with the niceties, Callie. I'm very busy. What do you want?"

Her tone took me by surprise. Pamela and I had known each other since high school, and though we'd never been close, there'd been no hostility between us.

I decided it was best to lay things on the table. "I, um, noticed Raul and Lynn here earlier and wondered what they wanted."

She tossed her head and started rearranging truffles on a tray. "I can't see why that's any of your concern."

As I gathered my thoughts, I studied her. Like me, Pamela was in her mid-forties, but with her slender and athletic build, she looked ten years younger. Her skin was clear and smooth, except for tiny laugh lines around her eyes and mouth. She wore her thick hair, dark as chocolate, pulled into a ponytail. The image of a happy, successful business owner. Only her eyes, red-rimmed and puffy, offered a contradiction.

I smiled, attempting a tone of lighthearted camaraderie. "Everything that goes on here is everyone's business."

She crossed her arms. "Callie, cut the crap. You're poking around trying to figure out who poisoned Brian Ratliff, and you're probably hoping to pin it on me."

I drew back, shocked. "That's not true, Pamela. I've always considered us friends."

"Friends?" She guffawed. "When's the last time you asked me to one of your little get-togethers? Was I invited to the dude ranch? Am I included in your girls' night out parties? Never. Don't insult me by pretending I'm your friend."

I touched my hand to my chest. "Pamela, I'm sorry. I didn't realize you'd be interested. You always seem so busy, so…"

"Aloof?"

I hesitated, then nodded. "Well, yeah. Whenever you and I have chatted, like at Chamber of Commerce meetings, you always seemed to be in such a hurry. I never thought…"

She smiled sadly. "Sorry. I sound pathetic. My counselor tells me I'm a card-carrying introvert with extrovert longings. I push people away, then get mad when they go."

Plucking a truffle from the tray, she put it on a napkin and handed it to me. "Truce?"

"Thank you." I popped the treat in my mouth and groaned in pleasure. "Sea salt and caramel?"

She nodded. "Heavenly," I said.

She passed me one more. "Anyway, you're not here to delve into my insecurities. There's another mystery to solve in our not-so-sleepy little village. And since you seem to be the one who gets things done around here, I might as well tell you what I know."

I suddenly felt a little seedy, like I was using her. "Only if you're comfortable talking…"

The corner of her mouth lifted. "It's fine. Raul and Lynn say it might have been my fudge that poisoned Brian."

My eyes flew wide. I'd speculated the detectives were questioning Pamela because someone else had witnessed the ferocity of her reaction when Brian and Desiree crashed the wedding. It hadn't occurred to me they were considering her as the source of the poison.

Pamela continued arranging confections as she talked. "They said they found one of my gift boxes on the nightstand beside Brian's bed. Apparently, he'd been eating the fudge over the course of a day or two. Most of it was gone, but they sent the rest in for testing."

"Did you give Brian the fudge?"

She threw her shoulders back. "Of course not. I wouldn't give that man CPR if he were having a heart attack."

And there it was again—the same fury I'd seen at the wedding.

"What did he do to you, Pamela?" I asked gently.

She spoke without lifting her eyes from the tray. "Nothing."

"It's not nothing. I could read it on your face at the wedding. He hurt you somehow. Maybe it would help to talk about it."

I waited as seconds ticked by. Finally, Pamela dabbed at her eyes with the hem of her apron and gave me a wry smile. "It's the same old story. I'm not unique. Nice girl falls for a bad boy. Believes she can change him. He uses her, then tosses her aside." She sighed. "It all happened months ago. I thought I was over him. But when he showed up at the wedding with Miss Blondie on his arm, the scar ripped open."

The pain radiated off her, but she waved it away. "Anyway, blah, blah, blah. Can we not talk about it? I'd rather not wallow. It's never been my style."

"Sure," I said. "But let me say one last thing, okay? I've been in your shoes, Pamela. Not your exact circumstances, but I've gone through all the same emotions. I've been humiliated, furious, even desperate. I thought the only way to handle it was to isolate myself and keep everything inside. But come to find out, the only way to get through it was to lean on others. If you want to, you can lean on me. When you're ready to talk, I'm here for you."

Her face manifested a series of expressions. First, suspicion. Then, confusion. At last, I saw what I'd been waiting for. Hope.

I reached out and took her hand. She looked down at our intertwined fingers, and I spotted a tiny shimmer in her eyes. She drew away and wiped her hand on her apron.

"Anyway," she said. "Back to the case of the poisoned fudge."

I nodded. "How certain did Raul and Lynn seem that the fudge was the source?"

"Well, they said they were exploring other options, but I got the idea they were pretty convinced."

"I assume you'd remember if Brian had come in and made a purchase."

Her eyes flashed. "I would remember my foot wedged in his posterior as I kicked him out the door."

"He could have bought it from one of your employees," I said.

She shook her head. "I've barely left the place over the past two weeks. One of my employees is sick, and another is out of town at her grandmother's ninetieth birthday party. I've been here on my own. Anyone who bought something from the Fudge Factory bought it from me. And I assure you that Brian Ratliff wasn't one of my customers."

"What about Brian's wife? Did Desiree come in?"

Pamela's face paled. "His wife? That woman I saw him with at the wedding…they're married?"

I winced. I'd forgotten the news Desiree had shared at the hospital wasn't common knowledge. "So she claims. When the doctor asked about next of kin, Desiree volunteered the information. The twins hadn't heard anything about it."

Pamela swayed on her feet and clutched the counter. A moment later, she started laughing. "I thought he was a tomcat who would never settle down after Victoria. Guess he just didn't want to settle down with me."

"I'm sorry, Pamela. I didn't mean to spring it on you like that."

"It's fine, Callie. Believe it or not, knowing helps. Gives me some of the closure I've been searching for. In fact, the only thing that would give me more closure would be if Brian actually died."

I cringed. "I wouldn't repeat that to anyone. If it turns out the poison was administered via fudge from your shop, you're already going to be a suspect. You don't need to add fuel to the fire."

She huffed. "I take your point, and I'll watch what I say. I didn't mean it, anyway. I don't want Brian Ratliff dead." She pulled out a knife and started whacking a pallet of fudge into rectangles. "I'd rather see him suffer. For a long, long time."

14

The sun glinted on the shop windows as I walked the half block from the Fudge Factory to Sundance Studio. The temperature had risen enough that, as predicted, any residual white stuff had turned to slush. But there'd be more. It was only March, after all.

The vitriol in Pamela's voice had unnerved me, along with the fire in her eyes. I'd observed murderous rage before, and if Pamela's demeanor wasn't a sister to it, it was a first cousin. If Raul and Lynn had witnessed that same attitude, she'd be their top suspect.

It made sense, too, especially if it turned out Brian had indeed ingested poison-laced fudge. Still, I couldn't see Pamela as Brian's attacker. For one thing, she'd appeared legitimately surprised when I mentioned Brian and Desiree's marriage. That didn't eliminate her motive, of course. Brian had dumped her, and she obviously carried a grudge. But if she'd wanted to kill the man, surely she would've tried before now.

Although…she'd mentioned that Brian's reappearance in the village had reopened old wounds…

One way or the other, when Monika and I created our suspect list later this afternoon, Pamela's name would be on it.

As I neared the studio, I turned my thoughts to the poison itself. I wasn't well-educated on the subject of toxins, so I was confused about how fudge could be used as a conduit. How would someone get the poison into a pre-baked slab of chocolate? Inject it? Dip the fudge into a puddle of poison? Wouldn't there be a residue? A smell? A taste?

I paused, letting my gaze soften as I imagined a scenario. *The unidentified would-be killer buys a box of fudge from Pamela's shop. They take it to an unknown location, somehow fill the fudge with poison, repackage it, and...*what? Present it to Brian as a gift?

I sighed. Those answers would have to come later. Right now, I needed to talk to Braden—before Raul and Lynn beat me to it.

***

I stepped into the studio and locked the door behind me. The only light seeped through the slats of the blinds, but even without that, I'd have been able to navigate the space. I walked across the polished concrete floors, catching glimpses of my photos hanging in the shadows: snow-covered Mt. O'Connell dotted with skiers; a majestic elk bugling; Rock Creek gurgling beneath a thin layer of ice. I glanced at the far wall, where I'd encouraged Braden to establish a presence for his work. Though he was a rookie, his photos were already attracting attention. His style differed from mine, which gave the gallery variety. Whereas I gravitated toward landscapes and wildlife, Braden's work centered on humans. I loved how he captured the spectrum of people's moods, from the whimsical to the very dark. The boy had talent and a drive I'd rarely seen in one so young. I needed to make sure nothing impeded him from following his dream.

Turning into the hall, I caught a familiar whiff of chemicals drifting from the darkroom. Usually, I found it to be a comforting smell, like the scent of my mother's perfume. Today, it offered a stark reminder of the trouble looming over Braden and Banner Ratliff. One of them, anyway.

Music played inside the darkroom. I rapped on the metal door before stepping into the circular cylinder and rotating it to lead me inside. When the door opened into the darkroom, I was greeted with a blackness so dark it was as if I'd dropped into a bottomless pit. I heard shuffling, followed by a snap that shut off the music.

"That you, Callie?" Braden's disembodied voice called out from the darkness.

"No, it's Santa Claus. Ho, ho, ho. I've come bearing gifts for all good boys."

"Christmas was months ago. You should have gone with the Easter Bunny. I could use a chocolate egg right about now."

The mention of chocolate gave me a shiver, as I remembered Pamela's fudge. But I managed a tentative laugh, not quite ready to broach the related subject of poison and a father in a coma.

"Give me thirty seconds," Braden said. "I'm about to drop a print in the wash. Then you can turn on the light, and I'll show you what I've done so far."

I listened to the sloshing sound of his tongs moving in the chemical tray. My eyes had already adjusted enough to make out his dim outline near the workspace at the far wall. As one of my photography professors had taught us, no matter how dark it is, some light exists. The philosophy of an optimist.

A moment later I heard the sound of running water, followed by a click. I blinked as white light illuminated the room. Braden turned to me, grinning like a proud little boy wanting to impress his teacher. And in fact, that was just what he was. For the moment, anyway, he'd been able to compartmentalize and shove aside the past thirty-six hours to focus on creating art. I knew the feeling well. I often lost myself in my work, in the process of making pictures. I'd intend to spend an hour in the darkroom and look up to find three hours had whizzed past.

Braden made his way to a clothesline strung across the width of the room and gestured for me to join him. A half dozen photos hung from clothespins, still damp. I leaned in to examine them. A couple were contact sheets—prints of negative strips that he'd use to choose which images to print. Then I noticed a couple of test prints, striped photos with a variety of exposure times. He'd spent the morning laying the groundwork to streamline his later efforts.

I mentally patted myself on the back. The boy had received some solid training.

"Very nice," I said, studying a test print of Tonya and David at the altar. "I'd say the third exposure is the one you want to go with."

"That's what I thought, too. Since the lighting was consistent throughout the ceremony, I can probably use the same exposure for all the altar shots."

"Agreed. Keeps you from wasting time and photo paper." I pointed to the trays in the long, deep sink. "Can I peek at the photo that's rinsing? Or is it some big secret?"

He grinned again. "I only work on secrets when I know you won't be interrupting me. You can look, but I warn you—you might not like it."

I bent over a photo swirling in the running water. Once I made out what I was seeing, I laughed aloud.

"You're a heathen," I said.

It was a picture of me standing near the altar in my gray satin dress. I looked elegant—the perfect Grande Dame.

From the neck down, anyway. Braden had snapped the shutter in the millisecond when my eyes were closed and my mouth dangled open. I looked bored—or worse, as if I'd dozed off. Truth be told, I resembled Weston Bouton.

"Destroy that at once," I said. "If Tonya catches sight of it, she'll run it on the front page of the *Gazette*."

"For your eyes only," Braden said. "But I can't promise I didn't snap a picture of it on my phone in case I need it for future blackmail."

We spent a couple of minutes studying the contact sheets, strategizing which images to print. At the wedding, Braden had shifted between film and digital cameras, so we'd have to go through those, too. Tonya and David's wedding was commandeering a lot of Sundance Studio resources. But it was worth it.

Braden was eager to get back to work and subtly tried to coax me to leave. Unfortunately, I needed to stay. There was a conversation we had to have. "I'll just keep you company," I said.

He went to the enlarger, placed a negative strip in the film carrier, fiddled with the filters, and pre-set the timer. When he'd focused the image, he turned off the overhead lights. In the darkness, I heard him pull a sheet of photo paper from the paper safe and position it on the easel. A moment later, the enlarger light beamed through the negative for a few seconds, then shut off.

As he carried the exposed paper to the sink, I followed him like a stalker in the night. "Listen, Braden, I need to talk to you about something."

He stayed quiet. I imagined him sliding the photo into the developer tray and using the tongs to swirl the chemical across its surface. After a few seconds, he said, "About Dad?"

I nodded, remembered he couldn't see me, and said, "Yes."

"Is he…?"

"Oh, gosh, no," I said. "I should have led with that, Braden. I'm so sorry. I don't have any updates about your father's condition. As far as I know, nothing has changed."

He expelled a breath. "Then what do we need to talk about?"

"Well, your father ingested some sort of poison."

"I already know that. The doctor told us yesterday."

He sounded impatient, but I figured he was just scared. My reticence was only making this worse. Best to pull off the Band-Aid all at once.

"Braden, the detectives think the poison may have come from a box of fudge they found at his bedside. Do you know anything about that?"

"Fudge? What are you talking about?"

"Apparently, the box came from the Fudge Factory. Did your dad mention buying fudge? Or getting some as a gift?"

"Not to me. The only thing Dad has talked to me about for the last few months was what a failure I am."

I fumbled in the dark for his shoulder, feeling him tense beneath my touch. "Is that all you wanted to tell me?" he asked.

"No," I said, dropping my hand. "Braden, when they searched your house, they found darkroom chemicals in your bedroom."

His breathing quickened, but he didn't respond. I let the silence drag out for a minute. The timer beeped, and liquid sloshed as he moved the print from the developer tray to the stop bath.

"Talk to me," I said softly.

His voice was hoarse. "They think I took darkroom chemicals home and put them in my father's dessert? Would I really be that stupid?"

He paused, and in a plaintive voice added, "Is that what you think?"

15

Braden, no. I could never believe you'd hurt your dad. Not in a million years."

"But Raul and Lynn suspect me, don't they?"

His voice was so small, so scared and sad, that I wanted to whisk him out of the village and hide him away somewhere until all this got worked out. But since none of us could escape this whole mess, I had to help him find a way through it.

"I'm sure they don't, Braden. But they're detectives. It's their job to examine all the evidence and find explanations. They're going to need to talk to you about why you had those chemicals in your bedroom."

He moved the paper from the stop bath into the blix, where it would remain for one minute. When I knew he'd made the transfer, I continued. "To be honest, I'm curious, too."

"It's no big deal," he said. "I've been setting up a makeshift darkroom in my bathroom, that's all."

"A makeshift darkroom?"

"You said you'd set one up yourself when you were in high school, so I decided to try it. I borrowed one of the old enlargers from the storage room. I have black trash bags to cover the window, and I planned to shove towels under the door to make it light safe. It'll only be for black-and-white prints, so it wouldn't be that complicated." After a pause, he added, "Are you mad?"

"No, of course not," I said. "I just don't understand why you didn't tell me. Besides, it seems like a lot of trouble when I've already said you can use this darkroom whenever you want."

He hesitated. Then he said, "I didn't tell you because I'm not proud of why I did it."

The timer interrupted him, and I waited as he moved the photo into the wash tray. There was a click, and the overhead lights came on. In the brightness, Braden's face appeared drawn. He'd sounded so young, but his face looked much too old.

"The truth is, I set up that darkroom to spite my dad. He hates that I'm a photographer, and he never misses a chance to tell me. I wanted to rub his nose in it, you know? I wanted him to see that bathroom door closed whenever I was home and to smell those chemicals when he passed my room. It was my way of flipping him off."

"I see."

His shoulders slumped. "Guess I'm as much of a jerk as he is."

I shook my head. "That's not true, Braden. You're the polar opposite of your father. You're compassionate, hard-working, funny—everything he's not. He just gets under your skin, that's all. This bit of…well, civil disobedience…was the only way you knew to stand up for yourself."

He turned back to the sink, to the work that comforted him. "Well, it's gonna end up biting me in the butt, huh? Now they think I took those chemicals home to poison my dad."

"It'll be fine. We'll go to Raul and Lynn, tell them what you just told me—"

"And they'll say, 'That makes sense. You're off the hook, Braden.' Is that what's gonna happen?"

"Okay, maybe it won't be quite that simple, but they'll see reason." I drummed my fingers on the counter. "It wouldn't hurt for us to figure out who did poison your father, though. Are you sure you have no idea who might've given him that fudge?"

"I'm sure. I haven't had much conversation with dear old Dad. You could ask Desiree, I guess. Unless…"

He didn't finish his sentence, but I knew we were on the same wavelength—*Unless Desiree had done the deed.*

***

Braden finished the photo—a stunning image of Tonya and David at the altar, framed by the floor-to-ceiling windows. The sunset, muted by the clouds, tinted the scene with a soft golden tone, and the falling snow looked like the gods were shaking gold flakes from the sky. I patted my protege on the back and told him good job. He said he wanted to keep working, and I understood he needed some time alone. I left the darkroom and headed to my office.

I fell into my chair and slumped across my desk, resting my head on my arms. My mind drifted to Brian, still lying in the hospital in a coma, struggling to fight off the poison that had invaded his body. To say I didn't like the man would have been an understatement, but I didn't wish that kind of suffering on him. And even though he wasn't the Father of the Year, losing him so soon after their mother might devastate those boys.

But I wasn't a doctor. I had no control over what happened to Brian, so I'd have to focus on what I could control—and that meant fully addressing the persistent investigative itch in my brain.

I had a good idea where to scratch.

Raul and Lynn believed laced fudge had poisoned Brian. As a journalist, I hadn't covered many stories involving deadly poisons, so I had a limited knowledge base. I needed to consult an expert: the oracle Google.

I sat up, turned on my computer, and began my research. Mostly, I was interested in whether darkroom chemistry contained a level of toxicity sufficient to lead to a coma. Or worse.

I entered a few inquiries into the search bar. At first, the results cautioned me not to drink darkroom chemicals or let my children drink them. Thanks, Google. But more refined questions led to more useful information. I skimmed a scientific paper on the neurological effects of ingesting photo chemicals. Though I didn't take the time to decipher the jargon, the summary made it clear: the introduction of these chemicals through the gastric system would cause symptoms such as dizziness, slurred speech, unconsciousness, and even, without treatment, death.

I leaned back in my chair. I realized Google was a lightweight research tool, vulnerable to misinformation, but this study appeared legitimate—and that didn't bode well for Braden. It meant he had means. He had opportunity. And after his public confrontation with his father, some might also say he had motive.

Anxiety pulsed in my chest, but before it could fully take over, the back door opened, followed by the sound of familiar voices. A moment later, Ethan, Renata, and Banner entered the office.

With his ruddy, outdoorsy glow, Banner appeared relaxed. "Looks like you guys had a pleasant walk," I said.

"Walk? More like a workout. These two are beasts. I barely kept up."

"Then you need more exercise," Ethan said. "I'm fifteen years older than you, sonny. You should be running circles around me."

"I can't compete with an old man," Banner groaned. "How humiliating."

I laughed. "Well, I bet you've all worked up an appetite. How about lunch at the Chow? My treat."

Banner rubbed his hands together. "I've been thinking about ChipMunch all morning."

"Go tell your brother to hit pause. We'll head down as soon as he's ready."

Banner darted out of the office, and I smiled after him, coveting the bottomless energy of youth. Renata and Ethan plopped into the visitor chairs facing my desk.

"He seems upbeat," I said.

Ethan shrugged. "He's okay, I guess. A little moody. One minute, he acts carefree, and the next, he's morose.

The hardest part for him seems to be the limbo. Not knowing how all this will turn out."

"He mentioned his mom a few times," Renata added. "I've never heard him talk about her before."

"What about Braden?" Ethan asked. "How's he doing?"

"Not great." I filled them in on the fudge and the darkroom chemicals.

Renata's brow furrowed. "Raul and Lynn can't really believe Braden poisoned his own father."

The storm in her eyes resonated in her voice, and I shushed her. "I'd rather they didn't overhear us talking about this."

She pressed her lips together. When she spoke again, her voice was softer, but her tone was still hot. "I'm going to have a talk with my brother."

"I wouldn't if I were you," I said. "You, of all people, know how he is. If you tell him to put on the brakes, he'll floor the accelerator."

"You have a point," she said. "I'll talk to Lynn instead. At least she can be reasoned with."

"Callie, you'll be doing your thing, right?" Ethan asked. "My thing?"

"You know, your unofficial investigation deal."

"I don't know what you're talking about," I told him. He responded with a smirk.

We heard footsteps then, and Banner called out, "Let's go! We're starved."

***

Lunch was a roaring success. We started with platters of a nacho beef mixture over potato chips, a dish Sam had named ChipMunch and that might have actually made me fall in love with him for the second time. The appetizer was followed by Beef O'Connell, an Irish beef stew with tender chunks of meat, cubed potatoes, carrots and onions, all swimming in a red wine sauce that left us licking our lips. Vanilla SnowShakes topped off the meal.

Sam joined us, and there was laughter and joking around the table. It was like a happy family get-together.

As the meal wound down, I saw the boys' spirits begin to decline as reality descended over them like a storm cloud.

They excused themselves and stepped outside to call the hospital. I'd offered to drive them to Pine Haven for a visit, and they wanted to make sure they'd actually be permitted to see their dad. When they came back inside, they wore identical smiles.

"The nurse said Desiree just left and told her she'd be gone at least a few hours," Braden said.

"Yeah, it's the perfect time to go," Banner chimed in. "We won't have to see Dad's bimbo."

He noted my look of disapproval. "Sorry," he said, in a clearly unsorry voice.

I put on my coat, kissed Sam goodbye, and handed my spare house key to Renata so she could swing by and pick up Terror. As we were about to leave, the front door whooshed open, and Raul and Lynn entered the café. Instinctively, I stepped between the detectives and the twins, like a mother bear protecting her cubs. Raul rolled his eyes, and Lynn looked annoyed.

I didn't care. I took the boys' arms and led them out. When I glanced back inside, Renata was standing toe-to-toe with her brother. I almost felt sorry for him. But not quite.

16

The boys were subdued during the drive through the mountains. I sensed their nervous tension, so I didn't even try to make conversation.

When we arrived at the hospital, we checked in at the front desk, where the attending nurse scanned our IDs. She allowed me to accompany the boys to the ICU waiting area, where another nurse greeted us. Through a window, we saw Brian lying inert on the bed, wires and tubes sprouting from seemingly every part of his body. It was the first glimpse the boys had gotten of him, and they both gasped. I'd witnessed my share of trauma over the years, but even I experienced a quiver of shock. The man had seemed larger than life two days ago, hurling insults and threats. Now, he lay weak and powerless in a hospital bed.

The nurse stated the obvious: Brian had not regained consciousness. His vital signs remained stable, though. She said the boys could visit one at a time, but since I wasn't family, I wouldn't be allowed in the room. Tough break for Brian. Surely my presence would have provided him great comfort. He might have rallied just so he could hurl more insults at me.

Banner asked the nurse about his father's prognosis. She dropped her eyes to a stack of paperwork and said they'd have to speak to the doctor about that.

The boys agreed Banner would visit their father first. Braden and I watched him ease around the bed and position himself near his father's shoulder. He reached out to touch Brian's arm, then jerked his hand back as if he'd been tased. Cautiously, he tried again, letting his hand linger this time. We saw Banner's lips moving as he bent to speak to his dad.

Watching such a private moment felt intrusive. I turned my head away.

Beside me, Braden sat with a straight back and anxious expression, like a teenager waiting to talk to the principal. I put my hand on his. "He'll be all right," I said.

"You don't know that." His tone was hard.

"You're right. But I do know this: no matter what happens, you'll be okay. It may take time, but you will."

He didn't move for a moment, then his posture relaxed. "Promise?"

"I promise."

I only hoped it was a promise I could keep.

***

Banner stayed beside his father's hospital bed for about fifteen minutes. Finally, he leaned over again, hesitated, then kissed Brian's forehead and left the room.

"I'm not sure I can go in there," Braden murmured.

"You don't have to," I said. "But I'm afraid you might regret it if you don't."

Banner's brow furrowed. "It's not all about you, Braden. Dad needs you. Get in there."

Braden flinched, but stood and moved toward the room. At the door, he paused and looked back at us. After Banner mimed a shove, Braden entered the room.

I frowned as Banner sank into the vacant chair beside me and stared at the wall.

"Maybe don't be so hard on your brother," I said. "He's having complicated feelings about all this."

Banner rolled his eyes. "Well, stop the freaking world from spinning. Braden's having complicated feelings."

His response left me stunned. He'd never spoken to me in that tone—at least, not since the *ubuntu*. In that moment, he'd sounded just like his father.

"Banner, I just—"

He jerked out of his chair. "I'm going to the cafeteria. Text me if the doctor comes before I get back."

I watched speechless as he strode away. But as I thought about it, I realized I shouldn't have been surprised. Identical as they were physically, the twins possessed distinct personalities, and they dealt with stress in opposite ways. Braden was vulnerable, even a little sensitive. Banner buried his emotions beneath a veneer of toughness. When I'd pointed out Braden's pain, Banner must have felt like I was favoring his brother. Both boys were struggling. Banner needed me, too.

This maternal thing wasn't as easy as my mom made it appear.

I turned my gaze back to the ICU room. Braden's face was unreadable as he stood beside the bed. He barely even looked at his dad. I ached for him.

At the sound of heels clacking fast across the tile, I turned to see Desiree approaching, indignation visible on her face.

The ICU nurse rushed from behind the counter and held up a warning hand. "Mrs. Ratliff, please calm down."

"Calm down?" Desiree shook a finger at the nurse. "That boy poisoned my husband. Get him out of that room at once!"

I leapt to my feet. "Braden did no such thing!"

Eyes blazing, Desiree turned her wrath on me. "This is all your doing. You brought him here, didn't you?"

"Braden has every right to see his father."

"He hated Brian. You heard how he threatened him. And the police found poison in Braden's bedroom. The idiot wasn't even smart enough to hide the evidence." She shot a venomous look at the nurse and took a step toward the room. "If you won't remove him, I will."

A fog of fury clouded my brain. I grabbed Desiree's shoulder. "If you even go near him, I swear, I'll—"

The nurse wrenched my hand away and stepped

between us. "Ladies, I insist that you control yourselves. This is an intensive care unit, and I won't have our patients disturbed. If need be, I will call security and have you both removed from the premises."

Desiree and I stared at each other for a long moment. Then, by unspoken agreement, we retreated to the chairs against the wall. I looked through Brian's window and saw Braden staring at us with a horrified expression. I felt a pang of guilt. This was the last thing he needed right now.

"I'm sorry," I said to Desiree. "I shouldn't have grabbed you."

She flipped her hair over her shoulder. "Apology accepted," she said, loud enough for the nurse to hear. But I could tell by Desiree's expression that she didn't mean it any more than I did.

The nurse resumed her spot behind the counter, raising an eyebrow at us as if to say, *I'm watching you.*

I pretended to gaze straight ahead, but I spent a moment inspecting Desiree with my peripheral vision. Her eyes looked puffy and her face extra-lined. Wearing little makeup today, she appeared old and tired. I'd written off her earlier histrionics as a solid acting job, but maybe I was wrong. Could the woman genuinely be worried about her husband?

I decided to take a sympathetic tack. "Desiree, you must be upset and frightened about Brian. But I know you can't truly believe Braden would harm his own father."

She snorted, glanced quickly at the nurse, and spoke in a hushed voice. "This stupid place. You're all a bunch of village idiots. I never should have come here."

I struggled to restrain my retort. In fact, I struggled to keep from slapping the contemptuous look off her face.

She smirked at my reaction, then swiveled her head. "Where's Brat 1?"

"Brat 1?"

"Weston and I refer to them as Brat 1 and Brat 2. Like that Dr. Seuss book. Thing 1 and—"

"I know the book," I snapped. I glanced toward the nurses' station and lowered my voice. "It's not very kind of you to refer to your husband's sons that way."

She waved a hand. "Oh, Brian agrees with me. He said the boys' mother coddled and pampered them from the day they were born. When she got killed, you took over where she left off."

I summoned my inner Raul and closed my eyes, silently counting to ten. When I opened them again, Desiree was sneering. I realized she'd been trying to bait me.

Well, two could play that game.

"So, you and Brian are married, huh? At least, that's what you're telling people."

"Are you questioning my word?"

I examined my nails. "You have to admit it's a little strange he never mentioned you to anyone. Almost like he was embarrassed."

Her face turned crimson. "He's not embarrassed. Not of me. He just wanted to wait for the right time to break the news to the brats. They're a little soft. He wasn't sure how they'd take it."

"Well, he's been gone so long, I suppose he doesn't really know them."

She uttered a humph. "Now I understand why he stayed away. You people. You're so cliquish. So judgy. Why would Brian want to live here?"

"Why did he come back then?"

She cocked her head toward his room. "Bet now he wishes he hadn't."

She sat back and folded her arms. I sat back and folded mine. We probably looked like two pouty toddlers. After a couple of minutes, Desiree pulled her phone from her bag and started scrolling. I looked at Braden through the window of the hospital room. He'd taken a seat next to the bed and glanced over at us every few seconds. I got the sense he was ready to leave the room but didn't want to face Desiree.

I leaned as far as I could toward her chair trying to sneak a look at her phone screen, but she tilted it away. I bit my lip. Here I was, sitting next to a woman I considered a prime suspect in the attack on Brian, and I hadn't asked her so much as a single probing question. What a wasted opportunity.

Still, I didn't want to create another scene. Not with the nurse's eagle eyes on us and with Braden already so vulnerable.

But staying quiet chafed against my nature. Every fiber of my being wanted to pressure this woman into a confession.

I opened my mouth but was saved from potential disaster by the sight of Banner loping toward us, a can of Coke in one hand and a candy bar in the other.

"Brat 1," Desiree muttered.

Inwardly, I fumed, but I plastered a pleasant smile on my face and rose to greet him. He was looking past me, though. When I followed his gaze, I saw Dr. Johannes marching down the hall, clipboard in hand.

Maybe now we'd get some answers.

17

D r. Johannes shook hands all around, then asked again if the family consented to my presence as she updated them on Brian's condition. Braden and Banner agreed. Desiree hesitated, but finally nodded grudgingly.

The doctor skimmed her notes. "The report is good overall," she said. We all looked skeptically toward Brian, prone in the bed.

"I realize his condition doesn't look that great," the doctor said, "but I'm pleased to report there's been no further deterioration. In a poisoning case, that's excellent news. We've run an MRI, an EEG, and several other tests, all of which show no signs of hemorrhage or stroke. No masses or tumors in the brain. His esophagus and his gastrointestinal system are intact. Kidneys and liver are functional. These are positive signs."

Each twin blew out a breath of relief. Desiree, however, appeared dubious. "If it's such good news, doctor, why is my husband still unconscious?"

"Unfortunately, that's the nature of comas. They are still the subject of medical uncertainty. We can map the brain and monitor its waves, but we can't probe its every fold and delve into its mysteries. I will tell you that most coma patients recover consciousness after a few days, maybe a week. In the meantime, we have summoned a prominent neurologist from Denver for a consult. He should arrive first thing tomorrow."

Braden nodded. Banner frowned. Desiree tapped her foot. No one seemed inclined to ask questions, so I jumped in with mine. "Dr. Johannes, have you determined the exact cause of Brian's condition?"

"As I said yesterday, we are fairly certain Mr. Ratliff ingested a toxin. Lab results support that diagnosis."

"Could it have been alcohol?" I asked.

"I already told you, Brian wasn't a drunk," Desiree said. "He'd enjoy a beer or two, but nothing that would cause alcohol poisoning."

"You said yourself that you'd confronted him about his drinking," I said.

"That was before we knew about the attack on his life," Desiree practically spat. "The poison explains the slurred speech and all the other signs."

The doctor cleared her throat, and we returned our attention to her. "From what we have ascertained, alcohol wasn't a factor."

"Ha." Desiree gave me a victorious smirk.

"What about carbon monoxide?" I asked, ignoring her. "It can result in unconsciousness and…" I trailed off, not wanting to use the word "death" in front of the boys.

"I'm told there was no residual vapor found in the home," the doctor said. "Since no one else who lived there was affected, we're prepared to rule that out."

Dr. Johannes clutched her clipboard to her chest. "We can't say with certainty how this happened. Believe me, it's as frustrating to us as it is to you. But my educated guess would be that Mr. Ratliff orally ingested a toxin via food or beverage."

"Like e coli or salmonella?" I asked.

Desiree huffed. "When did you get your medical license? Be quiet and let the doctor talk."

I felt an angry flush rise up my neck. Once again, I longed to throttle the woman. But I was a grownup, and the twins were watching. I faced the doctor. "My apologies. I guess the journalistic instincts never completely dissipate."

She nodded sympathetically. "No worries. You're asking relevant questions. But Mr. Ratliff's condition does not present as infectious or bacterial. Poison is most likely."

I'd been searching for a way to classify Brian's poisoning as an accident in order to remove suspicion from Braden, but it seemed that was not in the cards. The only thing left was to identify the real culprit.

We were quiet a moment, digesting the information. Then Banner broke the silence. "You're saying someone did this on purpose. They wanted to kill my dad."

The doctor squared her shoulders. "I can't speak to the why, only the what and the how. I'm afraid your question is better addressed to the detectives."

Desiree choked back a sob—another fake one, no doubt. "Brian…my husband… will he pull through?"

"We're hopeful," Dr. Johannes replied.

"If…when…he wakes up…" She hesitated. "Will there be brain damage?"

"That's doubtful. People who recover from comas may experience confusion at first, and possible persistent short-term memory loss. But rarely is neurological functioning permanently impaired."

The doctor paused and gave us all a compassionate smile. "I'd suggest we cross that bridge when we come to it. I encourage you to take this day by day. The hardest part for families—for those of us in the medical field, too—is the realization that there are some things we simply can't control. We are doing everything possible for your husband and father. We're administering fluids to flush out his system. Monitoring him constantly. Continuing to run any labs that might provide answers. We're bringing in the consulting neurologist. I understand you all are anxious to know what caused this, but at this point, we have a treatment plan in place. Identifying the exact toxin wouldn't alter it, so it isn't terribly important."

Not important to you, I thought. *But for Braden, it might be critical.*

"We are confident Mr. Ratliff's condition will resolve itself," Dr. Johannes continued. "Be patient. Easier said than done, I realize, but it's our best option right now."

"Thank you, doctor," Desiree said. "Please keep us apprised."

Dr. Johannes nodded, then headed down the hall.

As soon as she was out of earshot, Desiree leaned toward the twins. "I hope you're happy, you stupid brats. This is all your fault."

The blood appeared to drain from Braden's face and transfer straight into Banner's. Before either of them could reply, Desiree whirled and marched toward Brian's room.

"Boys, this is in no way your fault. You—" My phone vibrated, and I glanced at the screen. "Sorry. I have to take this. I'll just be a minute."

I hurried down the ICU hallway, through the door, and into the main waiting room. I held the phone to my ear. "Raul?"

He heard the tension in my voice. Either that, or he was clairvoyant. "What's going on?" he asked.

I filled him in on the afternoon's events—the boys' visit to their father, my confrontation with Desiree, the doctor's update. "Raul, Dr. Johannes confirmed this wasn't an accident."

When he spoke, his voice was gentle—never a good sign. "I told you yesterday we were investigating this as an attempted homicide."

"Well, you don't need to investigate Braden. You know him, Raul. You've seen the changes in him this past year."

Raul was silent. I pictured his brown eyes filled with compassion. Though he often projected a tough-guy demeanor—and could be stubborn as a mule—he had as many soft spots as the Pillsbury Dough Boy. Except Raul's were buried beneath a six-pack of toned muscle.

I forced my mind away from that image.

"Your father was chief of police. You understand how

this goes. We have to follow where the evidence leads. We're interviewing everyone who had negative interactions with Brian Ratliff—including Braden."

"So, you're interviewing yourself?" He didn't deserve my snippiness, but I couldn't seem to suppress it.

He took my attitude in stride. "If I wasn't already sure I hadn't done it, I'd make myself available for questioning. The twins should, too. If they're innocent, we'll clear them."

"Wait, you're looking at Banner, too?"

"He lives in the house." Raul paused. "Listen, Callie, you need to trust us. We will treat the boys with respect and consider them innocent unless we have proof that indicates otherwise." He sighed. "I thought you knew me well enough by now to realize that."

I swallowed. He was just doing his job, and I hadn't meant to hurt him.

"I'm sorry, Raul. It's just hard that you're freezing me out of the investigation."

"My hands are tied. You're way too close to all this."

I nodded, not trusting my voice.

"We need to speak to them, Callie. It'd be best if they came to us."

When I didn't answer right away, he said, "If we can clear them, all the better, right?"

"Is that likely?"

His silence spoke volumes. I bit my lip. "I'll tell them."

"Good. Thank you. How about nine tomorrow at the station?"

"I'll ask them, but I think that should work. In the meantime, is their house still off limits?"

"For another day, at least. I'll let you know when we're done."

When we hung up, I saw the twins huddled together in a corner of the waiting room, watching me. Their faces were a mixture of sadness, fear, and frustration.

I knew just how just how they felt.

18

The sun hung low in the western sky as we maneuvered the winding two-lane mountain road back to Rock Creek Village. A herd of elk grazed in a roadside meadow, chewing lazily as they watched us pass. A few miles later, we spotted a family of bighorn sheep hopping nimbly across the rocks. But after my disclosure that the twins needed to meet with Raul and Lynn in the morning, the mood in the car was gloomy.

As we turned onto my street, both boys' phones pinged. Once they read their texts, Banner turned to me from the passenger seat, wearing a hopeful smile. "Elyse says a group of our friends are driving into Boulder for dinner and a movie tonight. She wants us to come."

Braden leaned up from the back seat. "Is that okay?"

I smiled. "Of course you can go. You don't have to ask my permission. I'm not..." My smile faded. *Your mother.* "I'm just your boss at work, guys. After hours, you do as you please."

"But we're staying at your place," Banner said.

"We might be kinda late," Braden added.

"No problem," I said. "I gave you a key. Just keep it down when you get home. Carl gets testy if anyone interrupts his beauty sleep."

I pulled behind the townhouse and parked beneath the carport. The boys jumped out of the car, reinvigorated.

Inside, they took a moment to pet Woody and Carl, then darted up the stairs to do whatever boys do to prepare for a night on the town. I heard some good-natured squabbling, the bathroom door closing, and the sound of the shower.

Woody nudged my hand with his nose, and I slid to the floor, suddenly exhausted. My seventy-pound golden retriever wedged himself into my lap, wriggling to get comfortable. Carl piled on and issued a contented purr. I spent a few minutes petting, stroking, and cooing, allowing myself to release the stressors of the day.

After a few minutes, the creatures were done with the cuddles and switched into play mode. The two of them chased each other around and over the couch and up and down the stairs.

The shower stopped and a few minutes later started again. I pushed myself to my feet and checked my phone, noticing a couple of new texts. The first was from Sam, who said he'd bring dinner but probably wouldn't make it over until seven. Could I wait that long? I glanced at my watch. Four-thirty. My stomach growled in protest, but I ignored it.

You provide the dinner, you set the agenda, I typed.

My agenda doesn't happen until dessert. He added a devil emoji.

I sent back a heart emoji, then clicked on a text from Monika, who wanted to know what time we were getting together.

When can you be here? I asked.

5?

A thumbs up emoji served as a confirmation.

I tapped my phone against the palm of my hand. What was I getting myself into with that girl? Sure, Tonya had hired her. And yes, she'd passed Mrs. Finney's muster, not a simple task. But I wasn't certain the two of us would work well together. If, as my parents had suggested, Monika was the journalistic image of me in my younger years, maybe she wasn't so good at working as part of a team. I knew just how it felt to be a lone wolf. Prior to my ignominious resignation, I'd gained a reputation as a pioneer in convergence media, in which a solo journalist photographed, videoed, reported, and wrote a story.

Working alone had been my brand.

That had changed when my big-city career ended and I returned to Rock Creek Village. Here, a person couldn't get away with working alone. Everyone knew each other's schedules, habits...even their moods. For heaven's sakes, when I'd had my last cold, four villagers had offered me medicine before my first sneeze.

When I'd moved back, I'd initially found it all smothering. But as the months went by, I realized I liked it. Relied on it, even. I'd discovered the comforts of camaraderie, the benefits of friendship, and the efficiency of teamwork. I'd found community. And now I had to wonder how Monika would weave into that tapestry.

Woody and Carl trounced back into the kitchen, then scurried through the hall to the front door. A moment later came the knock. I headed to the door and opened it to find Elyse waiting on the stoop. She came in and fell to her knees, giggling, as Woody covered her face with kisses and Carl snaked across her legs. Then the twins pounded down the stairs, leaping off the last step with a flourish. They wore jeans and long-sleeved, button-down shirts and had combed their hair, still damp, back from their faces.

Elyse rose and assessed her half-brothers. "You two clean up good." She completed a little twirl. "Good brothers would repay the compliment."

"You look great," they said in unison.

After promising there'd be no drinking or otherwise inappropriate carousing, the three of them piled into Elyse's car. I waved as they pulled away.

Before I got the door closed, a blue Corolla rolled to a stop at the curb. Monika hopped out and reached into the back seat to grab a bag. She wore an expression that told me she meant business.

I smiled. Let the investigation begin.

***

We set up our workspace at the kitchen table. Monika opened her laptop, and I gathered my legal pads and pens. I'd poured us each a glass of wine to lubricate the cogs in our brains. Monika's blue eyes were bright with anticipation. Her taut skin was wrinkle-free, and I pictured myself pinching a bit of skin on her hand and watching it snap back into place. As a test, I pinched the back of my hand. The skin stayed tented for a good two seconds before sinking back into place.

Ah, youth. There were aspects of it you didn't miss until they were gone.

On the other hand, the file cabinets in my brain were packed tight with experiences, knowledge, and strategies. I possessed much more of a store to draw on than this newbie. So, there were also advantages to getting older. At least, that's what I told myself.

Monika lifted her glass. "To new alliances."

I tapped my glass to hers, and we both took a sip. "Tell me what you've learned so far."

She opened the notes on her phone. "First off, Brian Ratliff's work history is nothing to brag about. The man can't keep a job."

No news there. When I'd first moved back to Rock Creek Village, I'd been unimpressed with Brian's work ethic. It was obvious at the time that his wife supported the family. Apparently, even Victoria's death hadn't sparked a sense of fiscal responsibility. I wondered again how the family maintained that big house. I paid the boys decent part-time wages, but not enough to manage a mortgage.

Monika continued scrolling through her notes, the tip of her tongue poking between her teeth. It was a charming little quirk, not too different from how I chewed the inside of my cheek when deep in thought.

"Brian played professional hockey for a hot minute," she said a moment later. "A knee injury ended his career, but the Avalanche continued paying his contract for a few months. Then they released him, and I couldn't uncover any evidence of income for several years. After that, his wife employed him as a consultant for her business. When she died, Brian moved to Denver and lived with a woman for a while. No employment record, so he must have been mooching off her. Then he rented an apartment in Boulder and took a job as an assistant hockey coach at the university there."

"Elyse goes to school at the University of Boulder," I said. "She mentioned to the twins that Brian had been 'let go' a month ago. Were you able to find out why?"

Monika's lips curved into a smile. "Oh, yeah, and it's juicy."

"Tell me," I said, taking another sip of wine.

"I spoke to a person in the coaching office on the condition that I not reveal their name. But I can assure you it's someone in a position to be privy to pertinent conversations."

"You don't need to convince me," I said. "I'm not your editor. Just tell me what they said."

"Coach Ratliff was widely despised by players and staff."

"That's not earth-shattering news," I said. "Brian is despised by everyone who knows him."

"They described him as volatile and arrogant, always trying to one-up everyone, especially the head coach. My source didn't understand why the team hired Brian in the first place. Connections, they figured."

"It could have been as simple as his professional hockey career," I mused. "College teams can benefit from the exposure of hiring a former pro."

She shrugged. "I suppose, but in this case, the publicity didn't benefit them. Brian performed the minimum amount of work. He showed up late to practices, and my source said they sometimes smelled booze on his breath. He ranted at players, contradicted other coaches, and spent most of his time rambling on about his glory days."

"What cause did the school give for his dismissal?"

"You're going to love this," she said. "Apparently, Brian tried to seduce the head coach's wife—in front of the entire team."

19

I couldn't help laughing out loud. Brian Ratliff had tried to seduce the head coach's wife? The man either had the daring of a coyote or the stupidity of a wild turkey.

Monika grinned. "The coach fired him on the spot. Brian threatened to sue for wrongful termination, and the coach told him where to put his lawsuit. Brian hasn't filed a complaint—at least, not to date."

The whole thing would be comical if it weren't for Brian's kids. The twins had to live under the cloud of a loser father. And poor Elyse attended the school where all this had played out. Luckily, most people on campus weren't aware of their shared DNA. Sam was listed as father on Elyse's birth certificate, and Petrie had always been her last name. Unless Elyse—or Brian—had made their connection public knowledge, her peers and professors wouldn't associate the two of them. Still, it was a difficult situation.

On the positive side, Elyse and the twins had forged a genuine sibling relationship. They joked and teased as if they'd grown up under the same roof. They supported each other's dreams and seemed to truly like each other. Proof that, as my mother said, something good can be made even from a turnip.

"Some good stuff there," I said. "You've helped widen our suspect pool."

"There's more." She scrolled. And scrolled. And scrolled some more. My knee bounced. Reading from a phone didn't take any longer than flipping through a notebook, I supposed, but I still preferred good old paper and ink.

After a few seconds, she found what she'd been searching for. "I'm not sure what you already know about his late wife's finances…"

"We all thought Victoria had a lot of family wealth passed down to her," I said. "But when she died, it came to light that she and Brian had gone through all the cash and were at the point of accumulating debt."

"Did you know about her life insurance?"

I shook my head.

"The insurance company resisted paying the claim," Monika said. "Something about Brian being a suspect in her death."

"Well, he was cleared quite a while back."

"That's what his attorney said in the lawsuit," she said.

"Lawsuit?"

"Brian sued the insurance company and won. They issued the payment just last month. To the tune of a million dollars."

My jaw went slack. Brian was a *millionaire?*

"And the twins?" I asked.

"Nothing. The policy was issued when they were children. I'm sure the assumption was that Brian would provide for the boys, but there's nothing in the policy that stipulates he has to, not once they reached legal age. The money is all Brian's. No strings attached."

I rubbed the back of my neck. The twins could barely afford their tuition at community college. Now that their father was rich, had he even offered to finance their schooling? Not that I'd heard. No, I was certain he'd burn through the insurance money keeping himself and his wife in fine style. Even Desiree's brother was more likely to benefit than Brian's own sons.

*New wife…million-dollar payout…*My mind churned with heinous possibilities.

I drank more wine—a gulp this time. "Anything else?"

Monika put her phone on the table. "That's all I had time for. I plan on attacking again once we're done here."

"Well, I'm impressed. You gathered some important info. Tonya was right. You're the real deal."

She blushed, but her eyes sparkled. "Thank you. That means a lot to me, Callie, especially coming from someone with your reputation."

I cringed. "We'll discuss my reputation another time. For now, let's talk about suspects. And if it's all right by you, Grasshopper, I'll make the list on paper."

"Grasshopper? Yuck. Why am I an insect?"

I groaned. More evidence of the generation gap that yawned between us. I picked up my pen and pulled the legal pad in front of me. "Someday, after all this is over, you and I will sit down with a bucket of popcorn and watch *Karate Kid*. In the meantime, who should we place at the top of our list?"

While she considered the question, I drew four columns on the page, titling them: Suspect, Motive, Means, Opportunity.

She chewed her lip. "To me, the most obvious suspect is Pamela Ashton. If the poison was in the fudge, it's logical that she's the one who put it there."

"That's a big if. We can't say for sure that's how the poison was administered."

"Not yet," Monika said. "The lab report should be back in a day or two. Anyway, it's a viable option. That earns her a place on the list."

"Agreed," I said, jotting Pamela's name in the suspects column. I easily filled in means: *Makes fudge for a living*.

"What about opportunity?" I asked. "How did she get the fudge to Brian?"

Monika shrugged. "Offered it to him as a truce?"

"True. There are a dozen ways Pamela could have gotten the box into his hands. As for motive, she has a good one."

I told her about Pamela's ill-fated affair with Brian, and Monika's lips curved into a victorious smile. "We have a winner."

"Not so fast," I said. "It's not prudent to stop racing just as you've cleared the first hurdle. Most cases are not as simple as they appear." I considered writing that down for Mrs. Finney to use on her cups.

Monika sighed. "You're right. I tend to leap before I look."

I grinned. This might turn into a successful partnership after all, especially if the newbie journalist continued deferring to my wisdom and experience.

"My turn," I said. I wrote Desiree's name in big block letters.

Monika peered at the pad. "Is that because you really believe she's guilty, or because you want her to be?"

"Both, I suppose. I focused on Desiree as the prime suspect from the beginning. As I'm sure you know, the spouse is often the lead suspect in a murder." I stopped. I had to keep reminding myself that our victim wasn't dead. Otherwise, I might slip up in front of the boys. "The same is true for attempted murder, assault—all violent crimes."

"My criminal investigation professor drilled that into us."

"Desiree had a top spot on my list even before you told me about the life insurance policy, but now…"

Monika nodded. "Her motive is money."

"How convenient that she married Brian just after he came into a windfall—and just before he was poisoned. In fact, I'm adding Weston's name, too. Maybe the two of them plotted it together."

"I don't know," she mused. "It almost seems too obvious. Wouldn't Desiree worry everyone would be looking in her direction? Why would she chance it? Besides, that brother of hers doesn't seem capable of any intricate scheming."

"True. But I've watched him do her bidding without question. Maybe he was her henchman."

I felt confident Desiree was the person we should

target, but I knew we still needed to consider every option. "Who else?" I asked.

Monika suggested Coach Rick Montgomery, Brian's former boss. "Brian hit on his wife and made him a laughingstock in front of the team. Then he threatened to sue the man."

"Solid motives," I said. "But there's a problem with means and opportunity. He lives an hour's drive from Rock Creek Village."

The tongue tip reappeared as Monika thought. "Not insurmountable. Pretty easy for him to slip into town without catching anyone's attention. He buys the fudge, doctors it with poison, and leaves it on Brian's front porch."

I cocked my head, skeptical. "So many things might go wrong. What if someone recognized him? Brian, or even Elyse? And as far as doctoring the fudge, are you speculating he drove into town with poison in his trunk?"

"It's not all that farfetched," she responded.

"If he left the fudge on the front porch, how could he be sure Brian would be the one to eat the fudge?"

"That's true of all our suspects, though. How could anyone be positive Brian would be the one to eat it?"

"Well, there's one suspect who could have made sure of it," I said, tapping on Desiree's name.

We let our thoughts percolate for a moment. "You realize what the real problem is regarding opportunity?" I asked.

"I think so," Monika said. "Poisoning makes confirming alibis nearly impossible. The fudge might have sat on Brian's nightstand for a week before he ate any. There's no solid timing to clear a suspect."

"Bingo," I said. "It makes an investigator's job exponentially harder."

"But not impossible," she said with an optimism that came with youth.

I turned back to the list. "Okay, Coach Montgomery

seems like a long shot to me, but we'll keep him on the list. And I'm adding another coach: Trent Wallace."

Monika's brow furrowed. "The guy who tried to help Brian to his feet when Sam pushed him at the wedding?"

"That's him," I said. "You heard Brian yelling at Trent. We all did. Brian mentioned that they were rivals stretching back a couple of decades. He bragged that he'd taken Trent's position on the college team and then the spot he'd wanted in the pros. Brian even married Victoria, Trent's one-time girlfriend. Sounds like Trent had several reasons to hate him."

"But like you said, that was decades ago. Would Trent still be harboring grievances? He has a wife now, right? A good job? Wouldn't you say he's moved on?"

"Well," I said, "didn't Brian say something about going after Trent's job at the high school—and his wife? Those threats might have dredged up all the old resentments."

"His old nemesis comes into town," Monika mused. "Reminds him of all the ways he bested him. Then threatens to do it all over again. It's plausible."

"I hope it's not Trent," I said, even as I wrote his name in the suspect column. "He seems like a good guy—a loving husband. Renata speaks highly of him, too—says he's great with his players."

Monika pointed her phone at me. "Looks can be deceiving. We need to pursue every lead, no matter how distasteful."

I raised an eyebrow. Was I getting schooled by this rookie? "All right, smarty-pants. What should I put as means?"

"Trent lives in the village. It'd be a cinch to pop by the Fudge Factory. And, wait, let me have a look…" She tapped on her phone and stared at me, wide-eyed.

"Along with his duties as hockey coach, Trent Wallace teaches a few classes."

I shrugged. Small-town high school coaches often did double duty as teachers. "So?"

"Callie, he teaches chemistry."

My eyebrows shot up. I scribbled the information in the means column and chewed the inside of my cheek. My mind was feeling frazzled. My stomach churned, and I glanced at my watch. Six-thirty. "It's getting late. I'm about ready to call it a day. Have we covered everyone?"

She took a deep breath. "The only others…well, you're not going to like it."

I understood where she was going, and she was right. I didn't like it. But I also couldn't ignore it.

"Braden," I said.

She nodded. "But we also can't rule out Banner. He must be harboring some mixed feelings about his dad, too. And he has the same means and opportunity as his brother."

"But Braden's the one who works with chemicals," I said.

"It's true that Braden probably brought them into the house. But after that, Banner had easy access."

I shook my head. "I still can't buy that either boy would hurt his father. And I know Banner would never set up his brother."

"Not intentionally…"

She locked eyes with me, but I wouldn't budge. "You can put them on your list if you find it necessary, but I'm not writing their names on mine."

Monika didn't press the issue. I hunched over my legal pad and studied my list. "Should we add Kimberly and Parker Lyon? There's no love lost there. Parker and Brian have been on bad terms ever since…"

I stopped, realizing where this line of questioning would inevitably lead. Monika watched me and waited. I sighed, then wrote Parker and Kimberly's names. Motive? Brian's long-ago affair with Kimberly that had resulted in a child. Means and opportunity I left blank for the moment.

She nodded, then gave me a sympathetic but resolute

look. She turned her phone and showed me her own suspect list, identical to mine but with a few notable additions. Braden and Banner's names were present, as I'd expected. And at the bottom, one more name: Sam Petrie.

20

I reached out and pushed Monika's phone away. "You are out of line," I said.

But deep down, I knew she was right to add the names. If I hadn't been personally invested, Sam and Banner might be on my suspect list, too, and Braden definitely would.

But Monika was new to Rock Creek Village. I knew these people much better than the rookie reporter did. My knowledge, my instincts, my experience—they all counted for something.

Carl leapt onto the table and gave Monika a snarky look. He adored Sam almost as much as I did. Monika and I stared at each other in silence for a minute, neither of us ready to capitulate. Part of me marveled at her courage. Here I was, an accomplished former journalist, a Feldman Award winner, and her idol, according to her words, yet she'd stood up to me because she believed it was right.

I finally broke our little staring contest. "Monika, there's no way on earth Sam poisoned Brian. It's a ludicrous presumption. Same with Banner and Braden. I'd stake my reputation on it. Heck, I'd stake my life on it."

She opened her mouth, but I raised a hand to stop her. "You're right, though. We either conduct a thorough investigation or none at all."

Her face twisted in a mixture of emotions: relief, pride, gratitude. But mostly what I saw there was respect. She saw me as a role model, and—for the time being, anyway—I'd just lived up to her expectations.

Before I could be tasked with the unpleasant duty of

assigning motive, means, and opportunity to my own boyfriend, the front door opened. Sam's voice drifted into the room, followed by the tantalizing aroma of meats and sauces and spices. A moment later, the chef himself entered the kitchen. He graced me with a sexy smile before he noticed Monika. I saw a question float across his face, followed by instant understanding.

"Ah," he said. "I deduce I'm interrupting a crime-solving session."

I stood and pecked him on the lips. Then I gestured to the red-haired reporter. "Sam, you remember Monika Schiff, don't you?"

"Of course," he said. "The newest addition to the *Gazette*. Welcome to Rock Creek Village. We're all happy you're here."

"Thank you." She shifted in her seat. I noted the merriment in Sam's eyes. He had to realize he was on her suspect list, but he didn't care. A sure sign of an innocent man.

He headed to the island countertop, opened his thermal bag, and began extracting covered dishes. "Why don't you join us for dinner, Monika? I'm trying out a new Italian dish in honor of Tonya and David's marriage, and I made way too much for just Callie and me."

"As always," I said. Woody whined, indicating he'd be pleased to help with the leftovers.

Monika looked nervous. After she'd just thrown my boyfriend's name into the suspect ring, she probably wasn't sure I'd want her at my dinner table. I smiled at her. "You should stay," I said. "If you don't, I'll end up needing to buy bigger jeans."

"Well, I don't want to be responsible for unnecessary clothing purchases." Monika gave Sam a tentative smile and sniffed the air appreciatively. "If you're sure it won't be any trouble, I'd love to stay. I've been subsisting on canned Spaghetti-Os and chips since I moved here. A homemade meal would be a nice treat."

Another thing Monika and I had in common—an apparent lack of interest in culinary pursuits.

We cleared the table of our journalistic tools. I tucked the legal pad into the desk drawer as Sam gave a knowing half-smile. A couple of years ago, he'd been a person of interest in a murder, so he knew how things worked. I'd helped clear his name back then, and I was prepared to do it again, if need be.

But I didn't think it would come to that.

Sam filled three plates with creamy Tuscan shrimp served over pasta, along with crusty bread. I poured the wine, and we all dug in with gusto—none of us more than Monika. When she came up for air, she gazed at Sam, awestruck.

"You're an artist," she said, stuffing another bite into her mouth. "A true genius."

"Beats Spaghetti-Os?" he asked.

She didn't respond, just kept shoveling in the food.

The mood had officially shifted, and we spent the next half hour eating and chatting and laughing. Woody clearly adored the young woman—or perhaps he thought his big brown eyes would lure her into providing table scraps. Even Carl seemed interested in her. He stared at her with an intensity that told me he might just allow her into our fold.

She smiled at the creatures. "Woody and Carl. How'd they get their names?"

I cocked my head. "I expected you'd have figured that out. Would it help if I told you Woody is short for Woodward?"

"Got it. Bob Woodward and Carl Bernstein," she said with a grin. "How perfect."

Then, in true reporter form, Monika got Sam and me talking about our high school years and our first foray into dating. After dinner, I made a pot of coffee while Sam cut squares of tiramisu. We took turns telling stories about the little mysteries he'd helped Tonya and me solve during our early escapades as an investigative team.

Monika seemed dazzled, both by the dessert and the stories. "You were a couple back in the nineties," she said, as if she was referring to the ancient pyramid era.

I pursed my lips. "It wasn't all that long ago. It's not like we're AARP members or anything."

"A few more years," Sam said, slipping a leftover shrimp into Woody's mouth. I'd told the man a hundred times we should not feed the dog from the table, but both he and the dog refused to obey me. Sam gave me a slightly guilty look and slipped Carl a taste.

"What are you talking about?" I asked. "I'm barely in my forties."

"Callie, you can join AARP when you're fifty," Sam informed me. "And unless I'm mistaken, you turn forty-six in a few months."

My mouth gaped. "Doesn't AARP stand for something about retired people? I'm not exactly a senior citizen."

Monika tamped her fork against her plate to gather the last crumbs of tiramisu. "I wasn't even born in the nineties," she mused.

"Oh jeez." I massaged my temples.

Sam scooted his chair close to mine and put an arm around me. "I've always said I wanted to grow old with you—just didn't realize we were already doing it."

I smacked his chest. He and Monika laughed, and I couldn't help but join in. Monika wadded up her napkin and dropped it on her plate. "Tonya tells me you two are getting married. Have you set a date?"

I yelped and buried my face in my hands. "A girl—or should I say, an elderly woman—can't buy a break tonight."

I peeked at Sam through my fingers and saw him wearing an amused grin. Worming his way between us, Woody woofed. Carl stretched his limbs, arched his back, and purred, as if sanctioning the union.

Monika frowned. "Have I said something wrong?"

I got up and began toting dishes to the sink. "We're not quite ready to discuss marriage yet."

"*She's* not ready," Sam said. "Fortunately, I'm a patient guy." I returned for more dishes and paused, resting a hand on his shoulder. He reached up and patted it. "But patient doesn't mean long-suffering."

Monika cleared her throat and offered to help with the cleanup, but Sam and I assured her that wasn't necessary. "We have a routine," he said. "You know, like an old married couple."

I rolled my eyes.

"All right, then, I'm out of here," Monika said. "Thanks for dinner, Chef. It was a meal I won't soon forget."

He gave her a formal bow. "There's plenty more where that came from. Stop by Snow Plow Chow anytime you're sick of canned spaghetti."

I walked Monika to the door, with Woody trotting along behind us. Carl wasn't big on goodbyes, so he darted halfway up the stairs and watched us through the balusters.

"Sorry if I made things uncomfortable," she whispered as she slipped on her coat. "From the way Tonya talked, I assumed the two of you were engaged."

"Tonya's a busybody," I said. "She thinks because she finally took the plunge, I should, too. Like jumping into an icy lake and yelling to the person on the shore, 'Come on in! The water's fine.'"

Monika smiled, then dropped her eyes. "I'm also sorry for adding Sam's name to the list. Now that I've spent some time with him…well, it's obvious you were right. He doesn't have it in him to hurt anyone. Even Brian Ratliff."

"Everyone has it in them," I said. "One of my professors used to say every human being is capable of murder if faced with the proper circumstances. You were right to insist we chase every possible suspect." I paused.

"But let's consider this particular suspect chased and released. I think we're better off focusing our time and energy elsewhere."

She nodded. "Agreed."

I reached for the doorknob, but a sudden idea stilled my hand. "I may have a task for you, but only if you feel it's worth your time."

Her eyes shone with eagerness. "Sure."

She was like a puppy, waiting for me to throw the stick so she could chase it down.

"You might want to use your research skills to look into Desiree Bouton's past. There's something shifty about that woman. I can't put my finger on it, but there's more to her than meets the eye. She's hiding something. I know it."

Monika squared her shoulders like a soldier with her marching orders. "If she's hiding something, I'll find it. You can count on that."

21

Soon after Monika left, I snuggled into the crook of Sam's arm with a mug of hot cider, watching flames blaze in the fireplace. The smell of cedar and apples and cinnamon mingled pleasantly, along with the spicy scent of Sam's cologne. I sighed. A girl could get used to this. Or even an old woman…

Woody had contorted himself into a tight knot in the corner of the couch, while Carl stretched across the back. The scene was close to perfect—if not for the fact that some of the people I cared about were suspected of attempted homicide.

Sam trailed a finger down my shoulder. "Someone has a birthday coming up."

"Still a few months away. And I don't want to think about it, especially after your little AARP insight."

"Well, maybe the gift I have in mind will ease some of the sting."

I lifted my eyebrows, and he smiled mischievously. The lines around his eyes crinkled, and he looked so handsome it took my breath away.

"What is it?" I asked.

He took my hand. "Can't spoil the surprise, can I?"

The way his thumb ran across my knuckles gave me goosebumps—and not the cold-weather kind. Was Sam's surprise in the shape of a circle? One that would fit around my finger? My hand tensed.

"Relax," he said with a chuckle. "You'll love it."

We sat quietly for a moment, listening to the creatures' soft snores. "Heard anything from Tonya?" he asked

I sat up, placed my mug on the coffee table, and

grabbed my phone. "I have. Want to see the photos?"

He leaned his head close to mine as I scrolled through images of the happy couple in Florence. They posed in front of Il Duomo, on the Ponte Vecchio bridge that spanned the Arno River, and in the tourist-filled Uffizi Gallery. Tonya looked gorgeous, of course, and David was dashing. There was no doubt they were madly in love.

When the mini slide show concluded, Sam and I settled back against the cushions. He stroked my hair. "Heaven," he murmured.

"Yes, it's beautiful there. I'd love to go someday."

"Italy's not what I was talking about," he said.

I leaned over to press my lips to his neck.

*****

Sam headed home at ten-thirty, rumpled and flushed and smiling. I was warm and content, too—and sorry to see him go. Maybe having another human in my house on a permanent basis wouldn't be so bad after all.

The notion brought with it a familiar spasm of anxiety. Sam had hinted for months that the time for a proposal was drawing near, and I still didn't know how I felt about it. Yes, I wanted to spend the rest of my life with him— talking, holding his hand, loving him, facing life together. But I fretted at the idea of sharing my space forever. Moving his clothes into my closet. His toothbrush into my bathroom. Except for Woody and Carl, I'd lived alone my entire adult life. And I wasn't someone who embraced change.

I sighed. No need to think about that tonight. All I wanted right now were my pajamas and my cozy bed.

As I snuggled beneath the covers, I considered waiting up for the twins. I even opened my e-reader and tried to get lost in my latest whodunit, but my eyes weren't having it. By eleven, I was curled on my side with my golden retriever stretched out next to me and my tabby cat's paws buried in my hair.

Sometime later, Woody stirred against my thigh and Carl's tail flipped against my nose. I came awake just enough to note the footsteps padding up the stairs. Then I drifted back to dreamland.

***

At seven-thirty, I awoke to an unexpected sensory delight: the smell of bacon. Woody stood with his nose pressed to the bedroom door. I untangled Carl from my hair and sat up, still groggy. I looked at the other side of the bed. Sam hadn't spent the night, so who…

Ah. Realization dawned. Braden and Banner were making breakfast.

I took a quick shower and hurried to get dressed. Fifteen minutes later, I hopped down the stairs. Woody beat me to the kitchen and greeted the twins with a lolling tongue and doggie grin that said, *Feed me.*

I kept my tongue in my mouth, but barely. The sight of the feast laid out on the kitchen counter made my mouth water. Blueberry pancakes, scrambled eggs, crispy bacon, orange juice, milk, and coffee.

I squealed and pulled the boys into a hug. "This is so unexpected. And unnecessary. But much appreciated."

"You've done a lot for us, Callie," Braden said.

"Yeah, we just wanted to let you know we're grateful," Banner said.

"For everything," Braden added.

"Well, this is just the best surprise. I'm overwhelmed."

Banner winced. "You might not be so thrilled when you see the mess."

I glanced around the kitchen at the pots and pans piled in the sink, the wadded paper towels littering the counter, and the pancake batter congealing on the stove.

"Don't worry, we'll clean up," Braden said.

"Hey, I didn't agree to that." Banner gave his brother a gentle shove. Braden punched him on the arm. I was glad to see the boys in a playful mood—especially with the upcoming interview looming over their heads.

We piled our plates with food and ate heartily. They'd done a good job. The bacon was just the right amount of crispy, and the pancakes were fluffy. They'd developed some skills over the past two years they'd been forced to fend for themselves.

As we neared the end of the meal, I could feel the tension creep into the room. I glanced at the clock. The boys were due at the station in an hour.

After I'd mopped up a puddle of syrup with my last bit of pancake, I laid my fork on my plate. "Are you two nervous about meeting with Raul and Lynn?"

"Nah," Banner said, but his eyes told a different story.

Braden, always more forthcoming, wrinkled his nose. "Well, I am. I know how things look. I've been mad at Dad for a long time. Everyone heard me argue with him at the wedding. And the chemicals in my room…they must all think I'm guilty. But I didn't do it, I swear."

Banner put a hand on Braden's shoulder. "Don't get your panties in a wad, man. We believe you."

Braden's frown transformed into a grin, and he socked his brother's arm. "I don't wear panties, you jerk."

"Liar. I've seen 'em in the laundry. But hey, it's okay." Banner held his hands palms up. "They're nice."

Then Braden pushed Banner, Banner pushed back, and Woody hopped around them, smiling and wagging. Carl rolled his eyes at the antics and sashayed out of the room.

"Okay, enough." I plastered a fake sternness on my face. "These dishes aren't going to do themselves."

Side by side, the three of us cleaned up the kitchen, bantering and trying to ignore what was coming.

For the most part, we succeeded. But when the last plate went into the dishwasher, reality set in. "Grab your coats, guys," I said. "Let's get this over with."

22

I turned on the radio to mask the uncomfortable silence as the twins and I drove the few blocks to the station. The bright sunshine outside contrasted with the dark atmosphere inside the car. I found a spot half a block from Town Hall, which housed Rock Creek Village's city offices and the police and fire departments. We got out of the car and trudged toward the entrance. Braden's eyes didn't leave his feet.

"Best to go in looking confident," I said. "You've done nothing wrong. Let them see that."

He nodded, drew a breath, and threw his shoulders back. I gave him an encouraging smile and turned to Banner. "Doing okay?"

He tilted his head, his expression grave. "Ready to be done."

"Me too," I said. "So, let's do it."

Banner opened the door, and the three of us entered. Marilyn, the department's administrative assistant for over thirty years, was chatting with a man whose back was to us. Even before he turned around, I knew who the man was. My father.

He turned, and I was struck again by the chiseled good looks that had long ago inspired the nickname Butch, from the Paul Newman and Robert Redford film *Butch Cassidy and the Sundance Kid.* Though his hair was mostly silver now, and the lines on his forehead had deepened, he remained a strikingly handsome man—as well as one of the kindest humans I'd ever known. Though he dropped in at the station regularly, I realized today's visit was no coincidence. He'd come here to lend the boys—and his daughter—a bit of support.

He strolled over, shook each twin's hand, and pecked me on the cheek.

"Hi, Dad," I said. "Fancy meeting you here."

"Just passing through. Thought I'd stop by and bring Marilyn some decent coffee. If memory serves, the stuff they have here isn't fit for human consumption."

Frank Laramie, the current chief whom Dad had worked with for many moons, came down the hall then. Tall and lanky in his jeans and boots, he looked more like a rancher heading into a corral than the chief of police.

When she saw Frank coming, Marilyn lifted her cup and saluted Dad. "Thank you for the coffee, Chief Cassidy. It's always a pleasure to see you." She leaned across the counter and stage-whispered, "Things haven't been the same since you retired. But don't you dare tell my current boss I said so."

Frank stopped at the desk, thumbs in his belt loops, and gave her a somber look. "Marilyn, please phone the *Gazette* and tell them we're hiring. I'll be replacing my administrative assistant."

She responded with a mock scowl, and he rocked back on his heels and chuckled, clearly pleased with himself. Then his eyes fell on the twins, and his face turned serious, though still kind. "Boys, we appreciate you coming in this morning. The detectives are ready for you. We'll make this as quick as possible."

He looked at me, as if to convey the same message. "You waiting for them, Callie?" I nodded. "All righty. I expect we'll have 'em back in two shakes of a lamb's tail."

He gestured for the boys to follow him down the hall. Banner's shoulders were slumped, but Braden walked with his chest out and his chin up. A casual observer wouldn't have any idea how much he was dreading this—except for the flicker of fear in his eyes as he looked back over his shoulder.

I gave him a thumbs-up, but I felt queasy myself, like I was watching the twins being led down the green mile.

Dad took my elbow and led me to a row of visitors' chairs against the wall. "Try not to worry, Sundance. Raul and Lynn are only taking statements. You've given your share of them over the years, and here you sit, fine and dandy."

How did my father always seem to sense what I was thinking? I gave him a weak smile, and he took my hand. "You know how this works. Unless one of those boys confesses—"

I stiffened. "Why would they confess? They're not guilty of anything!"

He put a gentle hand on my knee, but his voice was firm. "Stop it, Callie. You're letting yourself get worked up, and that won't do those boys any good."

I inhaled, held my breath for four counts, and exhaled for eight. Once more, and my heartbeat returned to a normal rhythm.

Leaning my head on my father's shoulder, I said, "I'm sorry, Dad. I'm not sure where that came from."

"It came from that big heart of yours. You care about them, and you're worried. Been there, done that." He gave me a meaningful look. "There's nothing harder than knowing you can't fix problems for the people you love. But sometimes, the best you can do is to be present. Offer a listening ear and a shoulder to cry on."

"Sounds like one of Mrs. Finney's cups," I said.

"Maybe I'll copyright it and sell her the rights."

I sat back in my chair. "I'm surprised Frank took both of them," I said. "I assumed they'd interview the boys separately."

"I imagine they are. Raul will have one of them and Lynn the other."

Of course. It made me feel better, somehow, knowing the detectives weren't pulling the good-cop-bad-cop routine on the twins.

"So, what has Frank told you?" I asked.

Dad twisted his wedding ring. "Nothing much."

"Yeah, right." Dad and Frank were like twins themselves, though certainly not identical. The two conversed daily. Frank turned to Dad for advice on cases, and Dad—who, like me, still occasionally longed for his old investigative days—was more than happy to oblige. If Chief Laramie knew something about this case, former Chief Cassidy knew it, too.

Dad's eyes flicked toward the front desk. He caught Marilyn watching us with a smirk that said, *I know you're about to spill, but I won't tell.* He grinned at her, then leaned in close to me. "Lab reports are in. The fudge was the source. Ninety-nine percent certainty."

I nodded, unsurprised. "What was the poison?"

He shrugged. "They can't pinpoint it. That kind of sophisticated testing would take months and more money than the Rock Creek Village PD has in its coffers. They can't say for sure it was darkroom chemicals in Brian's system, but they also can't eliminate the possibility."

I sighed. Though it had been a long shot, I'd hoped the lab report would miraculously rule out the darkroom chemicals, thus pivoting the harsh light of suspicion from Braden. But as my mother said, if wishes were horses, beggars would ride.

"How do you think the poison got into the fudge? I mean, isn't the most likely scenario that Pamela added it during the cooking process?"

"I'm sure they're looking hard at her. But she allowed a search of the Fudge Factory, and nothing turned up. Anyway, the perpetrator could have dipped the fudge in poison, letting it soak into the chocolate. Or it could have been spread on, possibly in the icing. Even injected."

He chewed the inside of his cheek, and I saw where I'd gotten the gesture. "The problem with poison," he continued, "is there's no solid timeline. But you already know that."

I nodded. "The poisoning could take place over hours,

or even days, during which the guilty party could make sure she was seen elsewhere."

"She? You seem to have someone specific in mind."

"I do. But right now, I have no way of proving my theory."

Dad gave me a warning look. "Nor is it your job to prove anything."

"We're just spitballing here, Dad. Passing the time."

"Mm-hmm." He lifted his hand, examined his fingernails. "As long as we're shooting the breeze, I spoke with Brian's wife and brother this morning."

I sat up straight. "Desiree and Weston?"

"I was doing a little work on the property, and the two of them were heading toward the parking lot. Desiree stopped me to ask about staying on longer. Said she couldn't bear the thought of living in the house when Brian wasn't there. I told her the cabin was vacant for the next week, and I'd shuffle some things around if she needed it after that."

"Interesting," I said. "I got the idea she was slumming it by staying in a one-room shanty."

He shook his head. "There's something off about those two. I can't put my finger on it, but they're strange."

We didn't have time to plumb the depths of the Bouton family weirdness because Raul appeared, escorting Banner and Braden down the hall. When they got to us, the twins looked calm. Raul gave us a tentative smile. Dad made a lame attempt at a joke. I bit my tongue to keep from giving everyone the third degree.

"Callie, could I have a word with you?" Raul asked.

Dad stepped forward. "I'll take these two to the car and regale them with stories of my misspent youth."

I shot him a grateful look, and the three of them put on their coats and exited. I looked at Raul and lifted my chin. "So, did the big interrogation of two kids turn up any important leads?"

He closed his eyes and did his counting to ten thing.

When he looked at me again, I saw an expression on his face that made me regret my harshness. "I'm sorry," I said. "I know it's your job." I paused. "How are they?"

"They're okay. Lynn was in with Banner, and I spoke with Braden. He answered all my questions, thoroughly and succinctly."

"As an innocent person would."

"He didn't appear deceptive. But Callie, this isn't over. You know that. There's too much still in limbo. Until we get some concrete evidence, we can't clear him completely. Banner either."

"You really can't clear anyone," I said. "Dad and I were discussing the fact that no one can have an alibi, since there's no way of proving when the poison was delivered."

He ran a hand through his thick, black hair. His eyes looked troubled. "You're right. But one thing we can say is that the poison was almost certainly in the fudge."

I nodded, and he arched an eyebrow. "You don't seem surprised." He glanced at the door. "Of course. Your insider source."

I smiled briefly before turning back to business. "So, are you interviewing anyone else?"

"Of course we are."

"Desiree Bouton?"

"We've already interviewed her once, and she's coming in…" He shook his head. "How do you do it?"

"Do what?"

"Always manage to get me talking?"

"We make a good team," I said. "Just tell me what you have. I've helped you before, and I can do it again."

His mouth set in a resolute line. "Not on this case. Like I said before, you're too close. I'll tell you what I can when I can." His voice softened. "Nothing personal."

"Oh, it's personal," I muttered. "It could hardly be more personal."

23

As we pulled out of the parking lot, I glanced at Banner in the passenger seat and at Braden in the back. Banner was the older brother by a full two minutes, and he used that fact to pounce on every older sibling perk available. That meant he always rode shotgun.

"How'd it go?" I asked.

"I got lucky," Banner said with a grin. "Detective Clarke interviewed me. She's hot."

Braden reached up and smacked his brother on the back of the head. "Inappropriate, bro."

"Ow! Knock it off, Bray. You're just pissed you got the Grinch."

The tussling between the boys boded well. Neither seemed especially ruffled by the interrogation.

Braden fell back against the seat. "My interview went better than I expected. Detective Sanchez seemed chill."

I felt the knot of tension in my shoulders unravel. We weren't out of the woods yet, but we might have sighted civilization.

We. Maybe Raul had a point and I was too close to be objective.

"Raul said they're through with the house," I said. "The two of you can go home whenever you want."

The boys exchanged a strained look. "I don't want to be in the house with the bimbo," Braden said.

"Or the stoner dude," Banner added.

"Well, from what I was told, they won't be back anytime soon." I summarized my father's conversation with Desiree. "Seems like you'd have the place to yourselves again. At least for the time being."

There was a long silence, and I sensed some unspoken conversation pass between them, the way twins communicate. Banner was telepathically elected to speak on their behalf. "I get that we're a pain and a hassle, but…could we stay with you another coupla nights?"

His request evoked a flood of emotion I hadn't anticipated. I didn't respond right away because I didn't trust my voice not to crack. Then I caught sight of Braden in the mirror. Worry lines etched his forehead. "Never mind," he blurted. "We'll be okay at home."

I shook my head. "No! I'm just…well, I'm pleasantly surprised that you want to hang around." I sniffled. "I'm touched, that's all. Stay as long as you want. You're always welcome in my home."

The two of them breathed a sigh of relief. "If you insist," Banner said.

"But don't expect a gourmet breakfast every day," Braden said.

"No? If you're not going to pamper me on a daily basis, I may have to reconsider."

We pulled into the alley and parked behind Sundance Studio. The boys hung their coats in the hall closet and headed into the gallery. I peeked in and saw a few early customers milling around. Ethan stood behind the counter, ringing up a sale. Banner scooted in to take over, while Braden greeted a woman who was studying an array of canvases.

I made my way into my office, tossed my coat over a chair, and checked my watch. Ten-fifteen. Time to get packed up for my eleven o'clock photo shoot. I fought off a spasm of dread as I thought about the upcoming high school hockey team photos at the Ice Zone. Last time I'd been there…well, suffice it to say, things hadn't gone well. I'd ended up on the ice beneath a dead body, nursing a broken wrist.

But as my father said, you had to get back up on the horse. Or the ice, in this case. What were the odds of another traumatic incident on the rink?

I unlocked the metal storage cabinet in the corner of

my office and began assembling the equipment I'd need. My Nikon DSLR. Tripod. Portable tower light. As I packed everything into carrying cases, Ethan tapped on the open door.

"Attempting hockey pics again? Brave woman."

"Not sure about brave. I'm actually pretty nervous."

"Well, I have a word of advice," he said.

"What's that?"

"Duck."

"Ha ha. Does Renata realize how lucky she is to have such a funny boyfriend?"

"She should. I tell her every day." He dropped into a chair and jerked a thumb toward the gallery. "I've asked this a hundred times, but how are the boys holding up?"

"Not bad, all things considered. The interviews went well. At least, that's my impression. Raul is being tight-lipped with me, and Lynn won't speak to me at all."

"She knows she'd cave and tell you everything. Or that you'd put a major league guilt trip on her if she didn't."

"That's not true! I don't do guilt trips. I'm respectful of boundaries."

He snorted, then turned serious. "Callie, I've been hearing some rumblings from the gossip mill, and a lot of it centers on Braden."

"People think he poisoned his father?"

He shrugged. "It's one perspective. Most people don't believe it, but you know how it is. There's some chatter."

My fists clenched at my sides. "Well, I'll put a stop to it."

"Not a great idea," he said. "You'll stoke the fire. Just sit back and let everything play out. People in this town are quick to gossip, but also quick to support their own."

Between fight and flight, I'd always choose fight, but in this case, Ethan was probably right. If I jumped in to defend Braden, I could end up making things worse.

"It's a heavy load on two kids who have already been through a lot," Ethan said. "And I imagine we'll be getting some busybody tourists in the gallery who've heard the gossip and want to rubberneck."

My brow creased. "We could send the boys home, I suppose. But I doubt sitting around stewing would be good for them. Better that they keep busy. Besides, we can't protect them forever."

"I agree. But it's good for them to be among friendly faces. When they're not with you, Renata and I were planning to hang with them."

Tears pricked my eyes. I'd left the village following my high school graduation, hoping to find adventure and excitement in the big city—which I did. But what I didn't find was loyalty, love, or a sense of belonging. Here in Rock Creek Village, I was surrounded by a core of people who cared about each other, who'd jump in to help without even being summoned.

Of course, there was the occasional murderer, too.

But then, no place was perfect.

24

I arrived at the Ice Zone and sat in my car for a moment to gather my courage. I hadn't been inside the place for almost a year, and my last memories here were less than cheerful ones. My wrist began throbbing. I realized it was psychosomatic, but that didn't diminish the pain.

I forced myself to get out of the car. Equipment bags on my shoulders, I stepped across puddles of recently melted snow and slogged toward the entrance.

One more cleansing breath and I yanked open the door, bracing myself against the rush of frigid air. I made my way to the side of the rink and saw they'd once again set up a non-skid runner to keep me from slipping on the ice. Not that it had worked last time.

I opened the plastic door in the boards and stepped onto the runner. Boys on skates whizzed past me. A few recognized me and called greetings. Renata spotted me and waved. Trent blew his whistle, and the boys gathered around him. Renata glided toward me, took one of my bags, and accompanied me to center ice.

"How are the twins?" she asked.

It was everyone's first question for me these days. "Holding up. Your brother and Lynn interviewed them this morning. Banner mentioned he was lucky enough to meet with the 'hot' one."

Renata chuckled. "Well, he wasn't talking about Raul."

I swung the legs of the tripod open and positioned it on the runner. Then I set up the portable tower light and tested it while Renata rezipped the empty bags.

"Any news on Brian?" she asked.

Usually the second question I got. "Not that I've heard. The hospital brought in a neurologist from Denver who's running tests today, so we'll see. From what I can tell, he's not circling the drain."

"Callie!"

"What? That's a good thing, right?"

Renata just rolled her eyes. I asked her to stand in the spot where the team would line up so I could take a few test shots. When I was satisfied with the lighting, she whistled for the boys to take their positions.

Trent made his way across the ice to Renata. "You got this?" he asked her. "I need to make a couple of calls."

She nodded, and he skated off to the back of the arena.

I turned to the boys and held up my remote shutter release. "All right, gentlemen, on the count of three, everyone smile like you just won the championship. One…two…three…"

They responded with the stoic scowls I'd expected. I sighed. "Let's do a couple more." I leaned toward Renata. "Could you slip and fall or something so we can get a grin out of them?"

"Nah. They're fine. It's good when they look like they're ready to take someone's head off. The intimidation factor and all."

I shot a few more frames, flipped through the images on my camera screen, and said I had everything I needed. Renata told the team they had ten more minutes until the rink opened for public skate. Under her watchful eye, the boys began sprinting back and forth down the length of the ice.

When I'd finished repacking my equipment, I took one last glimpse up at the catwalk and felt my shoulders relax. I started toward the exit, but my eyes drifted to the back of the arena, to the office area where Trent had headed. He was on our suspect list, and I might never get a better chance to talk to him. No time like the present.

Moving past the bleachers, the concession area, and the

public restrooms, I arrived at a set of metal doors bearing a sign that read, "Authorized Personnel Only." I bit my lip. I was the team photographer, right? Didn't that make me authorized?

With an air of confidence, I pushed through the doors and walked down the narrow hallway until I found a door labeled "RCHS Coaches." I peeked inside and saw Trent hunched over a scarred wooden desk, scribbling on a legal pad. I tapped on the open door. He looked up, then put his pencil down and stood.

"Callie, come in. Everything all right? Did the boys behave?"

I wrangled my equipment into the office, tugged the straps off my shoulders, and piled the bags beside the door. "They were great, Trent. You and Renata have trained them well. This photo shoot proceeded much more smoothly than the last."

He smiled. "Well, it could hardly have gone worse, could it?"

He gestured to a chair and I sat, wrinkling my nose as I caught a whiff of the room. It smelled like sweat and feet.

Trent grinned. "Sorry about the odor. We keep air fresheners all over the place, but nothing masks the smell of teenage boys."

He resumed his seat, his expression placid but concerned. "How are Banner and Braden? I've been meaning to come see them…"

His voice trailed off, and I could tell he felt guilty, as if he'd neglected a duty. The twins had played for him through high school. During their senior year, when their mother died, he'd tried to help them through that difficult time.

"They're doing okay," I said, parroting my go-to line. "Keeping busy."

He nodded. "I'll call them. We have a tournament this weekend. They could come help."

"I'm sure they'd like that." I paused. The man was so kind it made me reluctant to treat him like a suspect.

Luckily, he saved me from having to start the awkward conversation. "Everyone in the village figures you're investigating," he said. "After the way Brian and I clashed at the wedding, I guess you must have a few questions for me. Ask away."

I gave him an apologetic smile. "All right. Thank you. Let's start with this. You and Brian weren't exactly friends, am I right?"

He gave an ironic laugh. "Brian wasn't the buddy-making type. He was a bully and a jerk—and a terrible father. So, no, we were never friends."

"Past tense," I said.

"What?"

"You're referring to him in past tense. Brian's alive."

He sat back, clearly rattled. "Of course…I only meant, any relationship we might've had, however antagonistic, was in the past. I've moved on, and I assume he has, too."

I shifted. "I don't know, Trent. The hostility between the two of you seemed present tense."

He shrugged. "Brian was drunk. Drunk guys gravitate toward confrontation."

"Maybe. But from what he said at the wedding, you had plenty of reasons to hold a grudge against him. He took your spot on the college team. Got the pro gig you were after. Even stole your girlfriend. It'd be hard to forgive all that. It must have bothered you when he returned to the village."

Trent's placid expression turned stormy. The still waters began to churn. "I didn't like the man back in the day, and I don't like him now. But I didn't try to kill him. Why would I?"

I paused, letting him stew for a moment. "Rumor has it Brian was cozying up to your principal, lobbying to get your job. After last season's losing record, they might've even considered it."

Trent's fingers curled into fists. The churning waves threatened to become a tsunami. But it only took him a second to compose himself and treat me to a pleasant, if not sincere, smile.

"I understand that you're trying to help Banner and Braden, Callie. And I hope you can. But you're wasting your time here. I have a wife to think of, and players who trust me. I'd never risk all that over a lowlife like Brian Ratliff." He stood. "Now, as much fun as this has been, I have a lot of work to do if I'm going to repair that losing season you mentioned."

"Of course." I rose and gathered my bags. But before I headed out the door, I pulled a Columbo and turned back to him. "One more thing, Trent…"

He sighed and rolled his hand in a gesture that said, *Go on.*

"What subject do you teach?" I asked.

He looked confused. "What?"

"What subject do you teach at the high school?"

He got it then. His face turned red, and his eyes shot laser beams at me. He knew I already had the answer.

Just then, Renata poked her head into the office. She looked from Trent to me and pressed her lips together. "Wanted to tell you practice is over, Coach."

Trent exhaled. "Thanks. See you tomorrow." He sat at his desk again, picked up his pencil, and started writing.

Renata took my arm and guided me down the hall. "What did I walk into?" she whispered when we were out of earshot.

I shrugged.

"You don't think Trent poisoned Brian, do you?"

"I don't know. He does have a motive." I saw the disbelief on her face, along with her annoyance. "Renata, I'm just doing what I can to help clear Braden."

She nodded. "And I respect that. But I think you're barking up the wrong tree. Trent is a good man."

"Good men have been known to do bad things," I said.

"Well, I wish you'd find a bad one to pin this on."

I stopped in my tracks. "Renata, I'm not trying to *pin* this on anyone. All I want is to protect the twins, and the only way I can do that is to figure out who really poisoned Brian."

She dropped her eyes, then looked at me with chagrin. "You're right, Callie. I'm sorry. I know you'd never railroad an innocent person." She gave me an apologetic smile. "Forgive me?"

I jostled the bags on my shoulders and hugged her. "You don't even need to ask."

We walked the last few steps to the metal doors in silence. When we reached them, Renata said, "You need something to cheer you up, my friend. And I think I have just the thing."

She grinned and pulled me toward the rink. "Take a look."

I scanned the ice. Free skate had begun. Parents held their little ones' hands. A few skaters clutched the railings at the side of the rink to keep steady.

Then I spotted the object of Renata's attention, and I gaped. In the center of the rink, a couple spun and jumped and twirled like professional figure skaters. The woman danced into the man's waiting hands, and he lifted her over his head in a move that rivaled the scene from *Dirty Dancing*.

If the movie couple had been wearing skates—and if they'd been septuagenarians.

"You've got to be kidding me," I mumbled. "Is that...?"

"Yup," she said. "You're witnessing the skating prowess and artistry of our own Mrs. Finney and her partner, Mr. Purdy."

25

Mrs. Finney wore a violet chiffon skating dress with a crosshatched back and a silver-sequined t-neck. Her light purple skate covers complemented the corkscrew curls on her head. Mr. Purdy sported formfitting lavender slacks, flared at the ankles, and a ruffled silver shirt. I shook my head in disbelief. Surely I was hallucinating.

Renata chuckled. "You can't make this stuff up."

Mrs. Finney noticed us and took Mr. Purdy by the hand. The two of them flew across the ice, sending up a spray of snow as they slid to a choreographed stop in front of us.

"Cease your gawking, dear," Mrs. Finney said to me. "It's unbecoming and even insulting. It's as if you've never seen anyone over the age of twenty on skates."

I snapped my mouth shut. "It's not that, Mrs. Finney. It's just…I didn't know the two of you were such talented skaters."

"You can't possibly believe you've plumbed the depths of my skill sets, now, can you?" she asked.

Mr. Purdy beamed at his partner. "It would take centuries to plumb those depths."

Renata and I glanced at each other, uncertain how to respond. "The two of you put on a great show," I said. "It almost looks as if you're practicing for a competition."

Mr. Purdy slid an arm around Mrs. Finney's waist and pulled her close. "Right you are. We're preparing for the annual Ice Extravaganza competition in May." He touched the tip of his finger to Mrs. Finney's nose. "But it's not all work. We're having fun, too, aren't we, Dumpling?"

Mrs. Finney giggled like a schoolgirl. "That we are, Sugarcube."

Dumpling? Sugarcube? This relationship was advancing at warp speed, and the gag factor was increasing at the same pace.

"Well, you look like old pros to me," Renata said.

Mrs. Finney raised a bushy eyebrow. "*Old* pros, dear?"

"No, not old," Renata said, flustered. "I didn't mean…I'm trying to say *experienced.*"

I stifled a snicker, and Mrs. Finney turned her stern eyes on me. "One must never succumb to the societal constructs of aging, my dears." She threw her arms wide. "There is so much life to be lived. So much to be reveled in and relished."

I wondered if that was an AARP motto.

Mrs. Finney stared at Mr. Purdy with starry eyes, and he returned the affectionate gaze. "This isn't our first venture into pairs skating," he said. "We've been doing this on and off for decades."

My interest level spiked. Maybe now I'd get some background information on these two. I'd been trying for months, to no avail.

"I'd love to hear more," I said, leaning on the boards.

Mrs. Finney waved me off. "Another time, dear. For now, we must continue our training. Our upcoming contest is quite competitive. If we're to make a good showing, we mustn't dally."

"Yes," Mr. Purdy said. "We're lusting after that silver cup. It would be our fourth."

Mrs. Finney took his hand and pulled him to center ice, where they completed a stunning sequence of fancy footwork, topped off with a few breathtaking twirls.

***

As I loaded my equipment into the car, my mind reeled with images of Mr. Purdy lifting Mrs. Finney into the air.

I knew tonight's dreams—or perhaps nightmares—would be populated with dancing dumplings and sugarcubes.

Before heading back to the studio, I made a pit stop at my townhouse to pick up Woody and Carl, who scrambled into the car, excited at the prospect of getting out into the world. They'd been home alone too much the past few days. The two of them thrived on the hustle and bustle of gallery life, and I even kept sets of beds and snacks and food in my office to make the little princes comfortable.

As soon as we arrived at the studio and I unlocked the back door, Woody tore off toward the gallery. "Get back here!" I yelled after him. He ignored me, so I closed the door and jogged after him, with Carl bouncing in my arms. Though the creatures were at home in the gallery, not all humans were at home with animals. The sight of a big dog, no matter how friendly, might spook some customers.

On the other hand, how badly did I need a customer who didn't adore my friendly golden retriever?

As I passed into the gallery, I saw Banner kneeling on the floor with his arms wrapped around the dog's neck. Woody was giving the boy's face a thorough licking.

"Bad dog," I said, but even to my own ears, the scolding lacked force.

I counted ten customers browsing the gallery. Too many for the animals to be allowed free rein. "Will you escort that naughty dog to the office?" I asked Banner. When he stood up, I tucked Carl into his outstretched arm. "This guy, too, please. I'll be along in a minute to provide their highnesses with their sustenance."

Banner stroked Carl's back, and Woody trotted beside them. I took off my coat and scanned the room. Ethan stood behind the sales counter, ringing up a purchase for two women about my age. At the far wall, a young couple gazed at one of my larger—and more expensive—photos of snowy Mt. O'Connell gleaming in the sunset. I silently calculated the potential profit margin as I watched an older man circle a free-standing display of wildlife shots.

Near the far wall, I noticed a cluster of four who looked familiar. It took me a moment, but I placed them—the professors on retreat at my parents' resort.

I approached and asked if they had questions. The tallest of the bunch turned to me and grinned. "Well, if it isn't the famed photographer herself."

He held out a hand, and I shook it. "Callie Cassidy, at your service," I said.

"I'm Scott Digby, and I'm pleased to meet such a talented artist. Allow me to introduce my colleagues. This is Bernard Mitchell." He pointed to a man with thick, black-framed glasses and thinning gray hair whose smile came across as a smirk.

Scott next gestured to the lone female. "This enigmatic lady is Judith Maginot." The slender woman sported a Cruella de Vil hairstyle, black shoulder length tresses with silver streaks framing her face. She sneered at Scott. "I didn't realize Prosper offered doctorates in etiquette."

Before Scott could respond to her snarky comment, the last member of the group stepped forward and sandwiched my hand in both of his. His palm was warm and slick, and it was all I could do to keep from rubbing my hand on my leg. "I'm Dr. Jerry Lofland from Big Pine U," he said with a leer. "And let me assure you that any Big Pine innuendo you might consider does indeed fit."

I felt a quick spasm of revulsion cross my face, but he didn't seem to notice. "I'm smitten with your photography. Perhaps you'll join me later for a drink and instruct me on your technique."

Scott nudged the man aside and gave me an apologetic smile. "Pay Jerry no mind. He's spent too much time in a lab and lacks the ability to interact in social situations. But he's right about one thing—your photography is stunning."

I felt a blush creep across my cheeks. Being a graceful recipient of compliments had never been my strong suit. "Thank you," I said. "I enjoy the work."

"It shows," Scott said.

I shifted on my feet and foraged my brain for something clever to say. "The four of you are staying at my parents' resort," was all I could come up with. "They mentioned that you are philosophers."

"Ah, Butch and Maggie Cassidy," Scott said. "Your parents are lovely. This entire village, and the people in it, are so…quaint. So charming."

I smiled, hoping they couldn't tell it was my tolerant smile. His condescending tone got my dander up. We weren't Mayberry, for heaven's sake. We were intelligent, three-dimensional human beings. *Quaint and charming* seemed to relegate us to country bumpkin status.

He leaned in like a conspirator. "That's why it shocked us to learn of the attempted murder that occurred over the weekend."

"Wasn't the first one, the little birdies say," Jerry cut in.

"This town is a regular Cabot Cove," Judith added.

"Oh, I wouldn't go that far," I said.

Scott stroked his chin. "They say you employ your considerable investigative skills in such instances. Can you spare us any details?"

"We're quite discreet," Bernard said. He made a locking motion across his lips.

I glanced over my shoulder. Banner had returned from the office and now stood beside Ethan at the sales counter. Across the room, Braden assisted a customer. Both boys were well out of earshot, thank goodness.

Scott followed my gaze. "Oh, dear, are they…?" He turned to his companions and whispered, "Those young men must be the victim's sons. We heard they worked here."

He looked at me for confirmation, and I gave him a quick nod. "So, you'll understand why it wouldn't be appropriate for me to discuss the situation."

"Of course," Scott said, appearing chastened. "I fear we're coming across as tacky tourists, prying for lewd details. I assure you, that's not our quest. We are philosophers by nature, and we enjoy discussing and debating such matters. We follow a number of true crime podcasts and have gained some insights that might be useful to your pursuits."

"Happy to help you out," Jerry added.

I frowned. "I'm afraid you've somehow gotten an inflated view of my role. I'm not a detective—just a Rock Creek Village resident, waiting for the police to solve the case, like everyone else."

Scott eyed me dubiously while Judith pulled on a pair of sleek leather gloves. "Gentlemen, we're not getting anything out of this one," she said. "I believe it's time to take our leave."

Jerry grinned. "Hopefully, I'll run into you at the Knotty Pine. We're here until Friday." He leaned close, and his hot breath wafted into my ear. "I'd love to have that drink with you. I'm in Cabin Three. Come by anytime."

The four of them left, and I let go of the shudder I'd been repressing. If I went anywhere near Cabin Three, it would be in a hazmat suit.

26

At one o'clock, we had our usual post-lunchtime lull in customer traffic at the gallery, signaling it was time for our own late lunch. I collected orders from Ethan and the twins, added my own and one for Monika, who'd left me a message that she was on her way, and placed a call to Dan. Snow Plow Chow always hit the spot—and besides, I got free delivery, usually from the proprietor himself.

As soon as I'd placed the order, Monika arrived. She pulled off her mittens and her beanie, unleashing waves of red hair. The twins watched in appreciation, and it occurred to me she was only a few years older than the two of them. I always thought of them as boys, but in truth, they stood on the cusp of manhood. They had one foot in each world, longing to be children and yearning to be adults. It was a tough navigation in the best of circumstances, and in the boys' situation, it had to be doubly difficult. No mother to dote on them, an absent father who, when he did show up, created chaos in their lives and ended up comatose.

I put that thought aside and led Monika into my office. As soon as we'd settled into our chairs, I started updating her on my conversation with Trent. Then my cell rang, and a glance at the screen told me it was a FaceTime call from Italy. I pressed a button and smiled as my best friend's face appeared on the screen, with her new husband at her shoulder. Behind them, the lights of Florence twinkled like an invitation.

"Look at you two, all happily married and hanging out in Italy," I said. "Living your best life."

Tonya kissed David's cheek. "Best life sums it up,

sugarplum." Her red lips parted in a contented smile. "It's perfect here. Especially when you get to sleep next to your own personal tour guide."

I turned the screen to Monika, who said, "Ciao, boss. You, too, Signore Boss."

At the sight of Monika, Tonya's perfectly plucked eyebrow lifted and her tone suddenly changed. "How fortunate that I've caught the two of you together. I've just been informed that Brian Ratliff is in a coma."

Monika looked like a guilty child who'd kept a secret from her mother. I turned the screen back to myself. "How'd you hear?"

"From my mother, naturally. You know how Lydia loves to be the bearer of bad news. Maybe you can explain why my best friend didn't see fit to inform me of this development. Or my new reporter."

"No way we were going to drag you into this mess," I said. "You're five thousand miles away, and who knows how many time zones. There's nothing you can do to help. And don't blame Monika. I told her there was no need to involve you."

Tonya tapped a finger against her lip. "Hmm. No need to involve me. You do recall that I'm editor-in-chief of the *Rock Creek Gazette* and, as such, Monika's boss, don't you? Unless you've staged a coup in my absence, that is."

"Save the outrage, girlfriend. You'd have done the same thing in my shoes."

David put his lips next to his wife's ear. "She has a point, *amore mio*."

She shook her head and sighed. "Am I correct in assuming the two of you are working on this together?"

"You are. Your new hire is a whiz kid." Monika's face lit up at my praise. "You have nothing to worry about. Just enjoy your honeymoon."

She studied me for a moment, then nodded. "All right. But everything goes through Phil. And I'm going to tell him I want final approval. He can email me the edited version of any story before it goes to press."

I opened my mouth to object, but she held up a hand. "Nonnegotiable, sweet potato. I may be in Italy, but I'm still in charge. Now, give me to Monika."

When Tonya got like this—which was almost always—it did no good to argue. She was as immovable as the Rockies. But to be fair, it was indeed her newspaper, and she bore the responsibility—and liability—for everything printed in it.

I held out the phone and Monika reached for it, her hand trembling. Talented and self-assured as the young reporter was, she was still green—and very young.

Tonya's voice softened, but her tone still made it clear she'd brook no dissent. "Monika, I realize Callie can be a force of nature. And we all know of her substantial professional experience. I imagine she's mentioned her Feldman Award more than once—"

"Hey!" I said.

"But I want to be clear that it was me who hired you, and it's me who pays your salary. Do you remember that?"

"Yes, ma'am. I do."

"None of this ma'am stuff. You're an adult, a professional, and a journalist capable of making her own decisions. Follow your instincts. Don't let Callie bully you into doing or writing anything I wouldn't approve."

"I object to this characterization," I said. "No way am I trying to push her around. I'm only—"

Tonya ignored me. "Are we clear, Monika?"

Monika's shoulders straightened. "Clear."

"Good. Now give me back to Callie."

When I took the phone, Tonya said, "Callahan Cassidy, you are the heart of my heart, the soul of my soul. But that does not give you license to strong-arm my reporter into any dangerous or otherwise questionable situations."

"I would never—"

"Uh-huh. Remember who you're talking to, sugarplum.

We'll be home in a week. Don't burn the place down while I'm gone."

David leaned into the frame and waved. "*Ciao, ragazze.*"

Tonya blew one last kiss and disconnected.

Monika gave me a look of wonderment. "Are the two of you always like that?"

"More or less." I cocked my head. "Is her lecture going to put a damper on the two of us working together?"

Monika shrugged. "Well, I won't do anything to lose my job. But Tonya told me to follow my instinct, and my instinct tells me we make a good team."

I smiled. "Good. Then let's proceed." I leaned across the desk and finished telling her about my conversation with Trent. Her fingers flew across her phone as she took notes. As I reached the end of the story, a knock came at my office door. "Come in," I called out.

Sam entered with a takeout bag. He rounded the desk, set the bag down, and kissed my cheek. "Lunch is served."

Monika pulled the bag toward her and began unpacking it. "Now, that's what I call service."

"It pays to have connections," I said, unwrapping my turkey and avocado sandwich. "What do I owe you?"

He winked at me. "Don't worry about the bill. I'll collect later."

He said he had to hurry back to the café. I remembered he had a catering job later and wished him luck. Monika had already begun chomping into her club sandwich on rye, and she mumbled her thanks around a mouthful of bread and meat.

We spent a few minutes gorging ourselves. Journalists often developed terrible eating habits, wolfing down meals in the limited time between interviews and deadlines. In no time at all, we'd polished off our sandwiches and started on the brownies.

"Were you able to dig up any information on Desiree Bouton?" I asked.

Monika wiped her mouth with a napkin and shook her head, looking frustrated. "I've hit a brick wall so far. She's a ghost. I can't find any DMV records under her name. Her only social media presence is very recent. No high school or college information. Nothing on her brother, either. It's as if they didn't exist before this year."

My antennae rose. In my experience, a lack of accessible background meant something nefarious. "Seems likely Desiree and Weston aren't who they say they are," I mused.

"That's what I think, too, but I can't figure out how to do a deeper dive." She popped the last bit of brownie into her mouth. "Not legally, anyway."

I sighed, recalling Tonya's warning. I couldn't encourage Monika to engage in illicit behaviors. If only I possessed the requisite hacker skills, I could pursue the leads myself. After all, I had no job to lose.

Monika's phone buzzed. She read the message, rose from her chair, and picked up her bag. "Duty calls," she said.

"Duty? What duty?"

"Reporter duty," she said. "I could tell you, but then I'd have to…"

I chuckled. "I see Mrs. Finney has used her signature line on you, too."

Monika smiled. "I'll keep digging, Callie. If you think of anything that might help, let me know. Otherwise, I'll talk to you tomorrow."

As she opened the door and headed out, someone else entered—a person I hadn't expected. Monika glanced at me and lifted an eyebrow at the sight of Detective Lynn Clark, but surprisingly, she didn't linger. Her "duty" must have been more pressing than I'd realized.

Once inside, Lynn closed the door. As always, she looked more like a fashion model than a stereotypical detective. She wore tailored tweed slacks and a cream-colored silk shirt with heeled boots that didn't hinder her from crouching to pet the creatures.

Once she'd paid homage to my furry friends, she settled into an empty chair and deposited her oversized leather tote at her feet.

"You and the new reporter were engaging in a social visit, I assume," she said.

Her sarcasm wasn't lost on me, but I played along. "We just got off the phone with Tonya and David," I said.

Her expression softened. "Well, that's nice. Are they having the time of their lives?"

"They are. But I'm guessing you didn't come here to talk about honeymoons and travel itineraries."

Her brows drew together. "You're right. I'm here on a bit of unpleasant police business."

Unpleasant? I braced myself for her bad news.

She reached inside the tote and pulled out an envelope, which she placed on the desk in front of me. "It's a restraining order."

"What? I didn't file for any restraining orders."

"It's not *for* you, Callie. It's *against* you. A judge issued Desiree Bouton an order of protection. You're not to go within one hundred yards of her for the next thirty days."

27

I jumped to my feet, almost knocking my chair over. Woody sprang to my side, the fur on the scruff of his neck standing up as he prepared to defend me against whatever unseen forces threatened. Carl jumped onto my desk and sniffed the envelope, then returned to his bed, disinterested.

"Desiree took out a restraining order on me? What the—?"

"She claims you threatened and intimidated her at the hospital, and she cited the ICU nurse as a witness."

"I did no such thing! If anything, she threatened and intimidated Braden and Banner. I was only trying to set her straight."

"So, you simply tried to reason with her and explain the error of her thinking," Lynn said.

"Exactly."

She shook her head. "Regardless of your interpretation of events, a judge granted the order. You are instructed to steer clear of Desiree Bouton. Please, Callie, obey the order. We have enough on our plates right now without having to haul you off to jail."

I sank into my chair. My heart was beating wildly.

Lynn stood and placed her palms on my desk. "I need you to acknowledge receipt of the restraining order."

"I acknowledge the order, Detective Clarke," I said stiffly.

She winced. Then she picked up her tote and slung it over her shoulder. "I don't expect you to like it, Callie. But I expect you to honor it."

She strode out of the room and shut the door.

***

My knee-jerk reaction was to charge over to the cabin where Desiree was staying and confront her about this ridiculous restraining order. I went so far as digging my keys from my bag and heading to the door. But as I grabbed the knob, I paused and bit my lip, my mind on the twins. Then Lynn. Raul. Sam. My parents. *Was my potential tantrum in anyone's best interests?*

Instead of darting to my car, I paced my tiny office, considering first one course of action, then the other, fully able to rationalize both sides. Every time I'd convince myself to take the high road, I'd look down at that piece of paper telling me where I could and couldn't go in my own village—my home!—and the indignation would bubble up again.

It was a battle I imagined most people fought from time to time—whether to heed what we knew was right or pursue the siren song of our baser instincts. Once upon a time, I wouldn't even have hesitated—I'd have succumbed to my combative urges without a second thought as to the consequences. But I'd learned the hard way that I often wasn't the only one those consequences affected. I sighed and sank into my chair, tucking the offending document into my desk drawer. I wasn't giving up, but I had to play this smart.

A tap at the door had Woody on his feet again. "Come in," I called.

My father entered. His smile couldn't fully conceal his concern. "Hey, Sundance." He took a seat across the desk.

I looked at him suspiciously. "What brings you here, Dad? And please don't tell me you're shopping for photos."

He raised his palms. "Isn't a father allowed to stop by his daughter's workplace once in a while?"

"Uh-huh. Frank called you, didn't he?"

Dad sighed. "All right, I suppose he did. He mentioned the restraining order. He was worried you'd bolt out of here in search of Desiree. To be honest, I was, too."

"So, you showed up to, what, put me in time out? I'm not a little girl anymore, Dad."

He shot a pointed glance at my bag on the desk, car keys lying beside it. "Then don't act like one."

I drew back, surprised at the sternness in his tone.

He took a deep breath. *Was he counting to ten like Raul?* When he spoke, his tone was tender. "I realize you're an adult, Callie. But I'm still your father. The instinct to protect you didn't fade away the moment you turned twenty-one. And no matter what age we are, we can all benefit from having someone step in before our impulses get the better of us."

I studied my dad's face. Wrinkles lined his forehead, eyes, and mouth. I wondered how many of those I'd caused—both the worry lines and the laugh lines. With a jolt, it occurred to me that my father was getting older. Yes, he'd celebrated his seventieth birthday recently, but I'd never thought of him as *aging*. If I was edging toward AARP status, my father had been living there for twenty years.

Suddenly, I wanted to reach up and smooth those worry lines away with a magic thumb. To turn back the clock. To make sure I didn't waste any time with him.

I blinked back my tears and smiled. "You're right. And so you know, just before you showed up here, I talked myself out of following those impulses you referenced. Maybe some of your good sense has rubbed off on me, Daddy."

He tilted his head. "Daddy? You haven't called me that in years."

I reached across the desk and covered my father's hand with my own. "Isn't a girl allowed to admit when her father knows best?"

He raised an eyebrow before giving my fingers a

squeeze. "Wonders never cease."

A wave of affection hit me so hard it nearly toppled me. "I hope you're right."

Then Dad told me Mom wanted me to come for dinner. I looked at my watch, surprised to see how late it had gotten—almost closing time. The hours fly by when you're contemplating a restraining order. I mentally consulted my social calendar. Sam had a catering gig tonight. The creatures were here with me. Ethan had said earlier he and Renata wanted to take the twins to dinner. Afterwards, the boys wanted to pick up a few things from their house, including their cars.

The promise of my mother's cooking made my mouth water. Nothing to deter me and plenty to lure me. "If you insist," I said. "I'll be over as soon as we close," I said.

***

Dad was waiting on the front porch of the lodge when I pulled into the parking lot. He still didn't entirely trust me to avoid Cabin One, I surmised. I gathered Carl in my arms and followed Woody to meet him, sparing only a quick glance at Desiree's current residence.

"They're not even home," Dad said, slinging an arm around me. "I checked before you got here."

I felt temptation release its grip. For now, I could relax.

We went into the lodge, where Mr. Farmington waved at us from the reception desk. Dad scanned the lobby, making sure everything was in order. A few guests stood at the buffet table, filling plates with hors d'oeuvres and ladling mulled wine into tall mugs. Beyond the glass wall, the setting sun painted Mt. O'Connell red and orange, giving it the appearance of an erupting volcano.

Dad said a few words to Mr. Farmington before opening the door leading to the private apartment upstairs. Woody darted up, and I followed more slowly, grasping the handrail while negotiating the squirming cat in my arms.

Before we even reached the top of the stairs, a heavenly aroma scented our path. From the way my stomach growled in response, it was hard to believe I'd eaten lunch only a few hours earlier.

Ahead of us, Woody made his way into the kitchen, and I heard Mom talking to him in the sweet, high-pitched voice she reserved for the animals. Then came the sound of an opening drawer, and I knew a snack was imminent. Sure enough, Woody pranced back into the room with a doggie bone clenched between his teeth.

Mom appeared at the door of the kitchen, wiping her hands on a dish towel. "I see your father intervened before you could be arrested. We can thank our lucky stars for that. I'm not up for a jailhouse visit to my derelict daughter. Not when there's a meatloaf in the oven."

She draped the towel over her shoulder, kissed me on the cheek, and reached out for Carl.

I handed him over and gave Dad my coat. "Dinner smells terrific, Mom."

"It's nothing fancy, darling, and it'll be another half hour. Why don't the two of you join me in the kitchen? Butch, will you pour us a glass of wine?"

We trailed her like ducklings into her nest. As I climbed onto a stool at the quartz island, she set Carl on the floor and rummaged around in the treat drawer, settling on a fish-shaped tuna treat. She held it out to Carl, who stared at it with contempt. Mom laughed. "Playing hard to get?" She dropped the treat on the floor, and as soon as she turned her back, Carl scooped it up in his mouth and dashed from the room.

While Mom washed her hands, Dad pulled two wineglasses out of the cabinet. "White or red?" he asked.

"Red, of course," Mom said. "I'm serving meatloaf."

"How silly of me," Dad said. "I'd forgotten you were such a connoisseur."

He retrieved the wine, along with a frosty bottle of beer for himself. He poured a couple of inches of crimson liquid into a glass, and I crooked a finger at him. "Keep it coming."

He poured a couple more inches, filled a glass for Mom, and popped open his beer. As he swigged, Mom and I sipped. The liquid tickled my tonsils and warmed my gut. I hadn't realized how tense I'd been all day—for the last three days, to be honest. It felt good to be hanging out with my parents.

But the peaceful moment wasn't destined to last, as I should have known. "So, Callahan," Mom said, giving me her teacher look, "what's this we hear about a restraining order?"

I spent the next few minutes defending myself while Mom bustled around the kitchen kneading dough for homemade rolls, mashing potatoes, and slicing green beans. Dad listened with barely concealed amusement. The creatures snoozed at our feet. Just another day in Callie Land.

After I'd completed my dissertation on how mistreated I was, Mom swirled the wine, looking thoughtful. "Well, darling, if it's any comfort, I'd have done the same thing in defense of those boys."

I shot a victorious look at my father. "Thank you."

"Besides," she said, "that Desiree and her brother… there's something strange about them."

"Now, Maggie," Dad said.

"Don't *now-Maggie* me, Butch. I'm entitled to speak my mind."

Dad smirked. "As if I've ever been able to stop you."

I nudged him. "Anyway, Dad, you said the same thing yourself at the police station."

Mom had gone back to mashing and pounding a poor defenseless potato. A strand of silver hair dropped across her eyes. She puffed her cheeks and tried to blow it away, but it stayed stubbornly put. My father reached over and tenderly brushed it back into place, then leaned in to kiss the spot on her forehead where it had rested. The simple gesture nearly leveled me. Forty-nine years of marriage and they were more in love now than I'd ever seen them. Suddenly, growing old didn't seem so bad. Could Sam and I be that lucky?

But right now, more important things occupied my mind. "Mom, why do you say the Boutons are strange?"

She shrugged. "Well, darling, you know I don't like to gossip…"

I rolled my eyes. "Whatever you say. But it's only us right now. It's not gossip if you're with family."

She raised her masher and heaved it into the helpless spud. "Well, you know that Felicia and her crew clean the rooms and cabins each morning…"

Felicia, the Knotty Pine head housekeeper, had been with Mom and Dad since they'd first opened the resort. She was approaching seventy herself, but spry as a baby goat. She usually hired a few temps during the busy times, such as spring break, but otherwise managed on her own. And unlike my mother, she had no aversion to loose lips.

"Today, Felicia mentioned that Desiree and Weston are terrible slobs. Clothes strewn about, dishes piled in the sink, wet towels on the bathroom floor."

"I'm not surprised," I said. "Desiree has entitlement issues, and that brother of hers always looks stoned."

Mom nodded. "Yes, Felicia mentioned a certain lingering odor." She turned to my father. "Perhaps you need to have a word with our guests about not indulging inside the cabin."

Dad took a gulp of beer and set the bottle down hard. "You bet I will."

I tried to get the conversation back on track. "Anyway, Mom, messiness is not that strange. I'm sure you've hosted plenty of guests who were messy."

She opened the oven door and removed the meatloaf. The room filled with the smell of tender meat and spicy sauce. "Yes, but that's not the interesting part. Felicia found it shocking that the two of them seem to be...well, sharing the bed."

Ick. An adult brother and sister in a double bed? Then again, I was an only child, so maybe it wasn't as weird as I thought. Besides, Felicia could be jumping to conclusions.

"Maybe Weston sleeps on the futon."

"I mentioned that possibility. But Felicia said she left extra sheets and a blanket, all of which appear unused."

"They could've folded them back up," I ventured.

"Amid such a mess? Doubtful."

Hmm. Mom was right, it was strange. But different strokes for different folks, right? In many cultures, it was the norm for families to share beds. Or maybe both of them had bad backs. Who were we to judge?

At that point, dinner was ready, which precluded further speculation. As we ate, we turned the conversation away from suspects and shenanigans, talking instead of our respective businesses. Dad said the lodge was almost completely booked for the next few weeks, and I mentioned that an uptick in customers meant Ethan and I already needed to restock the gallery. Business was booming for all the shop owners in Rock Creek Village right now.

I told my parents about yesterday's hockey team shoot. Mom shuddered. "Every time I drive by that rink, I picture you lying helpless on the ice. Your poor sweet wrist."

"Going back there was weird for me, too. But you want to know what made the visit even weirder?"

I told them all about Mrs. Finney and Mr. Purdy's skating routine. "I couldn't believe my eyes. She wore a purple and silver get-up, and he was dressed in tight slacks."

Dad laughed. "Those two never cease to amaze me."

"Well, I think it's sweet," Mom said. "You're never too

old to fall in love. Or to try something new."

"You are if that something new is ice dancing," Dad said.

"Butch, we should try it," Mom said brightly.

An image of Mom in a sparkly skating dress and Dad in a tight sequined onesie popped into my mind, and I nearly choked on a green bean.

Apparently, the idea didn't sit well with my father, either.

"I love you, honey," he said. "But that ain't happening. There are some lines you just can't force a man to cross."

28

I spent a few minutes reveling in the easy banter between my parents and the infinite adoration in their eyes. Then I cleared the table, insisting on doing the dishes as payment for my meal. Mom kept me company, while Dad headed into his study to do whatever he did there—probably phoning Frank to inform him he'd steered me clear of trouble.

When the dishwasher was loaded and running, I put on my coat, hugged my mother, called out a goodbye to my father, and corralled Woody and Carl. After a quick wave to Mr. Farmington, we stepped into the brisk, breezy night. Dinner with my parents had left me feeling better than I had in days. My nerves were soothed, and my heart and stomach were full.

Then I glimpsed Cabin One and remembered that wretched restraining order. My hackles threatened to rise yet again. I looked closer and noticed soft light gleaming through the slats of the blinds. The occupants had returned.

The familiar urge tugged at me, the desire to do something impulsive, but I tamed it. Before I'd left, I'd assured my parents they could trust me and there was no need to chaperone me to my car. Now, determined to honor my promise, I walked resolutely through the parking lot, opened the back door, and stood aside as Woody jumped in.

Then, in a quick move worthy of an Olympic gymnast, Carl contorted his body and performed a backward leap out of my arms, twisting in mid-air so that he landed on the pavement on four paws. He stared at me for a moment, meowed, and tore off toward Cabin One. I slammed the back door of the car, much to Woody's consternation, and took off after my cat.

"Carl, get back here," I demanded in my most authoritative whisper. He continued his dash along the path and up the cabin steps. Then he settled beneath the front window and calmly began to groom himself.

I skidded to a halt near the steps and crouched near the porch rail to stay out of sight while I caught my breath. As soon as I was confident my heavy gasps wouldn't alert the cabin's residents to my presence, I planned to tiptoe onto the porch, scoop up the defiant cat, and scurry back to the car.

But just as I put my foot on the bottom step, a thud echoed from inside the cabin. My pulse raced. My breathing quickened again. Carl looked at me as if daring me to act.

Shadows slithered across the porch. The wind caught the rocker, and it squeaked softly. Then came another thud. My hand shot to my pocket, searching for my phone, but I realized I'd left it in my bag in the car.

I considered my options. The noise was likely no cause for alarm. Desiree and Weston might be packing to move back into Brian's house. I'd probably simply heard a suitcase thumping on the floor.

I chewed the inside of my cheek. Despite my self-rationalization, I couldn't just leave. I had to be sure no one inside was in trouble. Creeping up the steps, I shuffled toward the window. Though the blinds were closed, the bottom slat rested about an inch off the sill. I positioned myself to the side of the window and bent at the waist. The muffled sound of Woody's barking from inside the car floated through the air. I glanced in that direction, tempted to grab the cat and dash to safety.

Another thud—this one softer—convinced me I needed to stay.

I summoned my courage and peered through the

opening. The light from the bedside lamp sent an amber cast across the room, revealing an empty kitchen. The bathroom door was open, and it, too, was vacant. The bed, rumpled and unmade, was likewise unoccupied.

Then I caught movement in the far corner of the room. I craned my neck for a better view. I made out Desiree…and there was Weston. Desiree's hands were wrapped around her brother's neck. *Was she strangling him?* But he was strong enough to fend her off. *Unless he was too high to defend himself…*

My shoulders tensed, and the muscles in my legs prepared to spring into action. Just as I made a move for the door, I saw Weston's arms wrap around Desiree's waist. In the next moment, they were kissing.

Ugh. I was pretty sure this wasn't how siblings expressed affection for one another. This steamy embrace was R-rated. And from the way Weston tossed Desiree onto the bed, it was about to turn NC-17.

That was something I didn't need to see. Carl remained silent as I snatched him up and crossed the porch, cringing as a board squeaked beneath my foot. When I'd descended the steps, I held him close as I sprinted down the path and across the parking lot, my breath huffing in frosty spurts. When I reached the car, I threw myself into the driver's seat, deposited Carl in the passenger seat, and locked the door.

Woody put his paws on the console and licked my ear. Carl curled up in a ball and snored. My panic dissipated, especially after a glance out the back window reassured me no one had followed us.

I ruffled Woody's fur and nudged him back into his seat. After a deep breath, and one more, I started the car and eased out of the parking lot. I didn't let my mind pore over what I'd seen until I'd safely turned onto Evergreen Way.

Either those two had the strangest brother-sister relationship in the world, or they weren't siblings at all.

***

My brain continued to whir as I reached home and pulled beneath the carport. I'd seen Ethan's Pathfinder parked out front, as well as Braden's car and Banner's truck. Party at Callie's house, apparently. I sat for a minute with my fingers gripping the steering wheel, collecting myself.

Should I tell the boys what I'd seen? Not the details, but what the scene revealed about Desiree and Weston's relationship? The twins already had so much on their plates. Did they need the thought of their father's brand-new wife's lover/brother/boyfriend piled on, too?

Another question occurred to me: was Desiree really Brian's wife at all? With Brian in a coma, we only had her word for it…unless Desiree had provided Raul and Lynn with that marriage license. I'd been told to stay out of the investigation, but I had to let the detectives know what I'd seen. Maybe when I disclosed my information, they'd feel generous and toss me a few scraps of their own.

I got out of the car, still undecided about whether to tell Banner and Braden about this latest discovery. But as the creatures and I walked into the backyard, I saw the boys through the window, sitting at the kitchen table. They were playing cards with Ethan and Renata, looking happy and carefree.

Decision made. I wouldn't tell them—at least, not tonight.

The animals and I entered to enthusiastic greetings. I tossed my coat over the back of the couch. "There's no illegal gambling occurring in my home, I hope."

"We're taking them for everything they're worth," Banner said.

"I'm a high school coach and teacher," Renata said. "That doesn't amount to much."

"Ethan's our actual mark," Braden said. "Partner in a fancy photography gallery. He has to be makin' bank."

"How'd you guess?" Ethan asked with a wink at me. "I've been hiding my Porsche in the garage, away from prying eyes."

They tossed red and black chips into the center of the table and continued joking around. I ambled over to the refrigerator and opened it. My eye fell on a bottle of pinot grigio, but I settled for Diet Coke.

At a lull in the conversation, I said, "How'd it go at the hospital?"

"Pretty good," Banner said. "Doc says things may be looking up."

"The neuro...neurowhatever said the brain scans show improvement," Braden said. "They're optimistic Dad'll come out of the coma."

"That's great! Any idea when?"

Banner shook his head. "Could be tomorrow. Could be next week."

Ethan frowned. "Remember, boys, the doctors are specu-lating. The brain scans are a positive indicator, but they're not absolute. The neurologist cautioned there were no guarantees. They're hopeful, but your dad is still in a coma. No one knows for sure when...or even if...he'll come out of it."

Banner shrugged. "He will. Our dad's a survivor."

I wondered what would happen to Brian's marriage when he regained consciousness. I didn't imagine Desiree would be eager to fill him in on the nature of her relationship with her so-called brother. Would that task fall to me?

I took a drink of my soda. "Was Desiree at the hospital?" I asked, feigning nonchalance.

"She was there when we met with the doctor," Braden said. "She left right after. Said she'd been at the hospital all day and needed a good night's sleep."

"Was...um...her brother there, too?"

Renata must have heard something in my tone, because she quirked an eyebrow at me. "Weston? No, we didn't see him. Why?"

"No reason. Old journalists never stop collecting useless information."

"You should be on *Jeopardy*," Ethan said.

"What do you guys know about Desiree and her…brother?" I asked the twins.

Now all four of them looked at me curiously. "Not much," Banner said.

"We didn't even realize that bimbo existed until Dad moved her into the house," Braden said in a bitter tone.

Banner shot him a glare. "Dad said he wanted to surprise us."

"Worst surprise ever." Woody trotted over and rested his head in Braden's lap. "Should have brought us a dog instead."

"Stop your whining," Banner said. "Dad is in the hospital. In a *coma*."

"You don't think I know that?" Braden's face turned red.

"Well, you're acting like an ungrateful moron," Banner said.

"Shut up!"

Ethan slapped his palm on the table. "That's enough! You two have too much going on in your lives to turn on each other."

The boys both sucked in a breath and hung their heads. "Sorry, bro," Banner said.

"Yeah, me too."

"You two want to hug it out?" Ethan asked.

"Nah, man, we're cool," Banner said.

"Not our thing," Braden added.

I thought of Desiree and Weston. Hugging it out was apparently only part of their "thing."

"Anyway, Callie," Ethan said, picking up his cards, "can we get back to our game, or do you want to treat us to more buzzkill?"

Woody scrambled down the entry hall a moment

before the doorbell rang. "It's okay, my work here is done." I threw the comment over my shoulder as I followed the dog.

I looked through the peephole to see Monika standing on the porch. Beneath the overhead light, her eyes shone. I recognized that look. She had news.

Before I'd even gotten the door halfway open, she wedged herself inside. "We need to talk."

29

I ushered Monika into the house and took her coat, trying to hide my eagerness to hear her news. At the sounds of the card game in the kitchen, she leaned toward me. "Privately would be best."

"We'll go upstairs," I said. "Just let me grab my drink. Want something? Wine, water, Diet Coke? Or I can make coffee."

She chose Diet Coke and followed me down the hall. Again, the twins' eyes bugged out when they saw her. She stood by the table and chatted casually with them while I poured her soda. Renata joined me at the fridge and folded her arms. "Thought Raul told you to stay out of it," she whispered.

"Since when has either of us done as your brother instructed?" I asked.

"Good point."

"Anyway, Monika's just here to run some ideas by me. She's a rookie, looking for sage advice from the wise old master. I'm going to offer a little journalistic guidance, that's all."

Renata smirked. "Sure, Callie. I was born at night, but not last night." She moved a step closer. "Just between us, I'm glad you're investigating. Those boys need some answers. Especially Braden. He's dealing with unresolved daddy issues in addition to a few people thinking he might be responsible for his father's condition. Raul and Lynn are great at what they do, and they're working hard on this, but it can't hurt to get as many eyes and minds on it as possible. And your eyes and mind are among the best."

I gave her a quick hug. "Thanks for the vote of confidence. And thanks for having the boys' backs. You and Ethan have been so good to them."

"We care about those kids," she said, her voice husky with emotion. "They've had some tough times. I'll do whatever I can to help them."

"We have that in common, then," I said.

Renata and I walked over to the table, and I handed Monika her drink. "Ready?"

She nodded, said her goodbyes, and followed me up the stairs and into a small sitting area in my bedroom.

"So, what did you find out?" I asked, as soon as I'd closed the door and we'd situated ourselves in adjacent club chairs.

She plucked a coaster out of the holder and placed her glass on the table. "The big news is that Detectives Sanchez and Clarke pretty much cleared Pamela Ashton."

I raised my eyebrows. "How'd you get that information?" Surely neither Raul nor Lynn had taken the reporter into their confidence.

She flicked her eyes away and shrugged. "A source in the department."

Well, that definitely got my interest. Monika had burrowed into the inner workings of the Rock Creek Village police force with remarkable agility. My respect for her increased daily.

"Who is it?"

"I can't tell you that," she said. "It's a confidential source."

I gave her a conspiratorial smile. "But we're partners, right? It'll be just between us."

She shook her head. It was the right answer, and I nodded my approval. Anyway, process of elimination left me with a pretty good idea of the person's identity. Aside from Frank, Raul, and Lynn, the only officers in the department with enough seniority to be privy to such information were Vicky Hardesty and Kevin Tollison. My money was on Kevin. He was a single male, and if Banner and Braden were any indication, he would be hard pressed to ignore Monika's entreaties.

"Did this source mention why they've concluded Pamela wasn't the poisoner? Did lab tests rule out the fudge?"

"No, they still think the poison was in the fudge. But my source confirmed that a search of the Fudge Factory and Pamela's home didn't turn up any poisons or chemicals consistent with what they found in Brian Ratliff's system."

I screwed up my face. "That doesn't seem definitive. We already knew the poison was in Brian's system prior to the wedding. The police didn't search the Fudge Factory until Monday. Pamela could have disposed of any incriminating evidence in the interim."

Monika nodded and pulled out her phone. "True. But combine that with the texts they discovered on Brian's phone…"

"Texts? Shouldn't you have led with that?"

"Saving the best for last," she muttered, scrolling.

"That's not very journalistic. You should start with what's most important and most timely."

"What can I say? I possess a flair for the dramatic."

I snorted. She sounded just like Tonya. "Well, now that you got my attention, spill."

"Give me a sec…just pulling up my notes. I want to be accurate."

I drummed my fingers on the table that separated our chairs. Finally, I opened the small drawer and extracted a classic, platinum coated ballpoint pen my former boss had given me when I'd started at the *Sentinel*. It had meant a lot to me at the time, but my life had changed, and I didn't need it anymore. Time to pass it on to the new generation. I held it out to her.

"You need to take notes the old-fashioned way," I said.

"Consider this my gift to you as you start your new career."

She took the pen and studied it. "That's really nice of you, Callie. And it's pretty, but it's not as efficient as this." She pointed to her phone. "Everything goes straight to the cloud, and I can access my notes on any device."

I shrugged. "Guess I'm old school, but nothing beats a notebook and pen in your hands. And no one ever said, 'The phone is mightier than the sword.'"

Her face creased in confusion. "What?"

I sighed. Another reference lost on the younger generation. "Never mind. Keep the pen. Give it a try sometime."

She tucked it into her bag and turned back to her screen. "Okay, here we go. My source said they found a series of texts between Pamela and Brian, in which she begged to rekindle their romance."

I was a little disappointed. Not terribly earth-shattering news. Besides, as I told Monika, wanting to get back together didn't eliminate Pamela's motive. In fact, if Brian rebuffed her advances and mentioned Desiree, it might have made Pamela mad enough to kill. The texts might make her an even more viable suspect than before.

"Yes, except Brian didn't reject her. He flirted back. The conversation between them turned…um, steamy. Here, read for yourself."

Monika's notes regarding the texts made even a seasoned pro like me blush. Brian and Pamela hadn't been shy in their anatomical descriptions. After I finished reading, I sat back and blew out a breath. I'd never be able to look at Pamela in the same way.

I remembered the wedding and the expression on her face when Brian and Desiree entered. She'd been furious. Was that the first she'd known of their relationship?

"When were the texts dated?" I asked.

"Last Friday."

The day before the wedding. "So, this spicy exchange

must have occurred *after* the fudge was in Brian's possession."

"Not necessarily, but probably. No one's sure exactly when he got the fudge. But the doc says Brian had likely been ingesting the poison for at least twenty-four hours prior to the coma."

The wheels spun in my head as I tried to create a plausible timeline of events. "Brian was stumbling and slurring his words at the wedding. We all thought he was drunk. But his physical deterioration was likely caused by poison building up in his system."

"The wedding was Saturday night," Monika said. "That means the poison had to be introduced by Friday night. Saturday morning at the latest."

"And if Brian and Pamela engaged in amorous texts on Friday, she either wasn't aware of his relationship with Desiree or believed it to be a short-term fling."

"She may have figured he'd dump Desiree for her. Women can be naïve about things like that."

She said it with such wistfulness that I wondered if she'd had personal experience in the matter. But now wasn't the time to chase that story.

"I'm guessing Pamela didn't know about Desiree until she saw her hanging all over Brian Saturday night," I said.

Monika nodded. "That's why the detectives dropped Pamela to the bottom of the suspect list. She's soft on motive—before the wedding, at least."

I chewed the inside of my cheek. The fudge still bothered me. "How did the poison get in the fudge if Pamela didn't put it there? Was someone trying to frame her? Or was it just a coincidence—an expedient delivery method?"

A long pause stretched between us as we considered the possibilities. "Okay," I said at last. "I'm not convinced any of this lets Pamela off the hook, but let's proceed as if it does. For now. Where does that leave us?"

Monika scrolled on her phone again and pulled up her

suspect list. "Trent Wallace. Desiree Bouton. Weston Bouton." She hesitated and met my eyes. "And of course…"

I held up a hand to stop her from mentioning Braden's name. "You don't even need to say it. His interview seemed to go well, but I'm sure he's still high on Raul and Lynn's list."

"At the top, according to my source."

"Well, he's still not even on mine." I leaned back and crossed my legs. My turn for a slow reveal. "Now, I have some information of my own to share."

She tilted her head and waited.

I started by telling her what the Knotty Pine housekeeper had told my mother about Desiree and Weston possibly sharing a bed. Then I summarized what I'd seen with my own two eyes as I spied on them through the blinds.

She pursed her lips. "Shouldn't you have led with that?"

I grinned. "Turns out this flair for the dramatic thing is kind of fun."

Monika twisted a lock of hair around her finger. "This puts a whole new spin on things."

"I knew there was something funky about the woman, but I never guessed that," I said. "We need more on her. Any progress?"

She shook her head in frustration. "Like I said, it's as if she has no past at all. I'm pretty good at finding back doors through firewalls, but these are bolted tight."

"Well," I said, "I may have a solution."

"What's that?"

"A source of my own. But unlike you, I'm happy to share the name. Mrs. Finney."

30

The next morning, I allowed myself another yawn as I relocked Sundance Studio's front door behind me. It wasn't even seven, and I'd never been a morning person. Today, though, I'd set my alarm and dragged myself out of bed without even the lure of frying bacon. All for the purpose of meeting Monika at Rocky Mountain High—to pester, cajole, and plead for Mrs. Finney's assistance.

I rubbed my eyes, and when I opened them, my fingers itched for my camera. To the east, the sun peeked above the distant mountain range, bathing the village in a tangerine glow. Orange and purple prisms shot through the wispy clouds.

With a slow spin, I soaked in my surroundings, basking in the sense that, for the moment, the village seemed to belong only to me. I marveled again at the perfect confluence that had resulted in this idyllic place. Rock Creek Village lay in a small valley at the foot of the Rocky Mountains. If this part of the Rockies was a resting arm, we were nestled in the crook of its elbow. To the west, Mt. O'Connell served as the bicep, while the forearm of the range extended upward to the north and then to the east. Our unique location gave us the kind of sunrises and sunsets poets expounded upon, and sheltered as we were in the crook of the arm, we were spared some of the extreme weather notable in other parts of the state.

I would have loved to run back inside and grab my camera, but I had promises to keep. A glance at my watch told me I was about to be late for the first of them.

I arrived at Rocky Mountain High to find Monika

leaning against the wall outside the door, her fingers pecking at her ever-present phone. So much for the pen I'd given her last night.

"Good morning," I said. "You're bright and early."

She slid her phone into her pocket and looked at the Apple Watch on her wrist. "Tonya told me you have a motto: If you're not five minutes early, you're late."

"That was the old me. The new, improved version is totally laid back. Ask anyone."

She chuckled and held the door open for me. The aroma of freshly brewed coffee mingled with the scent of whatever sugary concoction Mrs. Finney had created. When she'd first moved to the village, none of us could have predicted the stocky woman with a talent for sniffing out criminals would turn into a talented barista and baker. But as the already three-quarters-filled shop attested, her skills were the stuff of legends.

Monika and I piled our coats on a table to stake our claim and headed up to the counter. Mrs. Finney looked at me in surprise.

"Why, Callahan Cassidy, you're riding in on the fingers of dawn. I don't believe I've ever seen you before nine."

I stifled another yawn. "And there's a reason for that. Coffee, please. Pronto."

She turned to Monika. "What about you, young lady? Espresso?"

"You're a mind reader." Monika pointed to a stack of sweet rolls resting beneath a glass dome. "What are those? My mouth is watering at the sight of them."

Mrs. Finney looked delighted. "Ah, my new cinnamon date buns. They're already quite a hit."

She lifted the glass and selected one, lifting it with a pair of silver tongs and placing it on a plate. Her gaze flitted to me. "You'll try one, won't you, Callahan?"

I wrinkled my nose. "Dates? The only thing I know about dates is from that Indiana Jones movie. If I remember correctly, they killed a monkey."

Monika laughed. "Bad dates," she said in a fake accent.

Mrs. Finney tightened her lips. "I can assure you these dates are fresh. No one will die from my buns."

"Oh, no, I didn't mean…" Monika was flustered. "I was just quoting a line from the movie."

A wicked grin spread across Mrs. Finney's face. "I'm just messing with you, as the young people say."

While Monika recovered from the jolt, Mrs. Finney retrieved another pastry. "You'll give this a try, Callahan."

It wasn't a question.

"All right, but don't be upset if I don't like it." I eyed the fluffy, gooey bun suspiciously. "Anyway, we've come for more than caffeine and sugar. We want to request your help on a certain matter. Could you join us for a few minutes?"

Interest flared in her eyes. "Of course, my dear. Let me fetch Mr. Purdy. I'll be along in a moment."

Monika and I carried our plates and mugs to the table. As we settled into our chairs, Kimberly and Parker Lyon came inside and made a beeline for the counter. Since Mrs. Finney had disappeared into the kitchen, they were forced to wait. Kimberly slid off her coat and handed it to Parker as if he were a butler. Without a word of complaint, he took it and trotted toward a nearby table, where he draped the garment over a chair. By the time he returned to the counter, Mrs. Finney had reappeared to take the couple's orders.

As Mrs. Finney bustled about filling mugs and spurting cream, Kimberly looked around the coffee shop. Her eyes settled on me, and she smiled. Though we'd disliked each other throughout high school, we'd since formed a more cordial relationship. I wouldn't say we were friends exactly, but we got along fine—a good thing, since she and my boyfriend shared a daughter.

Kimberly pulled Parker over to our table. Her expression was serious. "Have you heard any updates on Brian's condition? Elyse says she doesn't have any news."

She listened intently as I filled her in on the doctor's hopeful prognosis. Beside her, Parker examined his cuticles. As always, he was dressed impeccably, his slacks neatly pressed and his loafers polished to a glossy shine. "That's too bad," he said.

Kimberly poked an elbow into his ribs, and he oomphed. "What? You're going to scold me because I can't summon up any sympathy for that beast? Seems only fitting he was poisoned, given his own toxic nature. Serves him right, if you ask me."

"Well, no one did," Kimberly said, "so hush. The two of us have already been accused of murder once. We don't need that in our lives again."

When she turned her back on him, Parker gave her a look of such petulance that I thought he might stick out his tongue. Instead, he muttered, "Don't know what you ever saw in that brute."

She heard him and flashed her husband a look. "Go get our coffee, dear. I'll join you at our table in a moment."

He trotted toward the counter. Her eyes followed him, and in them I saw affection.

"Elyse has been so worried about Banner and Braden," Kimberly said. "Is Braden…I mean, the police seem to think…"

"The twins had nothing to do with it," I said tersely.

"No, of course not. I just…I wish I knew how to ease my daughter's concerns."

I forced myself to tone down the defensiveness. Despite Kimberly's mean-girl antics in high school and the snobbishness she still occasionally exhibited as an adult, she was a loving mother. If my instincts were right, she might even be growing into a good person. I was prepared to give her the benefit of the doubt.

"It's a tough time," I said. "The detectives naturally have to rule out the twins. But I have every faith that'll happen soon."

Kimberly nodded, but she seemed unconvinced. "I

hope so. As you know, Elyse has become quite close to her half-brothers, and she'd be devastated if…well, if the worst-case scenario comes to pass."

"That won't happen," I said, with a confidence I didn't entirely feel.

Parker had carried two steaming mugs to their table, and Kimberly bade us goodbye. Tossing her hair over her shoulder, she took the seat next to him, and the two of them began whispering over their lattes.

"What's their story?" Monika said. "That guy has a definite attitude. Maybe we need to move him higher on our list. He seemed pretty unsympathetic about Brian's condition. And did Kimberly say the two of them had been murder suspects in the past?"

Mrs. Finney joined us, plopping into a vacant chair and scooting it toward the table. "Parker Lyon?" She waved a hand dismissively. "He's a spoiled pussycat."

"So's Carl," I said, "but if he had opposable thumbs…"

"Point taken, dear. Still, I can't picture Mr. Lyon concocting an elaborate poisoning plot. He doesn't possess the gray matter. But before we delve into suspects and schemes, we have a more pressing matter to discuss."

I gave her a questioning look, and she pointed at our untouched cinnamon date rolls. "Neither of you has so much as licked my buns."

After a moment of open-mouthed shock, Monika and I burst into laughter.

"What's so funny?" Mrs. Finney asked.

Monika composed herself before I did, and she took a big bite out of the pastry. Her eyes closed in rapture. "Oh. My. Gosh. This is the best thing I've tasted in weeks." She shot me a look. "Except the dinner Sam made, of course."

I grinned. "For the record, you're telling us you love Mrs. Finney's buns."

Monika chortled again, and crumbs flew from her lips.

When Mrs. Finney turned steely eyes on me, I stifled a giggle and picked up my own bun, sniffing it doubtfully. Hmm. Fragrant and cinnamony. I placed the edge between my teeth and tugged off a corner.

It was love at first taste.

I took a second, bigger bite. "I will always eat dates now," I murmured. "Every day for the rest of my life, if you provide them."

Mrs. Finney sat back, lacing her hands in her lap. "I'm delighted to hear it. We made the buns this morning from a secret recipe Mr. Purdy got his hands on." She looked toward the counter and gave Mr. Purdy a thumbs up, to which he responded with a fist pump.

After that, she scooted her chair even closer and leaned on her elbows. "Now, let's get down to business."

31

Monika and I spent the next few minutes summarizing our suspect list. Mrs. Finney absorbed the information, her brain processing the data like a computer. Despite being retired from the spy business, her sharp mind hadn't dulled.

When we mentioned Pamela, she frowned. "I'm not certain I'd clear her yet. Still waters run deep, as they say. Simmering rage often leads to the most spectacular of eruptions."

"That might be true," I said, "but can we classify what happened to Brian as an eruption? It feels more premeditated. If someone had bludgeoned him with a golf club, that would be a different story. But poisoning seems more calculated."

"You're thinking the would-be killer held a long-term grudge?" Mrs. Finney asked. "One that might have been building for years?"

"Actually, I'm leaning more toward a cold-blooded plot," I said.

"Ah." She leaned back. "You're referring to Desiree."

Monika gazed at her. "How did you jump to that conclusion?"

"Simple, my dear. The motives of everyone else on your list revolve around passion, lust, revenge, or pain. But I'm guessing Desiree and that perpetually baked brother of hers insinuated themselves into Brian's life for some as-yet unknown outcome. It's the only thing that makes sense."

I smiled, as much at her utterance of the word "baked" as from her spot-on assessment. "About that brother of hers…"

I told Mrs. Finney about the bedroom antics I'd witnessed, and she responded with a wicked snort. "Must say, I hadn't predicted that."

Then she steepled her fingers and turned to Monika. "Have you been able to employ your considerable computer magic to tap into their past?"

Monika scowled. "I've been at it for two days with no luck. I mean, Desiree Bouton is obviously an alias, but I can't uncover her real identity. She's constructed some serious security around herself. I don't have any legal methods of getting through."

I leaned forward, my elbows on the table. "But I bet you do, Mrs. Finney."

"Well, perhaps not legal, not in the traditional sense. And not me, of course, now that I'm retired. But I am still privy to a few resources…"

Her eyes flicked to Mr. Purdy, and I smiled to myself. With the two of them on the case, I predicted we'd get our answers by tomorrow.

***

Two minutes later, Mrs. Finney and Mr. Purdy stood with their heads together behind the counter, deep in conversation. She talked and gestured. He listened and nodded. I figured we were in capable hands.

Monika drained the rest of her coffee and reached for her coat. "I need to run back to the newsroom. Phil tells me it's time to sing for my supper."

I stiffened. "You promised you wouldn't write about any of this until we had some conclusive answers."

"Relax, Callie. Phil has me covering a school board meeting later this morning. I have to do some prep work, then show up at the meeting. The story itself should be a breeze—won't take me more than a couple of hours. Then I'll get back to our work. I'll be meeting with—"

She stopped mid-sentence, suddenly cagey.

"With whom?" I asked, curious.

She shrugged. "A potential source."

"Care to divulge?"

"You know I can't," she said.

I narrowed my eyes, but let it go, grabbing my own coat. We waved to Mrs. Finney and Mr. Purdy and exited, Monika turning toward the parking lot on the right, while I headed left toward Sundance Studio.

I felt optimistic about our investigation. With Mrs. Finney and Mr. Purdy on board, a resolution was inevitable. The sooner we uncovered Desiree's illicit past, the sooner we could expose her as the poisoner and get Braden and Banner back to their normal life.

The sun had risen in earnest by now. The day bloomed clear and bright, though still brisk enough that my fingers tingled in the cold. I reached into my coat pocket for my gloves and fumbled one to the ground. As I bent to retrieve it, a hard thud against my shoulder almost laid me out. When I straightened up, I saw that I'd collided with Pamela heading into her shop.

Or, more accurately, she'd collided with me.

"Sorry," she said disingenuously.

Where was this passive-aggressiveness coming from? I wondered. I tried for a diplomatic response. "No worries. Sometimes I get sidetracked and don't notice what's right in front of me."

"Is that supposed to be some sort of metaphor?" she said with a scowl.

I frowned. We obviously needed to address whatever was going on here. "Pamela, I thought we'd left things on good terms, but you seem stirred up. What's going on?"

"Nothing." A moment's silence. "You heard Raul and Lynn cleared me?"

"I did. I'm happy for you."

"But you're not convinced they should have, are you?"

"Raul and Lynn are two of the smartest people I've

met. I defer to their judgment."

A few more seconds ticked by. Pamela wrapped her arms around herself and shuffled from one foot to the other. I saw tears pooled in her eyes. "I hear Brian's still in a coma."

"Let's go inside," I said.

I took her arm and led her into her shop. As soon as the door closed behind us, she began sobbing. I was at a loss. Yesterday, she'd come across as angry but composed, and now she was a puddle of emotions. Awkwardly, I put my arms around her. By the time she pulled away, my shoulder was wet.

I went behind the counter, grabbed a handful of tissues, and tucked them in her hand. She swiped her cheeks and her nose. "Sorry about that."

"Nothing to apologize for," I said.

"I've been…well, having a rough time lately."

"I can understand that." I hesitated, but plunged forward. "Pamela, it's none of my business, but…are you in love with Brian?"

She barked a bitter laugh and wiped her nose again. "I wouldn't call my feelings love. Nothing as pure as that. I know what kind of man he is. He's no different than he's always been. But last year, I ran into him in Boulder, and he…well, he showed interest in me. Asked me out. We started seeing each other on and off. He paid attention to me, complimented me, listened to me. No one has done that in a very long time."

Her eyes drifted to the wall, and she gazed into the distance. "I hoped to build a relationship, hoped I might change him into a man I could love. Deep down, I knew that wouldn't happen. I realized he was using me. But I tried to convince myself we might make a go of it. So, when he ghosted me…"

She squeezed her eyes shut, fighting off another round of tears. "I'm just so lonely, Callie. It's like Noah's ark around here. Everyone is paired up. Everyone except me.

And I'm getting old. I don't want to die alone."

I chewed the inside of my cheek, wondering how to respond. My therapist would cite this as a prime example of catastrophizing. But in my experience, telling someone they're overreacting when they're in the throes of it only makes things worse. So instead of trying to pump out words of wisdom, I said what I felt. "I don't know what I can say that will help, Pamela. But I'm here for you. And I'm listening."

She turned her bleary eyes to me, as if assessing my sincerity. Then she nodded. Her eyes were glistening, but she appeared to be over the worst of it.

The door opened behind Pamela, and Willie Wright, the town's realtor and Chamber of Commerce president, strolled inside.

"Oh, Callie, I wasn't expecting to find you here." He looked at Pamela's back. "Am I interrupting?"

"No, it's fine, Willie." Pamela turned to face him. Her eyes were red and her cheeks splotchy, but when she smiled, it was barely noticeable. "I'm not open yet, though, and I'm running a little behind. I haven't even started on today's fudge."

He shuffled his feet. "Well, I'm not here as a customer. I was just passing by on my way to Rocky Mountain High and noticed your light on. I…um…wanted to see if I could bring you some coffee. Or anything."

Well, that was sweet. Pamela flushed and looked at him like she'd never seen him before. Could this be the beginning of a beautiful friendship? Maybe the old adage was true—there was someone out there for everyone.

"Listen, I need to get to the studio," I said, edging past them to the door. "I'll talk to you later, okay, Pamela?"

She nodded absently, and I hurried out the door, realizing as I left that I'd edged closer to Raul and Lynn's conclusion: I didn't think Pamela had poisoned Brian, either.

32

I worked in my office until Ethan got to the studio at nine-thirty. He reassured me he didn't mind handling the gallery until Banner and Braden arrived, so I headed off on my mission. I had news to share with Raul and Lynn—and I hoped they'd reciprocate.

At the end of Evergreen Way, I turned left toward the lower village. A handful of skiers schussed through the sunshine radiating off Mt. O'Connell's slope. Today was bright, with temperatures predicted to top out in the low forties, but the forecast warned of a late-season snowstorm headed our direction tomorrow. It wasn't supposed to be a blizzard, but even so, I hoped it would hold off until evening. I had a photo shoot scheduled for early afternoon tomorrow with a darling out-of-town family, and I didn't want to cancel.

As I braked at a four-way stop in front of Pinkerton's Place, I noticed the grocer sweeping the front stoop. I smiled and waved, and Mr. Pinkerton responded with his permanent scowl. But I saw the corner of his mouth twitch. Progress. The old curmudgeon was developing a soft spot for me.

Next, I passed the Ice Zone. Again, my wrist throbbed. Someday, perhaps, I'd drive by the arena without experiencing flashbacks. I wondered again about Trent Wallace. Could he be responsible for poisoning Brian? I didn't want to suspect the likable man, but I also couldn't dismiss him. Not yet.

Another left turn took me through the village's most upscale neighborhood, with its oversized chalets, party-sized hot tubs, wrap-around decks, and luscious mountain views. I drove past Kimberly and Parker's house, followed by the Ratliff home, where Braden and Banner had lived on their own for most of the past two years. Until Brian had returned, toting a new wife and her…whatever Weston was.

Five minutes later, I pulled into a parking spot near the town hall. I paused to ask the spirits to fill me with goodwill and soften my words. On occasion, my mother mentioned my tendency to come across as bullheaded and demanding. "Remember, dear, you catch more flies with honey than vinegar," she often told me.

Unfortunately, my stockpile of honey was usually in short supply.

When I entered the station, Marilyn looked up from her desk. "Morning, Callie. Are they expecting you?"

I gave her a sheepish smile. "Not exactly, but I have some important information for them. They'll want to hear it."

She raised an eyebrow, having listened to my song and dance more than once. "They've been holed up in Raul's office all morning. I doubt they want to be disturbed."

Then Frank appeared and headed toward me, a lopsided grin on his face. "Hello, stranger. Haven't seen you in at least twenty-four hours. Worried you might have turned in your Sherlock Holmes hat. Or sold it to that new spitfire reporter."

I grinned. Frank had been like an uncle to me since I was a child. He adored me, and the feeling was mutual. I also knew his affection for me wouldn't prevent him from kicking me out if it was best for a case.

"Just here to do my civic duty, Chief," I said with a little salute. "I've come across something that might be of value to you."

"That so? Well, you've caught me in a curious frame of mind. Let's go back and talk about it with my detectives."

He led the way down the hall to the third door on the

right—Raul's tiny office. Raul's head was bent over a stack of papers on his desk. Across from him, Lynn flipped through a file.

"Hey, everyone, look what the cat dragged in," Frank said.

"Carl would resent that," I said.

"Please convey my humble apologies for my faux pas when you see him next."

He leaned against a wall and gestured to the only other empty seat. Raul sighed. "Don't tell me. She's uncovered some juicy clue that'll solve our case for us."

Lynn tossed the file onto the desk, looking weary. "At this point, I'd settle for the win, however we get it."

"Things aren't progressing well?" I asked.

Raul ran a hand through his wavy black hair. "Never mind our progress."

"Or lack thereof," Lynn muttered.

Raul leaned back and laced his hands behind his head. "All right, you might as well fill us in."

I hesitated, looking at him hopefully. "Okay, but if I share my news, will I get something in return?"

He rolled his eyes. "What do you want, a reward?"

"Of course not. I want information."

Raul started to argue, but Lynn cut him off. "Honestly, Raul, what could it hurt?"

The two detectives glanced at Frank, who shrugged. "A fresh set of eyes might be what we need." He looked at me. "You'll have to promise to keep whatever you hear confidential, though."

"Absolutely," I said. "I'm the soul of discretion."

"Can we get on with this?" Raul asked.

"Sure," I said. "Let me start with this: my money is on Desiree Bouton."

I spent the next five minutes telling my now well-worn story about Desiree and Weston and their unsibling-like embrace. When I finished, I folded my hands and waited for their gratitude and accolades.

Instead, Raul narrowed his eyes. "One question. How did you happen to be close enough to witness this little entanglement? You know, considering the restraining order and all."

The three of them stared at me, and I flinched under their gaze. Maybe I hadn't completely thought this through. But sometimes, the best defense was a sense of humor. "Well, I can assure you I wasn't within a hundred yards of that bed."

No laughter, no chuckles, not a single smirk. I crossed my arms and stared right back at Raul. "My purely accidental peek into their personal activities may have broken your case. Honestly, you could just say thank you."

"Broken the case? How do you figure?"

I turned up my palms. "It's obvious. Desiree has secrets. Her relationship with her not-brother is the tip of the iceberg. Why else would she be so determined to keep me at arm's length?"

"Maybe she just doesn't like you," Raul said.

I ignored him and turned to Lynn. "I mean, are she and Brian even married? We only have her word for it."

Lynn shook her head. "We haven't been sitting around twiddling our thumbs, Callie. We interviewed the woman, and she provided us with a copy of the marriage license."

"Oh," I said. "Well, did you make sure it was legitimate?"

She sighed. "The license was issued out of state. We've requested records, and the info should be forthcoming soon. Are you satisfied that we're capable of conducting an investigation?"

I huffed. She was sounding like Raul.

Frank cleared his throat. "I think we can all agree Desiree Bouton is a top suspect. But let's talk about anyone else we need to be considering."

They looked at me. "Well, I would have said Pamela Ashton, but she told me you'd cleared her."

"She's not cleared," Lynn said. "Everyone stays on our list until this case is solved. But she's definitely on the periphery."

"Why's that?" I had to ask. I couldn't let on that Monika had already given me the details. Otherwise, I'd risk compromising her source.

"When we went through Brian's text history," Lynn said, "we found a conversation time-stamped Saturday morning indicating her desire to renew their relationship. It was obvious she didn't know at the time that Brian was married. And he didn't mention it. In fact, he encouraged her interest in a rather…graphic way."

I stroked my chin, pretending to process this news. "What about the fudge?"

"What about it?" Raul asked.

"I heard the fudge was the source of the poison. Wouldn't that point to Pamela?"

Lynn shook her head. "We're speculating someone used a Fudge Factory box but replaced the contents with their own version—one that included poison."

I reached into my bag and pulled out my legal pad, skimming the names. "Well, if you're sure Pamela didn't do it, what about Coach Montgomery? I assume you've already looked into him."

Raul and Lynn glanced at each other, obviously surprised I knew about Brian's former boss.

"There was friction between them," I continued. "Brian made a pass at the coach's wife in front of the team."

"There's a bit more to it than that," Lynn said. "Brian threatened to sue his boss and the university for wrongful termination. The coach was furious, and not shy about expressing it in his texts." She reopened her file folder and shuffled through the pages. "Here we go. 'I'll see you in a shallow grave before you get one red cent out of me, you…' You can imagine the series of expletives for yourself."

"Stupid thing to put in writing," I said. "But it sounds more like a tantrum than premeditation. If Brian had gotten his brains bashed in, we'd be looking hard at Coach Montgomery. But sending a batch of poison fudge?"

"Exactly," Raul said. "When we interviewed him, I didn't get a murderous villain vibe."

"Vibes don't constitute evidence," Lynn said.

"That's why we're looking for something more concrete," Frank interjected. "We're having Montgomery's phone records analyzed to see if he pinged off any nearby cell towers. Should have answers in the next day or so."

"Until then, we're still looking at a few others," Lynn said.

"Like who?" I asked.

"Brian had confrontations with several guests at the wedding," Raul said. "Trent, Parker, Sam."

Before I could protest, he held up a hand. "Don't go into a tizzy. Sam's no more of a suspect than you are."

"Or you," I pointed out. "I seem to remember more than one altercation between you and Brian."

"She's got you there, Sanchez." Frank grinned. Raul simply shook his head.

"So, is that everyone?" I asked, knowing full well it wasn't. A look like storm clouds passed between the three of them. I waited. It fell to Frank to say it aloud. "Callie, we can't clear the twins yet. At least, not Braden."

"But it sounded like the interviews went well," I said, trying not to whine. *Honey*, I reminded myself. *Flies and honey.*

"Just because we didn't charge Braden doesn't mean he's no longer a person of interest," Raul said. "You heard him arguing with his father at the wedding."

"And then there are the chemicals we found in his bedroom," Lynn said.

"They were for a home darkroom," I said, my resolve

to stay calm slipping. "Also, fathers and sons argue all the time. You don't know Braden like I do. The kid doesn't have it in him. Besides, he's devastated about his father's condition. He wouldn't—"

Suddenly, something clicked in my mind. "Wait, you found something else on Brian's phone, didn't you?"

Another look passed between them. "Might as well show her," Frank said.

Lynn pulled a sheet of paper from the folder, passing it to me. "This is a text conversation between Braden and Brian. Dated Thursday, three days before the coma."

As I skimmed the page, my heart rose to my throat. I went back and read it again, more slowly this time. No doubt about it, this was damaging.

The texts began with Braden berating his father for bringing Desiree into their home. The names he called her made "blond bimbo" sound like a compliment. Brian responded with equal venom, referring to Braden as a "sissy punk" and telling him to either shape up or ship out.

If you can't show Desiree and me the respect we deserve, pack your things.

Braden replied: *I AM showing you the respect you deserve, you (expletive).*

That's it. You're outta here. You got one week to find someplace else to live.

My shoulders drooped. Braden hadn't breathed a word of this to me. It was difficult to run defense when you had no idea what was coming.

"Listen," I said, "I understand you have to investigate him. But please, promise me you won't focus on Braden at the expense of other suspects. Keep looking at Desiree. I'm begging you. As Brian's wife, she's the one with the most to gain if he dies."

Raul spoke in a gentle voice, which almost made things worse. "Unless, as you said earlier, the two of them aren't married after all. If that's true, the twins would be Brian's heirs by default. They'd be the ones to benefit from Brian's death."

The implication was too much. I sprang to my feet. "Neither of those boys tried to kill their father. I'd stake my life on it. If you want answers, check into Desiree."

I stalked out of the office. None of them came after me.

As I passed through the reception area, I spotted Officer Tollison at his desk. When he saw me, his cheeks turned pink and he dropped his eyes, pretending to be immersed in paperwork. Apparently, I'd guessed right about Monika's source at the police department.

At least I'd solved one mystery. But the bigger one hung over my head like an axe.

33

I sat in the car, waiting for my hands to stop shaking enough to enable me to drive safely. The reasonable side of me knew I couldn't blame the cops for suspecting Braden. Between the argument at the wedding and the newly revealed texts, his antagonism toward his father was public record. They had no choice.

That made it even more incumbent on me to prove Braden's innocence. And that meant proving someone else guilty.

A quick call to Mrs. Finney showed that wouldn't be as easy as I hoped.

"Good morning, dear," Mrs. Finney answered, her voice chipper.

"Hi, Mrs. Finney. I was wondering what you…or rather, your colleague, had come up with regarding Desiree's background."

She clucked her tongue. "Contrary to popular belief, Callahan, I don't hold The Man's ear. When I whisper, answers aren't immediately forthcoming. There's a process, especially now that I'm retired. Give me a little time, dear."

I tamped down my impatience, said goodbye, and dialed Monika. "Have you uncovered any information about Desiree?"

"Callie, I already told you I'm on the school board assignment." She sounded distracted. "I've spent the entire morning prepping. After the meeting, I'll have to write the story, submit it to Phil, and complete any edits. Don't you remember how this works?"

"Okay, but it's a school board meeting. What you and

I are chasing is important. I need—"

"Are you implying that keeping my job ranks low on your priority list?"

"No, that's not it. But if Tonya were here—"

"Well, she's not. Phil is in charge, and I'm in no position to refuse his assignment. I'll talk to you when I'm done."

She hung up. I tapped my fingers on the steering wheel. What was my next move? I couldn't go near Desiree, not if I wanted to stay out of trouble myself. Pamela had been cleared, more or less. I doubted I'd get anything else from Trent. There was nothing to be gained by driving down to Boulder to spy on Brian's former boss. And I couldn't question Brian himself. I was stymied.

Nothing left to do but wait. And I didn't do waiting well. Work would have to serve as my distraction. I took off for Sundance Studio.

***

When I entered the gallery, Braden was bent over the computer behind the sales counter, while Banner leaned against a nearby wall, staring at his phone. There were no customers in sight. No surprise. Wednesdays were often a bit slow.

Banner looked up at the sound of my footsteps, but Braden stayed focused on the computer. "Been like this all day?" I asked.

"Nope. This is actually the first break we've had," Banner said.

I looked at my watch. Eleven. "Where's Ethan?"

Banner jerked his chin toward the office. "Interviewing. Second one of the day. He has two more this afternoon."

I'd forgotten my partner was on a quest to hire a new employee. We'd been talking about it for months, but I'd been hesitant. Aside from the twins, our last employee hadn't exactly worked out—and that was an under-statement.

Ethan was insistent, though. Running the gallery was getting to be too much for the two of us, even with the boys working part-time. Ethan wanted a full-time employee hired and trained before the busy summer season.

Banner tucked his phone in his pocket. "Listen, Callie, we were wondering…Would it be okay if we left early today? A buddy of ours got tickets to the Avalanche game tonight. He wants to leave here at five, and Braden and I were hoping to visit Dad before we go. If it's all right with you, we'd need to take off about two."

"Sure. I have nothing scheduled for this afternoon."

"Thanks," he said, but he seemed subdued.

I glanced at Braden, who hadn't made eye contact with me since I'd arrived. "Everything okay, guys?"

He still didn't meet my eyes. "Yup. As long as it's not busy, do you mind if I work in the computer lab? I'd like to go through the digital shots from the wedding."

"I think it's a great idea," I said. He got up and left the room without another word.

When his footsteps had receded down the hallway, I looked at Banner. "What's up with your brother?"

He shook his head. "Our father is in a coma. Some people believe Braden put him there. What do you think is up with him?" He caught himself. "Sorry, Callie. I'm just bummed. Braden's been mopey all morning, and he won't talk to me about it. Maybe you could try. Sometimes he'll open up to you."

"Of course," I said. "As soon as Ethan finishes the interview, I'll go to the lab. In the meantime, you're okay, right? Do you want to talk?"

The door opened, and a cluster of giggling women entered. "I'm fine," Banner said with a sigh, and he walked over to greet them.

***

A few minutes later, Ethan emerged from the office, accompanied by a perky woman in her twenties. He hurried her out of the gallery and clucked his tongue as he made his way over to me. "Not a good fit. This may have been the first time she'd seen a photo that wasn't a selfie."

I laughed. "Good help is hard to find."

"Yet I persevere."

"Better you than me."

He said he was hopeful about the two afternoon interviews, but I remained unconvinced. Still, I'd defer to his judgment. I was our partnership's creative force, and he was in charge of the business end. We consulted on everything, but there was a reason I'd asked him to be my partner. I wasn't about to interfere.

I told him I'd be in the computer lab helping Braden with wedding photos. "Text if you need us. By the way, the twins are leaving at two, so I'll handling customer service while you're finding us the next great employee."

I trotted off down the hall. In the lab, Braden sat in front of an oversized monitor and shuffled through a digital photo album. I took the chair next to his and watched as he cropped, color corrected, and resized photos, impressed yet again by how quickly his skills had developed.

He slid his eyes to me but said nothing. I moved my chair a little closer. "Talk to me," I said gently.

His fingers froze on the computer mouse. "There's just a lot going on. I'm a little stressed. No big deal."

"Braden, I know it's difficult to open up. Trust me, I get it. But it's a lot easier than pushing everyone away and trying to fight your way through life alone. Please, let me help."

He swallowed hard. "I...I heard you went to see Raul and Lynn this morning."

I nodded, but stayed quiet.

"Did they…tell you about the texts?"

His voice caught, and I immediately understood. He'd been hoping I wouldn't find out about the texts between him and his dad. I didn't want to compound his embarrassment, but I owed him the truth.

"They showed me a transcript. I can only imagine how much your father's words must have hurt you."

He turned his head away. I waited.

"I know it looks bad, Callie. But I swear, I didn't hurt my dad. You have to believe me."

"I do, Braden. My faith in you hasn't wavered. That's one thing you never have to worry about."

He stifled a sniffle and turned away. Vulnerability came hard to me, too, so I tried to lighten the mood.

"So," I said, "hockey game tonight, huh?"

Smooth, Callie. Braden managed a weak smile. "Yeah, Pascal won free tickets off some radio contest."

"Which one is Pascal?"

"Oh, you remember him. He's the one who took off his shirt and danced in front of the gallery window that time. You almost gagged."

I groaned. "The one who pressed his belly against the glass? Ugh. I can only imagine the shenanigans you guys will get up to. Promise me you'll keep your shirts on."

He laughed. Then his smile faded. "Thanks, Callie. Everything you're doing for us…it means a lot. We may not say it right, but we both feel the same."

"And I may not say it right, either, but the two of you are very important to me. You'll always have me in your corner." I stood up and brushed my hands together. "Enough sentimentality. If you're leaving early, you'd best get some work done. Our coming home party for Tonya and David is only a week and a half away, and this slide show isn't going to finish itself."

He bent back to the screen. "I'll be ready. You don't need to worry about me."

34

After an uneventful afternoon and evening, capped off by a decent night's sleep, I sat at the kitchen table the next morning, nursing a cup of coffee as I read through Monika's school board story in my online copy of the *Rock Creek Gazette*. As she'd predicted, the content wasn't riveting—a group of townspeople deciding whether to spend budget money on textbooks or sports equipment. Still, she'd crafted a readable and informative story. It was the first piece of hers I'd read, and it confirmed what I'd already suspected—the girl had writing chops.

Woody's ears rose at the sound of footsteps on the stairs. I, too, was surprised. It wasn't quite seven-thirty, and the boys couldn't have gotten back from the game before midnight. Besides, it was spring break, meaning no classes, and Thursdays were their day off work.

The twins plodded into the kitchen, looking a little worse for the wear and making gross boy noises.

"Coffee?" I translated their grunts into affirmatives and poured them each a cup as they slumped into chairs.

"Thanks," Banner mumbled, grimacing as the hot liquid touched his lips.

Braden, always the more cautious of the two, blew on his coffee before sampling it.

"You're up early," I said, stating the obvious.

"Just saying good morning before you left," Banner said.

"We'll go back to bed in a few minutes," Braden added.

"Better go easy on the coffee, then."

"Caffeine doesn't keep us from sleeping," Banner said.

They were quiet, eyes drooping, and I feared they were about to prove the point by dozing off at the table. "Sam and I watched the game," I said. "We saw some shirtless hooligans, but you two weren't among them."

They graced me with sleepy smiles. "Got the win," Braden said.

"Close game," Banner added.

Quite the conversationalists.

"How's your dad?" I asked tentatively.

Banner perked up. "Better than we expected."

My eyebrows lifted. "Has he regained consciousness?"

Braden shook his head. "Not yet. But the doctor said he's responding to stimuli, like a pinprick on his foot."

"Doc says that's a good sign," Banner said.

"I'm so happy to hear it," I said with sincerity. Much as I disliked Brian Ratliff, and especially the way he treated his sons, I hoped he made a full recovery—for their sakes. Who knew? Maybe a near-death experience would be what the man needed to turn his life around.

Hope springs eternal, as my mother would say.

"We didn't stay long," Braden said.

"Yeah, the bimbo showed up, so we hightailed it outta there."

Braden glanced at me and nudged his brother. "What?" Banner said. "Just telling it like it is." He took another sip of coffee. "We'll go back today. The nurse said if we call first, she'll tell us if the vulture is hovering."

"The vulture?" A small smile played at my lips.

"Yeah, you know about vultures," Banner said. "Just hanging around waiting for roadkill. Well, Desiree's not getting her claws into Dad. He's gonna wake up any day now. I feel it."

"I hope you're right," I said. We were quiet for a moment, lost in our thoughts. "I'd go with you to the hospital, but I have a photo shoot this afternoon."

"The Scanlon family?" Braden asked. I nodded. "Hope the snow holds off."

The three of us gazed out the window. The sky was robin's egg blue without a cloud in sight, but we'd all lived in Rock Creek Village long enough to know that could change in a heartbeat.

"Fingers crossed," I said.

A few minutes later, the boys took their empty cups to the sink and went back upstairs. As I loaded our mugs into the dishwasher, my cell rang. I glanced at the screen and smiled.

"Mrs. Finney," I said.

"Yes, dear, it's me. I have an update. Would you mind stopping by the Ice Zone on your way into town? Mr. Purdy and I are here for an early session."

Oh, goody. Another glimpse of Mrs. Finney in a bedazzled skate dress and Mr. Purdy in skintight pants. How could I resist?

I assured her I'd be there, and she suggested I invite "that sterling young reporter" to join us. When we hung up, I called Monika, who agreed to meet me at the rink in ten minutes. I scribbled a note to the boys, refilled the creatures' water bowls, ruffled their fur, and headed out.

***

I heard the beep of a horn as I got out of my car. Monika pulled into the parking space next to mine, and we walked together toward the Ice Zone entrance. She babbled on about the school board story, and I pretended to listen. Truth be told, I didn't miss those banal assignments one bit. I'd outgrown them about two years into my career and couldn't imagine how I'd ever survived them. Monika seemed energized, though. Ah, to be young and eager again.

When we reached the door, I said, "Before we go in, I have to warn you: what you're about to see…well, you won't be able to unsee it. It may stay with you for the rest of your life."

She stiffened. "What is it? Did something happen?"

I shook my head solemnly. "You'll have to experience it for yourself."

Without another word, I opened the door and gestured for her to follow me. We walked to the boards and stood scanning the rink. It didn't take long for me to spot our quarry. I nudged Monika and pointed.

Today, Mrs. Finney wore a violet mini dress with silver piping. The snug-fitting bodice sported a scandalously low-cut neckline, and the woman's ample bosom bulged at the seams. She skated like a gazelle toward Mr. Purdy, clad in yet another onesie pantsuit.

Mrs. Finney leapt into Mr. Purdy's outstretched hands. As he held her aloft, she spread her arms outward and crossed her feet at the ankles in what I now realized must be their signature move.

Monika's hand flew to her mouth. I snickered. "See? This image will haunt you forever."

We burst out laughing. Mrs. Finney, now back on solid ice, spun a circle around Mr. Purdy and curtsied. He responded with a deep bow.

"They're remarkably graceful," Monika whispered.

I nodded. "And agile."

"How old are they?"

I shrugged. "I've been trying to figure out Mrs. Finney's age for as long as I've known her. She won't tell, and her background is sealed up tighter than Dwayne Johnson's glutes. My best guess is that she's about my parents' age."

Mrs. Finney spotted us mid-spin. Ice flew from her skates as she ground to a halt. Then she glided toward us with Mr. Purdy close behind.

"Looking good out there, you two," I said. "I'm thinking that silver cup is yours for the taking."

Mr. Purdy looked pleased. "I believe you may be right."

"Let's not get ahead of ourselves, Sugarcube," Mrs. Finney said. "The fates don't favor unchecked egos."

"Very true, Dumpling. And may I suggest we consider that bit of wisdom for the coffee cups?"

She nodded and turned to Monika. "I read your story in the *Gazette*, my dear. You highlighted the important nuggets of an otherwise tedious meeting. Well done."

"Thanks. It was pretty easy to write. But to tell you the truth, I'm ready for something a little…well, meatier."

"Great segue, Grasshopper," I said. "Mrs. Finney, what have you learned?"

"Ah, yes. I think you'll find this interesting," she said. Then, to our horror and Mr. Purdy's apparent delight, she reached into the bodice of her skating dress, rummaged around in her cleavage, and retrieved a piece of paper. She held it out to me.

I wrinkled my nose as I held the paper gingerly between my finger and thumb. Mrs. Finney rolled her eyes. "It doesn't have cooties, dear."

"It's…damp," I said.

She folded her arms, further augmenting her hefty bosom. Beside her, Mr. Purdy smiled. "Of course it's damp," she said. "Mr. Purdy and I have been working up a sweat." I cringed again, and she put her hands on her sequined hips. "Oh, for heaven's sake, just read it."

I unfolded the paper. Monika peered over my shoulder at a list of names—five of them, to be exact. Mrs. Finney leaned on the boards and recited them from memory. "Birth name, Amy Templeton. First alias, Patricia Wooten. Next, she becomes Caroline Beale. Then Heidi Forsythe. Her most recent iteration, of course, is Desiree Bouton. There may be others, but these were the ones our contact could uncover for now."

I skimmed the details beside each name. The Templeton entry included a birthdate and location, high school graduation, and a few other insignificant facts. Only cursory information accompanied the next two names. There was a little more for Heidi Forsythe, including a brief employment history, but still not much to go on. "I was hoping for something more incriminating," I said. "Or at least more thorough."

Mrs. Finney's eyebrow shot up. "My friend at the Company…" Mr. Purdy cleared his throat, and she patted his arm. "*Our* friend at the Company is not in our employ, nor does he exist to do your bidding, Callahan. He's busy attending to a minor coup in South America. He'll dig deeper when he can. In the meantime…"

She gave Monika a pointed glance, and the reporter responded with barely concealed glee. "I'm on it! Now that I have these names to work with, hacking into Desiree's past will be a lot easier."

Mrs. Finney nodded. "I'm certain you're up to the task, dear."

Mr. Purdy cleared his throat. "Shall we get back to practice, Dumpling? Mustn't let the ice melt beneath stationary blades."

She gave him a tender smile. "Absolutely, Sugarcube." Her expression turned stern as she looked back at Monika and me. "Ladies, I trust you'll take care of business. It's time for the two of you to wrap up this investigation and pluck our boys out of the crosshairs. See to it."

35

While Mrs. Finney and her paramour sailed across the ice, Monika and I sat in the bleachers and discussed how to proceed in light of this new information.

"Phil said he won't assign me any more stories today," Monika said, "so I can start researching all these aliases."

"Sounds good. Let me take another look at that list first."

She handed the sweaty paper to me, and I skimmed the information again. The details about Heidi Forsythe generated a familiar niggle in the back of my skull. Some piece of the puzzle wanted my attention. I sensed it, but I couldn't yet get a fix on it.

"It says here Heidi worked as an adjunct professor at Prosper University," I mused. "Why does that school sound familiar?"

"Well, it's in Cheyenne," Monika said. "That's only a couple of hours from here. It makes sense you would have heard of it."

"Maybe," I said, but I had a feeling there was more to it. Was Prosper one of the colleges Elyse had considered before settling on the University of Boulder? Or…"Wait, did Brian coach there at some point?"

"Not ringing any bells, but I can check. Do you think it's important?"

I rolled my shoulders, trying to loosen the cogs in my brain. "Probably not. I may be searching for connections that don't even exist. But one thing I've learned is that the details I write off are the ones that come back to bite me."

Monika nodded and tapped a few words on her phone. "I'll check it out. This is all going to take me at least a few hours. How about if I call you this afternoon with an update?"

I glanced at my watch. Ten a.m. "I have a photo shoot at two, assuming the weather holds. It should last a few hours. We'll finish on the bridge behind the Knotty Pine. Why don't you meet me at the lodge at five for drinks?"

"Sure. I'd love that."

"Five o'clock, then. In the meantime, I'll call Raul and Lynn and fill them in on everything we've learned."

She made a face. "Um, Callie, can you hold off on that? Maybe let me do some research first?"

A battle played out in my head. On the one hand, I should inform the detectives about Desiree's aliases, right? On the other hand, I saw the determination in Monika's eyes. She wanted to figure this out for herself. I remembered that feeling—still experienced it myself occasionally.

Like right now.

I sighed. It wasn't as if we were hiding anything, not really. Raul and Lynn had access to the same information we did—might actually already possess it, in fact. At least, that's how I rationalized my decision.

"Okay," I said. "But we have to call them before the day is out."

"Of course," she said, her eyes gleaming. "Thank you, Callie."

As we gathered our things to leave, the door to the Ice Zone whooshed open and Trent ambled in, whistling a cheerful tune. As soon as he caught sight of me in the stands, the whistle died on his lips. He shoved his hands in his pockets and hurried toward his office without a backward glance.

"I don't think he likes you," Monika said.

I pulled on my gloves. "Quite the reporter's instincts." I paused. "Hey, Mon, where did Trent go to college?"

Her brow furrowed. "I'm not sure we ever heard. Why?"

"Remember how Brian mentioned beating him out for a spot on the college team?"

Her eyebrows flew up. "Prosper University?"

"I'm not sure. But it's worth looking into, don't you think?"

***

My plan had been to head straight to Sundance Studio after I left the rink, but as I passed the Knotty Pine, I decided to stop in for a quick chat with Dad. He'd likely have spoken to Frank today. Maybe I could wheedle some insider information out of him.

I stepped cautiously through the doors, camouflaging myself behind a potted plant and peering into the lobby to make sure Desiree wasn't around. No need to violate my restraining order at this point. There was no sign of her, but I still crept across the entry like a deer evading a hunter.

At the desk, Mr. Farmington looked up at me, amused. "In hiding?"

"Just trying to avoid Desiree and her…brother."

"Can't say I blame you," he said. "Strange pair, those two."

I cocked my head. "Why do you say that?"

"Well, I've only seen them a few times—always during happy hour. They load their plates and mugs and head back to their cabin. Never a word, or even a smile. Of course, with all that's going on with her husband, I guess I shouldn't expect them to be social butterflies."

He dropped his voice to a whisper. "That Weston character carries a distinctive odor. Every time he walks by, I fear I might get high myself."

I chuckled. "Now, Mr. Farmington. Why would you recognize that smell?"

"I was a high school teacher, remember?" He looked nostalgic. "Aside from that, I was a teenager in the sixties."

I tried to picture a young Mr. Farmington at Woodstock, jamming to the music and indulging in forbidden activities. That led to images of my parents at the same age. Then Mrs. Finney and Mr. Purdy. I had trouble imagining them all as young and carefree.

I wondered if Elyse and the twins—and Monika, for that matter—thought the same way about Sam and me.

The door slid open behind me, and a resort guest approached the desk. "I'll let you get back to work, Mr. Farmington. I'm just going to pop upstairs and say hi to my parents."

"You'll only find your mother there," he said. "Butch is out. Said he had a few errands to run."

So much for dragging information out of my father. Still, since I was here, I decided to visit with Mom for a few minutes.

I headed upstairs and followed the sound of Mom's humming into the kitchen. She was using a spatula to slide cookies off a baking sheet and onto a paper towel.

"Mmm," I said, reaching out to snatch one.

She smacked my hand. "These are not for you, Callahan. In fact, they're not for human consumption at all."

I squinted at the small cookies and realized they were shaped like little mice and miniature squirrels. "What are they?"

"Animal crackers, for actual animals. I found a recipe, and I'm making them for Woody, Carl, and little Terror."

I rolled my eyes. "As if the creatures aren't spoiled enough."

She laughed, then suddenly her eyes turned misty and a small smile flitted across her face.

I settled onto a stool at the island and rested my chin on my hands. "Penny for your thoughts."

Mom placed a new set of shaped dough onto the baking sheet and slid it into the oven. "Just reminiscing, darling." She smiled. "Do you have any idea why you call Woody and Carl your creatures?"

I considered the question. "Not really. It started when Woody and I first found each other. He was a puppy still, and I saw someone dump him out of a car and drive off. I scooped him up and took him back to my apartment in D.C. I remember cuddling him in my arms, and the word just popped into my head. 'You are the perfect little creature,' I told him. 'And now you're mine.' But I don't know where the thought came from."

"Well, I do. When you were a baby, I used to rock you every night before bed. I'd cradle you in my arms and gaze into your tiny face. My little Angelface. I'd say, 'You are the perfect little creature. And you're all mine.'"

I put a hand to my chest. "Oh, Mom. I don't remember that. But I guess somewhere in my subconscious, I do. It passed from your lips to mine."

She picked up a chunk of dough and began rolling it. "From my soul to yours."

I hopped off the stool and wrapped my arms around her, resting my head on her shoulder. "I'm not sure what I did to deserve you as my mother, but I'm the luckiest daughter in the world."

She wiped her hands on her apron and hugged me. Then she went to the refrigerator. "Those kind words have earned you a treat of your own."

"Human animal crackers?"

"Better, if I do say so myself." She pulled out a covered dish and pulled back a corner of the aluminum foil. "Chicken parmigiana with rigatoni. Leftovers from our dinner the other night. Your father said it was better than even Sam could prepare—though perhaps not Jamal."

I laughed even as my mouth watered. "And you're giving it to me?"

She tucked the aluminum foil back on top. "It'll make

a nice lunch. There's plenty for Ethan, too. Just heat it up in the microwave. I have some fresh Caesar salad as well, and a few cannolis."

She reached under the counter for a canvas bag and began packing it with dishes. The cooking gene wasn't one I'd inherited, so I gave silent thanks for the chefs in my life who kept me well-fed. Left to my own devices, I'd probably subsist, like Monika, on Spaghetti-Os and the Golden Arches.

"Thank you, Mom. And I'm certain Ethan sends his thanks, too." I glanced at my watch. "Speaking of, I should get back. I have a photo shoot this afternoon, and I need to finish some prep work."

"Hope the weather holds," she said. "They're saying this last snowstorm of the season might be a doozy."

I looked out the window and frowned. A few fluffy clouds drifted overhead, with a cluster of darker clouds lying in wait across the mountains.

Mom pulled out her phone. In Colorado, a weather app was as crucial to existence as a heater. "Temps are already dropping," she said. "Chance of precipitation starts around three, but it looks like the worst of it will hold off until later tonight. Your shoot should be okay."

I hoped so. At this point, I needed something to go right.

36

With the bag of food slung over my shoulder, I left the Knotty Pine, glancing at Cabin One on my way out. No sign of Desiree and her brother, but I didn't look too closely. I had no desire for a sequel to the scene I'd witnessed yesterday.

I tried to banish that image from my mind as I made the short drive to the studio. When I walked into the gallery, Ethan looked up from the computer, wearing a sardonic grin.

"Hmm. The face is familiar." He snapped his fingers. "Now I have it. The elusive Callahan Cassidy, rarely spotted in her native habitat."

"Ha ha. I'm so glad to bear witness to more of your comedy routine." I placed the insulated bag on the counter. "Perhaps you won't be so flippant when you get a glimpse of the gift I'm bearing. Lunch, courtesy of Maggie Cassidy."

He peeked in the bag and sniffed. "Your tardiness is forgiven. What's on the menu?"

As I began listing the culinary delights in his immediate future, Braden appeared at the arch separating the gallery from the back hall. "I thought I heard you come in."

"What are you doing here?" I asked. "It's your day off. I thought you were going back to bed."

"Couldn't sleep."

"Where's Banner?"

"He's the reason I couldn't sleep." He made an exaggerated snoring noise. "Besides, I wanted to work on the prints for Tonya and David's wedding album. As you reminded me yesterday, I only have a week and a half to get everything ready. I still have prints to finish, plus digital photos to select for the slide show. Then I need to assemble them into a video. I'm getting stressed."

"Welcome to the life of a professional photographer," I said. "Trust me, though, it'll all get done. I have a photo shoot this afternoon, and I'll need to spend a few hours tomorrow on those images. But after that, I'll pitch in on the darkroom work. The digital part won't be difficult. We can knock it all out in a few days." I noticed him eyeing the bag on the counter. "Want some lunch?"

Ethan held up a hand. "Hold on. I assume you're sacrificing your portion and not mine."

"You know my mother. There's plenty for all."

A young couple entered the gallery and began browsing. "I'll see to them," I said. "You two take the first lunch shift."

"Don't have to ask me twice," Ethan said. He snatched the bag and hurried toward the kitchen with Braden hot on his heels.

"Save some for me," I called after them. I walked over and introduced myself to the customers and, twenty minutes later, rang up a substantial sale.

Ethan and Braden returned from their lunch breaks wearing enormous smiles. I microwaved my chicken and ate with gusto, topping off the meal with a crunchy, creamy, chocolate chip cannoli. I only hoped I'd be able to keep my pants buttoned during the photo shoot.

Just before two, the family arrived: a husband and wife in their mid-thirties and three rambunctious little boys with unruly, straw-colored hair. The oldest declared he was eight and his brothers were six and three. While I chatted with the parents, the three boys raced each other around the gallery, jumping and hollering and making me simultaneously wish I'd had children and glad I hadn't.

We began with a few formal photos in my portrait studio, after which we drove our respective vehicles to the park to begin the outdoor portion of the shoot. The temperature had dropped into the thirties, and as the family hailed from Arizona, they were unaccustomed to the cold. It didn't bother the boys, who'd have run around in their boxers if permitted. The parents weren't quite as enthusiastic, but they were troupers, shrugging out of their coats for however long a portrait took and pulling them back on tight between shots. I situated them by the lake and on the playground, with mountain backdrops and forest settings.

Last, we drove to the Knotty Pine and made our way to the Rock Creek Bridge leading to the trail behind the lodge. By this time, the gray clouds that had clustered earlier in the distance dropped over the village like a puffy wool blanket. Fat flakes of snow sifted from their folds, leading to squeals of delight from the boys.

I arranged the family on the bridge with the creek bubbling across patches of thin ice below them, and the snow-capped mountains rising behind them. With its reflective nature, snow created numerous challenges for photographers, so I snapped a range of f-stops to be sure I captured the right exposure, occasionally adding a filter for variety. Once I'd finished with the children, they raced off the bridge and threw themselves on the ground, sweeping their arms and legs to make snow angels in the light dusting. Those made for some nice candid shots I knew the parents would treasure. Then I took a few photos of the husband and wife gazing into each other's eyes.

When our session concluded, the parents shooed the boys toward the parking lot. My watch said I had fifteen minutes before my meeting with Monika. Looking around at the landscape, dazzling in the falling snow, I couldn't resist capturing the scene.

After a half dozen shots, I called it a day. As I tucked my camera into its protective case, Pamela Ashton and Willie Wright strode off the trail and onto the bridge, fresh from a hike. I grinned. Were they edging toward couplehood? I'd always thought of Willie as kind of a doofus, but maybe that was just what Pamela needed. A doofus was a definite upgrade from a jerk.

"Hey, Callie," Pamela said. She slung her foot on the bottom rung of the bridge to stretch her quads. Willie echoed her greeting and mimicked her move.

"Hi, you two. Out for a hike?"

"Three miles," Willie said with pride.

"Good for you." I gestured to the sky. "Looks like you got back in the nick of time. It's about to—"

A cracking sound from above interrupted me, followed by what sounded like a muffled scream. The three of us swiveled our heads and craned our necks as a boulder hurled from the mountain overlook to the left of the creek. It landed hard about a hundred feet away, then rolled and bounced down the slope.

But wait. When the boulder crashed to a stop against the trunk of a pine tree, I saw that what had tumbled down the craggy mountainside wasn't a rock at all.

It was a human.

Pamela's hand flew to her mouth. Willie gasped. I quickly shook myself out of my momentary stupor. "Pamela, call 9-1-1," I said. She nodded and reached in her pocket for her phone.

I turned to Willie. "Run to the lodge and get my father." He dashed away, moving faster than I would have thought possible.

Then I scrambled up the slope to render aid, my feet slipping in the wet snow. As I drew closer, I started to make out details. The figure was a woman, and she'd landed headfirst against the tree. Her face was turned away from me, but I saw a mane of blond hair. A puff coat covered her slender figure. Blood had pooled in the snow around her and splattered across the tree trunk. She couldn't possibly have survived the fall.

Still, I had to be certain. I dropped to my knees beside the woman and placed a finger to her neck. Nothing.

I moved my finger a half inch one way, then the other.

Still nothing.

When I looked back at Pamela, I shook my head. She nodded gravely.

Then I rolled the woman onto her back, harboring one last bit of hope that she might somehow be revived.

That's when I realized whose broken body lay before me—Desiree Bouton.

37

I twisted into sitting position and curled my arms around my shins. Moisture from the thin layer of snow seeped through the seat of my jeans. The scent of pine that whisked past on a gust of wind couldn't entirely mask the coppery odor of blood. I pulled my legs tighter to my chest. A quick glance at Desiree's body and I turned away again, unwilling to look at her wide, unseeing eyes a single moment more. I rested my head on my knees, trying not to think at all.

Then came the sound of footsteps pounding on the wooden boards of the bridge. I heard Pamela call out, "Braden?" and my head shot up.

The boy hesitated for a split second, looking from Pamela to me. I scrambled to my feet. "Braden? What are you doing here?"

He took off at full speed then, running off the bridge and down the path past the cabins, finally veering into the copse of trees.

As soon as Braden had disappeared from sight, I saw my father running toward me from the lodge with Willie behind. Dad sprinted up the slope and skidded to a halt beside the body. He bent to check Desiree's pulse, just as I had.

"It's no use," I said. "She's gone."

He stood and pulled me into his chest. "What happened?"

I wriggled out of his grasp and pointed to the rock outcropping that marked the scenic overlook. About ten stories above the creek, it was a place where hikers could bask in a panoramic view of Rock Creek Village and the valley to the south.

"She came from up there. I thought she was a boulder at first..."

He squinted upward through the snow. "They installed a railing at the edge of the overlook years ago. Hard to believe she'd fall over it by accident."

Sirens wailed from the parking lot, and Dad took my arm and steered me toward the bridge. "Shouldn't we stay with her?" I looked over my shoulder at Desiree, lying still and alone.

"Nothing we can do for her, Sundance. Best if we get off the mountain so the medics have room to maneuver."

I trudged beside him, grateful for his presence, for the comfort of his hand on my arm. The shakes were beginning, the result of adrenaline and cold and trauma. Dad's steadfastness helped me stay calm.

Pamela stood near the end of the bridge, her face so pale it gave her a ghostly quality. Willie was beside her, their shoulders touching. At the other end of the bridge, a crowd had begun to gather—looky-loos, some with phones lifted to document the scene for their social media feeds. A flicker of movement to the left caught my eye. Through the falling snow, I noticed Weston on the porch of Cabin One. He saw me looking at him and hurried back inside.

Then Monika jostled her way through the crowd, looking a little frantic. "Callie, are you okay?" she asked breathlessly.

"I'm fine," I said. "But Desiree Bouton can't say the same."

***

Moments later, two paramedics appeared, their gear bags bobbing as they trotted across the bridge—Maddie and Roland, who had tended to my broken wrist last year at the Ice Zone. Dad directed them toward Desiree's body. Officers Hardesty and Tollison showed up just after that and spoke to the small crowd, which then began to disperse. We spotted a cowboy hat, indicating the arrival of Chief Frank Laramie. He calmly made his way toward us, stopping to say a few words to Pamela and Willie and point them to the lodge. Officer Hardesty led them away to wait inside.

When Frank reached Dad and me, he rocked back on his boots and looked toward Desiree's body. "Fill me in," he said grimly.

"It's Desiree Bouton," Dad said. "Callie witnessed her fall from the overlook. Pamela and Willie saw it, too."

"Accident?" Frank asked.

Dad shrugged. "Could be, I suppose. Though there's a railing…"

He trailed off, and Frank nodded.

I looked toward the parking lot for the two people I'd expected to see by now. "Where are Raul and Lynn?"

"They're on the way," Frank said cryptically.

"What's taking them so long?"

He hesitated, then turned to Monika. "Ms. Schiff, I'm not issuing any statements. Why don't you run along? I'll call when we have something to share with the press."

I winced. Telling a reporter to run along was like throwing gasoline on a smoldering fire. Monika's shoulders tensed. Her cheeks reddened. "Thank you, Chief, but I'll stay put. I have the right to—"

She was interrupted by the ping of her cell, indicating an incoming text. She skimmed the message and glanced up with shining eyes. "There's something I need to attend to. I'll check in soon."

I studied her, trying to transmit an unspoken question. *What could be more urgent than a dead body?* She shook her head and hurried to the parking lot.

I turned back to Frank. "Now that the press has left, will you tell us where Raul and Lynn are?"

"At the hospital in Pine Haven. They should be here in

twenty minutes or so."

"The hospital? Is Brian…?"

"He's alive," Frank said. "He's come out of the coma."

***

Half an hour later, we waited in the warmth of the lodge. Pamela and Willie huddled together on a couch facing the fireplace. Dad and I sat nearby in large leather armchairs. Mom fussed over me, draping an afghan over my legs and plying me with snacks from the buffet. I asked for wine, but she brought me hot cider instead, giving me a look that told me not to bother arguing. When resort guests approached, hoping for the inside scoop, she shooed them off in a friendly but nonnegotiable way.

I couldn't stop picturing Braden running from the trail. *What had he been doing up there?* I searched in vain for an innocent reason that he'd run away from the scene as he had. I had to be missing something. If only I could talk to him. But when I tried calling, he didn't answer. My anxiety level began to spike, and my hands trembled as I lifted the cider mug to my lips.

I'd defended the boy so hard. *Surely I hadn't been wrong about him…*A sliver of doubt began worming its way into my mind.

Then I thought of the Braden I'd come to know these past two years—the photographer, the brother, the friend—and I forced the doubts away. *No. Absolutely not.* I had to trust my gut on this one, and it was telling me Braden couldn't be responsible for any of this. There had to be another explanation.

Still, I couldn't keep this information to myself. For one thing, Pamela was sure to tell the detectives Braden had been on the scene. Even if she didn't, concealing the information ultimately wouldn't help Braden. It was time to come clean.

"Dad," I whispered, "I need to tell you something."

He caught the expression on my face, the worry in my voice, and leaned forward. I spoke low, in case of inquisitive ears that might be hovering nearby. When I finished, Dad sat back and rubbed a hand across his face.

He thought for a moment and had just opened his mouth to speak when the front door slid open. We looked toward it, anticipating Frank, Raul, and Lynn. Instead, the professors, the ones who called themselves philosophers, swaggered inside, swirling a trail of snow across the threshold. They swarmed toward us like bees, not even trying to mask their macabre interest.

"We saw the ambulance," Scott said. "What happened?"

Mom delivered her well-rehearsed response. "We've had an unfortunate incident behind the property. That's all we're able to tell you. We'll make more information available as we are permitted."

She used her best don't-mess-with-me, English-teacher voice, but it held little sway over the college professors. They moved past her, undeterred.

Dad stood up and blocked them. His voice was low but fierce. "As my wife said, we're not free to discuss details. Please step away."

The expression on his face would have stopped most people in their tracks, but not this group. "We're paying guests," Bernard said. "We have a right to be here."

"There's plenty of room at the inn, as the saying goes," Dad said. "We have lots of open seating on the other side of the lobby. The game room is available, too, as is the media room, if you'd like to watch a movie. Feel free to help yourselves to the buffet. I'm told the mulled wine is especially good this evening. All we're asking is that you respect the delicacy of our current situation."

"Humph," Judith said. "I hope you're not expecting a positive review on Yelp." She turned to the men in the group. "This entire backwoods village is wretched."

"Oh, I don't know," Scott said, rubbing his hands together. "This could serve as a fantastic topic for debate."

"Well, I'm with Judith on this one," Bernard said. "I'm glad this is our last night here."

Jerry caught my eye and grinned. "In my opinion, Rock Creek Village offers a lot of amenities, including some rather stimulating scenery." He gave me a suggestive wink and joined his friends as they shuffled toward the buffet table.

Dad turned back to me, but before we could resume our conversation, the door swooshed open again. Frank spotted us and headed over.

"Raul and Lynn are here," he said. "They'd like all four witnesses to join them outside."

38

The four of us got our coats and followed the Chief out the door. No sign of the ambulance. I hadn't heard it leave, but there'd been no need for a siren.

Snow continued to fall, spreading like a sequined bridal veil across the path. Our shoes crunched as we walked across it. Dusk had settled, with darkness riding its coattails. The snow and the wind would make it too difficult to set up lights on the overlook, so the police wouldn't have much time before they'd have to suspend the investigation for the night. A sense of urgency hung in the air, superseding the scene's apparent peacefulness.

Footsteps, heavy and hurried, broke the silence. We swiveled to see Sam striding from the parking lot, his face determined. Two young officers—rookies, I surmised—were positioned at the start of the path leading from the lodge to the bridge. They'd likely been instructed to keep anyone from passing.

I didn't envy them the coming encounter.

After a few seconds of raised voices, Dad had a word with Frank, who hollered to the officers to let Sam by. Without a backward glance, Sam brushed past officers and came to my side, wrapping an arm around me.

"Are you okay?" he whispered into my hair.

"Better now that you're here," I said, leaning into him.

We waited near the bridge as Raul and Lynn descended the slope. Bright yellow crime scene tape looped around the tree where Desiree's body had been. Officers Hardesty and Tollison came down the trail from the mountain, where I figured they'd been dispatched to seal off the overlook and conduct a cursory search.

Frank asked Pamela and Willie to wait and led me onto the bridge. Dad and Sam followed, and no one tried to stop them.

Raul looked at me and shook his head. "Why am I not surprised you're in the middle of this?"

"I was simply in the wrong place at the wrong time."

"Yet again," he muttered.

"Look, Raul, I don't have the emotional bandwidth to tolerate a lecture right now. Just tell us how Brian is."

Raul gave me a look I chose to interpret as an apology. "He's awake but not yet lucid. Looks like he'll recover, but the doctor says it may take a day or two before he can string thoughts together, much less remember anything about last weekend."

"Truth is," Lynn added, "he may never regain those memories. We'll have to wait and see." She glanced to the west and pulled her notebook from her bag. "Let's get these interviews done before we lose the light."

She flipped her long ponytail over her shoulder and locked eyes with me. "Tell us what happened."

I chewed the inside of my cheek, replaying the scene in my mind. "I'd just finished a photo shoot. After the family left, I shot a few scenic photos. The lighting was gorgeous this evening, with the snow—"

"Move it along," Raul said. "We're investigating a death, not taking a photography class."

"Okay, okay. Pamela and Willie came down from the trail. They'd been hiking, and we all said hello. They stopped to stretch. I was packing up my equipment, struggling with a stuck zipper on my camera bag, when I heard a cracking noise. I followed the sound to the overlook in time to see something hurtle off the ledge. At first, I thought it was a boulder." I gestured to the rocks lining the creek. "But once it got closer, I could tell it was a person tumbling down the slope, then slamming headfirst into that tree."

All eyes followed my outstretched finger toward the immense pine tree, draped with yellow crime scene tape.

"I told Pamela to call 9-1-1 and asked Willie to go inside and get Dad. I ran over to see how badly the person was injured. When I checked for a pulse, I got nothing. Then I rolled her over to check whether she was breathing. That's when I recognized her. Desiree Bouton. The top of her head was crushed. Blood was everywhere."

I dropped my eyes. Sam tightened his arm around my shoulder.

Lynn scribbled into her notebook. "Anything else you can remember?" she asked.

When I hesitated, Dad cleared his throat, and I gave him a sidelong look. "Well, yes actually," I said. "There's something else I need to tell you. But I don't want you to jump to any conclusions..."

Everyone watched and waited. I took a deep breath. "Pamela and I saw Braden running from the trail."

Lynn and Raul stared at me. Frank raised an eyebrow.

"You're referring to Braden Ratliff," Lynn said.

"Yes, I mean...well, I didn't see him at first. I was over there..."—I pointed to the tree—"...with Desiree. I heard Pamela say Braden's name. Then I looked toward the bridge and saw him. I called out to him. He stopped for a second, then took off running."

There was a long pause. Lynn shook her head. "Callie, why didn't you give Chief Laramie this information right away?"

I bit my lip and blinked hard. "Everything was so chaotic. I wasn't thinking straight."

Raul's jaw clenched. "So, what I'm hearing is that Braden Ratliff—whose father is in the hospital after being poisoned, who was found to have toxic chemicals in his bedroom, who publicly declared his hatred for his stepmother—*that* Braden Ratliff was seen running from the trail. The trail leading to the overlook from which

Desiree's body fell. And you failed to *mention* it?"

Dad widened his stance, just slightly, but enough to make a statement. "She's telling you now," he said.

"I know it looks bad," I said, my voice quavering. "But I still believe in him. He didn't do this. There's another explanation. I just...I don't know what it is yet."

Everyone was silent for a minute. Then Lynn tucked her notebook into her bag and looked at her partner. "Let's pick him up," she said.

I took a step toward them. "I'll go with you."

"No, you won't," Raul said through gritted teeth.

"But things will go easier if I'm there." I could hear the plea in my voice.

Sam took my fingers in his. Dad put a hand on my shoulder and spoke into my ear. "That's not going to happen, Sundance. Let them do their job."

I pulled my hand from Sam's and shook off Dad's grasp. "Braden did not do this." My eyes darted around. Panic threatened to consume me. I pointed at Cabin One. "What about Weston? He was standing on the porch watching when the paramedics arrived. Why aren't you questioning *him*?"

Frank adjusted the brim of his hat. "After you all headed into the lodge, I went to the cabin to notify him. He wasn't there. The Boutons' car is gone, too. I have officers trying to locate him."

"Well, that's convenient," I said. "Seems awfully suspicious that he'd flee the scene just after his girlfriend plummeted to her death."

My breathing was labored. I feared I was on the verge of hyperventilating. Raul saw me struggling, and his face softened. "Your dad is right, Callie. Let us do our job."

He turned and strode toward the parking lot. Lynn followed him. Every fiber of my being wanted to run after them, but it wouldn't do any good.

Braden would have to face them. And he'd have to do it alone.

39

Shortly after Raul and Lynn's departure, Frank conducted a brief interview of Pamela and Willie and sent them on their way. Then he rounded up the troops and headed out. The rest of us went to Mom and Dad's place, where Dad worked on securing a lawyer for Braden.

I was usually the stoic, tend-to-business type, so it surprised everyone, including me, when I turned to mush, crying first in Sam's arms, then onto Mom's shoulder. She tolerated my emotional outburst for a few minutes before holding me at arm's length. "Callahan Maureen Cassidy, that's quite enough. Braden needs you, so pull yourself together. Have you spoken to Banner?"

I reared back. *Banner.* I was ashamed to admit he hadn't even crossed my mind. Was he still at the townhouse? Had Braden contacted him? This turn of events would devastate him—and he'd already endured enough trauma to last a lifetime.

With a shaky hand, I pulled my phone from my pocket and pressed his contact button. The call went straight to voicemail.

I tried again. Same result.

As I was about to press the button yet again, Sam folded his hand over mine. "Maybe we should try something else. Why don't you see if Ethan has talked to him?"

I nodded and dialed Ethan's number. He answered on the first ring. "Callie, I just heard. Are the boys—?"

"Is Banner with you?" I cut in.

"What? No. What's—?"

"Braden was at the scene of Desiree's death, Ethan. Raul and Lynn are looking for him now to take him into custody. I don't have time to go into details, but it doesn't look good. We need to reach Banner. I've tried calling, but he's not picking up. If he contacts you, please have him get in touch with me right away."

Ethan's voice was steady. "I will, Callie. If there's anything I can do, just call."

I thanked him and hung up. Mom was on her phone, and she mouthed that she was talking to Mrs. Finney. I was grateful she was handling that notification. I couldn't endure one of Mrs. Finney's intense interrogations right now. Sam had stepped aside to call Elyse in Boulder and fill her in.

When Dad returned from his study, Sam hung up, and Mom ended her call. We all regrouped in the middle of the room.

"I talked to Frank," Dad said. "They found Braden in the darkroom at Sundance Studio. They have him at the station now."

"Did they handcuff him?" A lump rose in my throat.

"Frank didn't say. I called my lawyer friend in Boulder, and he'll come first thing in the morning. He's calling the station now to instruct them not to question Braden until he arrives."

"Has Braden been charged?" I asked.

"No. But they can hold him for twenty-four hours without charging him." Dad rested a hand on my cheek. "Frank assured me they'll do everything they can to make him comfortable, and I believe him."

My heart sank at the thought of Braden spending the night in jail. The accommodations at the Rock Creek Village Police Department were hardly medieval. They would house Braden in a private space with a door, a cot, and a small bathroom. No bars, no bucket for bodily functions—more like a dorm room. Still, he'd be locked in. And alone. It was almost more than I could bear. If I didn't do something, I was afraid I was going to lose it.

Reaching for my coat, I said, "I'm going to the station."

"They won't let you see him, Callie," Dad said.

"Then I'll camp out in the reception area. I'm going, and no one is talking me out of it."

The three of them exchanged knowing glances. "I'll drive," Dad said at last.

***

Mom remained home to field calls and continue trying to locate Banner. At the station, Dad exchanged pleasantries with the night clerk, Eugene, an older officer he'd worked with when Dad served as chief of police. He told Eugene why the three of us were there. The man looked uncomfortable as he picked up the phone and spoke into the receiver. A moment later, he told us Raul would be out shortly.

"Great," I said. I'd been hoping for Frank, or Lynn.

"Stay calm," Dad advised. "Act professional. You and Raul tend to butt heads. It'll go better if you behave like a journalist rather than a rabid mother bear."

A few minutes later, Raul came out, accompanied by Lynn and Frank. Clearly, they were going to present a united front.

To my surprise, Raul's manner was gentle—kind, even. "Braden is being well cared for, Callie. Go home. Come back in the morning."

"I can't do that, Raul," I said quietly, feeling the tears leak from my eyes. "The kid lost his mother, and then his father ran off. I won't abandon him, too."

He locked eyes with me for a long moment. I held my breath. Then he glanced at Lynn and Frank, both of whom nodded.

Raul held up his hand, fingers splayed. "Five minutes. And we'll be listening."

I exhaled. "Thank you. Can I see him now?"

"Give me a minute," Raul said. "I'll put him in an interview room, and you can meet with him there."

He headed down the hall. Dad and Frank stepped aside to talk. I slumped into a chair, and Sam sat beside me with his hand on my knee. My energy was sapped, but I knew I needed to channel my reserves. I couldn't let Braden see me so afraid. He needed a rock right now, and it had to be me.

Lynn took the chair on my left, and I looked at her out of the corner of my eye. "Despite how it looks, I still believe Braden is innocent," I said.

"If he is, we'll find out," she responded. "We'll get to the truth, Callie. You have to trust us."

She stared at me, her eyes unwavering. After a moment, I nodded. "I do."

Raul reappeared and crooked a finger at me. I followed him to the interview room. At the door, he paused and spoke quietly. "Remember, we'll be listening."

He gave me a cautionary look, and I realized he was trying to protect Braden, too.

Then Raul opened the door, and I stepped inside. Braden sat in a metal chair, hunched over a metal table. It all seemed so cold, so austere. He clasped his hands in front of him. His hair fell across his forehead as he peered up at me. "Hey, Callie," he said.

"Hey," I responded, dropping into a chair across from him. "How are you holding up?"

"I'm okay. Don't worry about me."

It was the second time today he'd told me not to worry.

"You're kidding, right?" I rested my elbows on the table. "Listen, we can't talk about details because our conversation isn't private. But I want you to know my father has arranged a lawyer for you. Don't say anything, don't answer questions, until you've consulted with him. That won't be until morning. Will you be okay?"

He nodded. "I told you, I'm fine. I'm ready to face what I've done."

My gut clenched. *Face what I've done?* It sounded almost like…a confession.

"Hush!" I said, my eyes darting around the room. I didn't know where they'd positioned the mic, but I was sure it had picked up his words. "You need to keep quiet and sit tight. Whatever you have to say, talk to your lawyer first."

He sighed, looking deflated. "Callie, I appreciate your concern. Honest. But right now, I'd just rather be by myself."

I sat back, stung. I'd come here to protect this boy, to serve as his advocate, and he wanted me to leave?

Then I narrowed my eyes. This wasn't like Braden. He was too smart to purposely incriminate himself. And trying to drive me away? Nope. Not his style. Something was up. My instinct told me this situation wasn't what it seemed.

Three sharp taps at the door signaled our time had ended. I reached across the table and squeezed Braden's hand. "One last thing. We haven't been able to locate your brother. Any idea where he might be?"

Braden's face immediately darkened. "Leave Banner out of this," he said sharply. "I don't want him involved."

I didn't even try to conceal my surprise. But before I could reply, the door swung open. Raul stuck his head in, telling me time was up. I glanced at Braden one last time, but he'd buried his head in his hands and didn't look up.

40

The rest of the night rolled past in a haze. Frank told Dad they'd issued an APB on Weston, and I was relieved they were still looking at other suspects. Even so, things looked bad for Braden. Really bad. What he said about facing what he'd done? I couldn't explain it, and I couldn't shake it off.

Sam and I returned to my house, where he poured us both a glass of wine to help us relax. Woody and Carl sensed something distressing was happening—or more accurately, Woody sensed it and Carl knew. My golden retriever clung to my side, while the cat jumped into my lap and stared into my eyes, as if he'd solve the mystery himself if I'd only provide the relevant information.

The news spread fast, as it always did in our little village—all the way to Moonglow Ranch, where my friends Jessica and Summer were visiting. Even in texts, I could detect their alarm. I tried to be as upbeat as possible, but I was scared, too. When they said they were returning home tomorrow, a day early, I didn't try to dissuade them. The twins needed all the support they could get—and so did I.

Still, I hoped the news wouldn't travel all the way to Italy. I didn't want recent events casting a pall over Tonya and David's honeymoon. But I held little hope they'd remain ensconced in ignorant bliss. Tonya was owner and editor of the local newspaper, so Phil—or Monika— would likely consult her about how to proceed.

The thought of Monika triggered more questions. *Where was she? Why hadn't she tried to get in touch with me?* She'd left the resort after receiving some mysterious text and hadn't contacted me since. When Sam got up to tend the fire, I tried calling her again, but she didn't pick up.

As I pondered reasons for her absence, my phone buzzed with a text—Monika, responding to the unanswered call.

In the middle of something right now. Talk to you tomorrow.

Irritation gripped me. Braden was in custody, Banner was missing, and Monika didn't have time to speak to me? I tossed my phone onto the coffee table.

Sam came back to the couch, shooed Woody aside, and sat next to me. "Want to talk? Or would you rather not?"

I kissed his cheek, grateful the man understood me so well. "I'm talked out for tonight. After I drain this glass of wine, I'm going to call it a night and try to get some sleep."

"Sounds good." We both took a long drink of the pinot. I laid my head on his shoulder and tried to clear my mind. It was no use, of course. My monkey brain wouldn't stop leaping and cartwheeling. Sleep was as likely as Raul handing me a badge and asking for my help.

***

When Sam stirred beside me at five the next morning, I was wide awake, staring at the ceiling. Woody snuggled between us, and Carl curled atop my head with his tail draped over my face.

Sam leaned over, brushed Carl's tail aside, and kissed my cheek. "Go back to sleep. I'm going to call Rodger and tell him I won't be in this morning. I'll be right back."

"No, don't do that," I said. "You have that realtors' group from Pine Haven coming for brunch this morning. I didn't sleep much last night—"

"No surprise."

"Anyway, I'm going to catch a few hours before I face the day. No need for you to babysit me. I'll be fine."

Even in the semi-darkness, I saw him grappling with

the decision. On one hand, he was as worried about me as I was about the twins and didn't want to leave me. On the other, he knew how much my self-sufficiency meant to me. On the third hand—was there such a thing?—he did have a busy day at the café and didn't want to dump all the work on his two chefs.

I stroked his cheek. "I mean it, Sam. All I'm going to do is lie here and try to sleep. Go cook and create. Save me some leftovers. I'll be by later to collect."

He gazed at me for a long moment, then gave me a tender half-smile.

"Okay, but call me if you need me," he said. "Even if you just want a little moral support. I can be here in three minutes."

"I promise."

He got out of bed, and a minute later I heard the shower running. The sound lulled me into the sleep that had been eluding me.

***

After three hours of uninterrupted slumber, I felt as refreshed as I was going to for the day. First thing, I checked my phone. I had a text from Sam reminding me he loved me, one from Dad informing me the lawyer was on his way to see Braden, and another from Mrs. Finney suggesting I find my way to Rocky Mountain High ASAP. Nothing from Monika. And even more distressing, nothing from Banner.

I rolled out of bed, showered, and stumbled down the stairs in search of coffee. Woody headed through the doggie door, and I watched him bounce around in the yard. Yesterday's snowstorm had ended, and the sun sparkled on the thin blanket of snow. As the coffee brewed, I scrounged through the pantry and discovered an old box of Pop-Tarts tucked behind the healthy stuff I kept for show. I'd just ripped open the silver foil and bitten into the strawberry pastry when Woody started yipping outside.

My pacifist pup must have caught sight of a ground squirrel and was trying, as usual, to entice the poor creature into a playdate. When I turned toward the window, I nearly choked on my Pop-Tart at the sight of Banner peering inside.

Throwing open the door, I stepped into the brisk morning air. "Banner, where have you been? We've been trying to reach you since yesterday."

He craned his neck and squinted past me. Carl scrambled outside and clawed at Banner's shin until he bent down and lifted the cat into his arms. "Are you alone, Callie?"

I cocked my head. What was with the cloak and dagger?

"Except for Woody and Carl."

Banner shivered, and I realized he wasn't wearing a coat. He had to be freezing. I pulled him inside, closing the door behind us.

I poured coffee and handed it to him. "Drink this," I said. "It'll warm you up."

He wrapped his hands around the mug, then drank. His face was pale, and the skin sagged beneath his eyes.

"Sit down," I said. "Tell me what's going on."

He sank into a kitchen chair and stroked Woody's ears. I took a seat across the table. Carl climbed into my lap and onto my shoulder, swishing his tail as he scrutinized Banner.

"Have you heard about my dad?" Banner asked.

I nodded. "He's out of the coma. That's wonderful."

"Sounds like they're expecting a full recovery," he said.

"More great news," I replied.

He sipped his coffee again and squirmed in his chair. The seconds ticked by, and I couldn't take it any longer. "Banner, I'm sure you've gotten the news about Desiree. About Braden."

He nodded, but didn't look at me, didn't speak. I'd had

enough. Time for some tough love. I pounded my palm on the table, causing Banner to jump. "There's something going on," I said, "and you need to tell me what it is. Right now."

He put his hands over his face. Beside him, Woody whimpered.

I lifted Carl from my shoulder, set him on the floor, and circled the table to kneel beside Banner's chair. "I'm sorry, kiddo. I've just been so worried. It's obvious you're hiding something. It's time to let me help you with whatever it is."

He looked at me with bleary eyes. "He made me promise not to tell. But Callie, I don't think I can keep that promise."

41

I went back to my chair. "Banner, some promises shouldn't be kept. Promises made under duress. Promises that can only end up hurting someone."

He stared out the window, his fingers still stroking Woody's fur. I stayed quiet, letting him work his way to a decision.

At last, he looked me in the eye, his gaze unflinching, expression resolute. I tensed, waiting for whatever bombshell he unleashed.

"It was me," he said.

I tilted my head. "What?"

"It was me running from the trail. Yesterday, after Desiree…you know."

I sucked in a breath. I'd been too far away to notice the small telltale scar on Braden's lip—or the lack thereof— that I often used to differentiate the twins. I'd just assumed Pamela had named the right Ratliff.

Now Braden's unwillingness to talk at the station made perfect sense. He'd been protecting his brother.

Momentary panic flashed across Banner's face, but he composed himself. Still, his next words rushed out in a torrent. "I didn't push her, Callie…I swear to you…I heard her scream…saw someone standing there…I don't know who."

"Banner, breathe. I believe you. But you need to—"

He shook his head. "I'm a coward. I saw Desiree arguing with someone, and I just stood there behind a tree. When the person pushed her over the guardrail, I didn't even move. I hid while the guy made a break for it. Then I freaked out and ran away, too."

His pain pierced me, but I stayed quiet, knowing he needed to get it out.

"I always thought I was the kind of person to step up in a crisis," he went on. "Now I know who I really am. A chicken. A weakling. A sissy."

I shook my head hard, figuring those words came straight from his father's mouth. "Banner, you're wrong. You've proven your strength and bravery countless times since I've known you. Anyway, what could you have done? There was no way to stop the person. You'd only have put yourself in danger."

He hung his head. "Only a coward would let his brother take the blame," he mumbled.

I realized I wouldn't be able to talk him out of his self-blame, not right now. And we had more pressing matters to attend to. "Why didn't you come to me? Or go to the police? Tell someone what happened?"

"After she…after it happened, I panicked and ran to your house. Braden was in the living room, watching TV. I told him what happened, that Pamela thought I was him. He told me not to say anything to anyone. Made me swear I wouldn't. He said the police already suspected him of poisoning Dad, so it would be better if just one of us was in their sights." He ran shaky hands through his hair, making it stand on end. "I shouldn't have agreed. I wasn't thinking straight."

He swallowed hard. "Braden told me to get out of town for a couple of days. He sounded really sure of himself, and I was so freaked out. I just did what he said. I drove to Valley Ridge and spent the night at a friend's house. Early this morning, I found out Braden was in jail, and I knew I had to come back. To tell you." He looked at me with wild eyes. "You have to help him, Callie. Get him out of there."

Woody whined and nudged Banner's hand. Banner took a few deep breaths and resumed petting. I hoped he was getting comfort from the dog, but I couldn't spend much time thinking about Banner's emotional state right now. What he'd told me was too important. It could break the case wide open—and get Braden out of custody.

"Banner, listen to me. You did the right thing coming back. Now, I need you to tell me who you saw on the overlook arguing with Desiree. Who killed her?"

"Don't you think if I knew that, I'd have told someone right away? I barely glimpsed the guy from behind." He threaded his fingers back into his hair and tugged, as if performing penance.

"Okay, calm down. Close your eyes. Describe what you did see. Was the man tall or short? What color was his hair? Any detail might help."

He shut his eyes and searched his memory. "A few inches taller than Desiree. Dark blue coat and one of those knit hats pulled low. Couldn't see his hair. And he was wearing gloves." Banner's eyes shot open. "It's not enough. I'm useless."

My heart ached for him, but I refused to get distracted. Not yet. "Banner, now's your chance to be strong. You need to tell Raul and Lynn what you saw. I'll call—"

As I reached for my phone, Banner's hand shot out and swiped it off the table. He jumped to his feet, upending his chair and startling Woody, who darted to my side. Carl arched his back.

"No!" Banner shouted. "I came to you for help, not so you'd turn me in. I made a promise to my brother."

"We already talked about that," I said, trying for a soothing tone. "We agreed some promises need to be broken."

He shook his head. "I don't know what's right anymore. I'm sorry, but I can't..."

Without warning, he sprinted out the back door. I ran after him, but by the time I got outside, he'd jumped the fence. A moment later, an engine revved. I hurried to the front of the house in time to watch Banner's truck tear off down the street.

Dejected, I trudged back inside and slammed the door.

Woody's tail drooped between his legs, as if he'd let me down. I crumpled to the floor and took the big hulk into my lap. Carl was not as solicitous of my feelings. He sat on his haunches nearby, scowling and mewing, as if expecting me to take some sort of action. "What do you want me to do, cat? I'm not going to engage in a high-speed chase." I sighed. "Besides, I believe him. He didn't push Desiree off that overlook. I only wish he'd gotten a better look at the person who did."

Leaning against the cabinet, I kneaded Woody's ears, calculating my next move. "I have to call Raul and Lynn. It's the right thing to do." Carl let out a hiss. "Yeah, not my first choice, either. But when I picture Braden in custody…" I wasn't often indecisive, but in this situation, it seemed like whatever action I took meant choosing one twin over the other. If I told the detectives about Banner, they might free Braden—but Banner would be in trouble.

It was a choice I couldn't make—at least, not on my own.

I nudged Woody off my lap and struggled to my feet. "Come on, you two. We're going to the lodge. It's not for nothing my father is a former police chief, and my mother is the most moral person I've ever known. They'll help us figure out what to do next."

***

A few minutes later, I pulled out of the carport and headed toward the Knotty Pine. I felt a sense of relief at the prospect of unloading this secret onto my unwitting parents, but a sense of foreboding countered it. Intuition told me they'd advise me to call Raul and Lynn right away. My conscience agreed. But it would be so hard.

The stoplight at the intersection of Evergreen Way and the park turned red. As I rolled to a stop, my phone rang on the seat beside me. I glanced at the screen, hoping it was Banner. When I read Monika's name, I almost ignored the call. But as always, curiosity got the better of me. I hit speakerphone.

"Been a while," I said frostily.

"I realize you're mad," Monika said, "but I need to talk to you."

The agitated tone in her voice put me on alert. "What is it?"

"Can you come to my apartment? There's something…well, I need to talk to you in person. It's important. Urgent."

"Tell me where you live," I said. "I'll be right there."

42

When we arrived at Monika's apartment complex, I put Woody on his leash and carried Carl upstairs. She opened the door before I knocked, looking harried and tired.

"I had these two in the car with me when you called," I said. "Okay for them to come in?"

"We're supposed to get advance permission from management, but I don't care. Animals on the premises are the least of my worries."

She took my coat and draped it across the back of a threadbare couch. Then she led me to a scarred wooden table in the kitchen, where her laptop sat open. "Want something to drink? I only have coffee or water."

"Coffee works," I said.

While she poured, I scanned her space. Monika's apartment looked like that of every rookie journalist I'd known—sparse, undecorated, no frills. She'd obviously rented it furnished, and aside from the few pieces of furniture, the place was bare. No artwork, no decor, no personal touches. Right now, Monika lived for her work.

She came to the table bearing two chipped mugs. I'd taken Woody off his leash, and he curled up next to my feet, while Carl climbed into my lap, ready for action.

Steam rose from the coffee—still too hot to drink. I stared at Monika, waiting for her to speak. But with Banner on the run and Braden unable to run, my patience was thin. I didn't wait long.

"So, I don't hear from you for eighteen hours, and now you're in crisis." I failed to keep the bitterness out of my voice.

"I'm sorry for going off the grid, Callie, but I had good reason. Something happened, something I thought would break the case wide open. I still think it might, but…I'm not sure how to handle it. I may be in over my head."

I straightened in my chair, every journalistic nerve ending in my body tingling. "Tell me. Between the two of us, I'm sure we can figure it out."

She hesitated, fidgeting with a crumpled napkin. I blew out a breath. "Monika, the clock is ticking. I'm in the middle of a crisis of my own. Let's get on with it."

Her eyes sparked with interest. "What's your crisis?"

"Nope. I'm not letting you get off course. You called me here, so tell me what's going on."

She nibbled at a cuticle and sighed. "Okay. It all started with that text I got yesterday after Desiree was killed."

"I remember. You barreled out of there, and I didn't hear from you the rest of the day."

"Right. The text was from Weston."

"Weston?" I asked, incredulous. "Do you know where he is? The police are looking for him. He might be the person who actually killed Desiree, who poisoned—"

Monika held up a hand. "Hold on a second. Let me get through this. Then you can ask whatever questions you have."

I crossed my arms, nodding for her to continue. She took a breath. "The past few days, I've spent a little time with Weston, talking, getting him comfortable with me with the goal of pumping him for info about Desiree. I was still in the early stages of establishing rapport and hadn't gotten much out of him yet, other than the fact that the two of them had been on-again-off-again lovers since high school."

"He admitted they weren't brother and sister?" I asked.

She nodded. "He told me it was a fun game for Desiree, passing him off as her brother and keeping him around under the noses of her current boyfriends. Anyway, yesterday, after Desiree's death, Weston contacted me saying he had something of Desiree's, something that might reveal her killer's identity. He wanted the person punished, but he said it was too risky for him to go to the police. He'd give me the evidence, but only if I followed a few rules."

I stared at Monika in awe. I'd viewed Weston as a mere stoner, of little value to the investigation. Meanwhile, she'd been grooming him as a source.

"So, what did you do?" I asked.

"I left the bridge, went to my car, and called him. He'd already loaded up his stuff and taken off. He was freaking out, sure the police wanted to pin Desiree's death on him, along with everything else."

"What did he mean by everything else?"

"He wouldn't tell me on the phone, but I assumed he meant Brian's poisoning."

"You agreed to meet him?"

She nodded. "He said he was on his way to what he referred to as his safe house. If I wanted the goods, I had to meet him at a rest area about three hours from Rock Creek Village. He said he'd be there at ten o'clock. If I didn't arrive by ten-fifteen, he'd leave and never contact me again."

I stared at her in disbelief. "You drove three hours to meet a veritable stranger at an isolated rest stop? And you told no one where you were going? That was immensely foolish. What if Weston was the killer?"

"He said if I told anyone or talked to the police, he'd vanish." She paused, gnawing her cuticle again. "To be honest, I didn't consider the danger. I just wanted the story. It may sound ambitious and arrogant, but it's the truth."

I had to admit I understood how she felt. I'd have done the same thing twenty-five years ago. Who was I kidding? Given the circumstances, I'd have done it yesterday.

"I get it, Monika. Believe me, I do. But here's the

problem: aside from the potential for physical danger, which luckily you avoided, your actions might land you in legal trouble. Dad told me there's an APB out for Weston as a person of interest in a murder investigation. If it turns out he's the killer, the police could charge you with aiding and abetting. Or at the very least, withholding evidence."

She nodded grimly. "I didn't think of all that until later. And I honestly don't believe Weston killed Desiree or poisoned Brian. But we can analyze my mistakes later. Right now, you need to see what he gave me."

She got up, hurried down the short hallway to the bedroom, and returned a minute later with a sturdy looking gray box, which she placed on the table in front of me. I reached toward it, but Monika grabbed my wrist. Then she retrieved two sets of latex gloves from a drawer in the kitchen. Impressive forethought. I wriggled my hands into the gloves.

I turned my attention back to the box. It was metal, probably eighteen by twenty-four inches, roughly the size of a document storage case. But this one was built to be semi-secure, with a latch and a cylinder lock requiring a three-number entry to open.

"What's in it?" I asked.

She shook her head. "Weston wouldn't say—just told me the box belonged to Desiree and contained everything I'd need. He said some of the documents might incriminate him in as a participant in some of her illegal activities, so he didn't want me to open it until I got back to Rock Creek Village and he was safely in the wind."

I nearly salivated at the prospect of opening that box. It might contain evidence that would clear the twins. I pressed the silver release button, but the latch held firm.

"Did he give you the combination?" I asked.

"No. He didn't want my access to be that easy or immediate."

I turned the box around, searching for another point of entry. "Do you have a flathead screwdriver? We might be able to wedge it in the crack and bust the thing open."

"I'm sure we could. It's not the caliber of a bank safe or anything." Monika drummed her fingers on the table. "And that was my original plan. Heck, I almost pulled over on the shoulder of the road and used the tire jack on it. But something made me hesitate—some, I don't know, moral dilemma. I've been wrestling with it for the last few hours."

I cocked my head. "Explain."

"Well, you just said I could be in legal trouble for even meeting with Weston. How much worse would it be if I messed with potential evidence? And what opening the box hurts any case the police might build against the killer? I don't want to be responsible for a guilty person going free."

"Let's hope the guilty person isn't Weston, then."

She winced. I sighed and stared at what could turn out to be Pandora's box. Should we, or shouldn't we? The answer, if I asked Raul…or Lynn…or Dad…was obvious. This was a police matter and should be handled by the detectives. On the other hand, I wanted to know what the box contained. I wanted to know bad.

Still, Monika made a solid point. It was too risky. We needed to turn this over to the authorities.

Before I could say just that, Carl climbed off my lap and onto the table. On dainty paws, he circled the box, sniffing and studying it. Then, without warning, he wormed a single claw beneath the latch and jiggled it back and forth. The lock popped open. Carl gave a satisfied meow and calmly licked his paw. Just another day at the office.

I looked at my cat in wonder. He might not have opposable thumbs, but he possessed a talent for safecracking. He was the true definition of a cat burglar.

43

Are you sure about this?" Monika asked, nervously studying the partially open lid.

I thought about it, then nodded. "The fates have decreed it—in the form of a four-legged oracle, that is."

She looked skeptical, but for me, that ship had sailed. The box was open, and I was diving inside. "Look, Monika, Braden is in custody. And Banner…well, I'll tell you about him later. But if something in this box can help them, I'm willing to face whatever consequences I have to. We can figure out a way to keep you out of it, though. We'll say Weston dropped the box off at my house. You don't have to go down with me."

"No way." She shook her head with finality. "If you're in, I am, too."

"All right," I said, and gestured toward the box. "Your source, your honors."

She pushed the lid wide open, and we peered inside the box at a stack of manila envelopes. With her gloved forefinger and thumb, she plucked out the first one and opened the flap.

She removed a birth certificate in the name of Amy Templeton—Desiree's original identity, according to Mrs. Finney's source. We read through the information. Birthplace: Kingston, Iowa. Parents' names: Donald and Janet Templeton.

Monika put the birth certificate aside and removed the rest of the contents from the envelope. A few photos of a skinny, wispy-haired baby, later a serious-looking child wedged between two unsmiling parents. No "brother" in sight. Next came a high school diploma. Finally, her parents' death certificates, dated not long after Amy's graduation. Causes of death: injuries sustained in a car accident.

"How sad," Monika mumbled.

She gestured to the box, indicating it was my turn. From the next envelope, I pulled out five passports, each issued in a different name, but all displaying Desiree's picture. We also found driver's licenses in the same names, all from different states, along with other minor forms of identification: a Costco card in one name, a Starbucks card in another. Desiree—or Amy, Patricia, Caroline, Heidi—had done her due diligence.

The third envelope contained statements from seven bank accounts, five in the United States and two overseas. I didn't bother to get out my calculator, but a little mental math told me that, while Desiree wasn't a millionaire, she was over three quarters of the way there when she died.

"The woman was proficient at her scams," I said.

The next few envelopes compiled the history of each persona. Desiree had lived all over the country, conning and swindling at least a dozen institutions and individuals—mostly men—over the past twelve years. Truly a remarkable feat.

"Wow," Monika said. "If Desiree had been caught instead of killed, she could have made a fortune publishing her memoirs."

"Well, someone will write that story." I grinned at the young reporter. "Might as well be you."

A spark gleamed in her eyes. "An interesting thought. But first, let's see this through."

She took the next-to-last envelope from the box and removed its contents. This one served as the Brian Ratliff dossier. We found the marriage license that had been the subject of so much speculation. I wasn't an expert on counterfeit documents, but to my eye, it looked legitimate. Interesting.

Next came a pair of wills, computer-generated from an online legal site, signed and notarized. Brian's will left all his worldly assets to Desiree, and hers left everything to him. Then there was a copy of Victoria's million-dollar life insurance policy. Taken together, the documents confirmed my early theory: Desiree poisoned Brian, intending to kill him so she could get her hands on his estate.

I felt vindicated, but Monika bit her lip. "I hate to say it, Callie, but this might end up being bad for Braden and Banner."

"How so?" I asked.

"Think about it. Brian's condition was touch and go. If he died, Desiree would inherit everything. The boys would have been left in the cold. But then Desiree dies. Who's next in line?"

My gut clenched. Monika had seen a side to this I'd missed. Between the chemicals in Braden's room, Banner running from the scene of Desiree's death, and now Brian's will, the motive against the twins seemed to be solidifying. Instead of helping to clear Braden and Banner, this box may have helped incriminate them.

"Last envelope," I said, pulling it from the box. "Let's hope this one contains the evidence that will prove the twins' innocence."

I pulled out a stack of papers, spreading them on the table. They were documents relating to the Heidi Forsythe pseudonym, the most immediate precursor to Desiree's current identity. We shuffled through the pages, pausing at a contract detailing Heidi's employment as an adjunct professor starting last August and continuing through the current term. The college? Prosper University.

There was that niggle in my brain again. I still hadn't figured out why Prosper aroused my interest. I'd creep close to an answer, only to watch as it faded away.

I sighed and turned to the next page: Heidi's grant

award from the university. My eyes widened at the amount. Seventy-five thousand dollars, scheduled for payment this past January. Since Heidi had morphed into Desiree and moved to Rock Creek Village, we could conclude she'd absconded with the grant money without honoring the terms of her contract.

Pointing to Monika's open laptop, I said, "See if you can find anything relating to Heidi Forsythe at Prosper University."

While Monika began tapping on the keyboard, I flipped through pages until I found the grant project summary. Heidi Forsythe had proposed a study of the psychological effects of climate change on the current generation of college students. How did the increase in wildfires, floods, tornadoes, and other weather disasters influence students' stress levels and productivity? Were their grades affected? Their quests for jobs?

An intriguing concept. Too bad "Heidi" never planned to pursue it.

Beside me, Monika grunted. "Here's an article from the Prosper U. newspaper dated last month. It covers the investigation into Professor Forsythe going AWOL from the university. Few details. And no major media outlets seem to have picked up the story."

They will soon, I thought.

Monika continued searching, then turned the laptop toward me. "Here's a brief article from last November covering the grant award—and there's a picture of Desiree. Heidi, I mean."

I squinted at the screen. In the photo, Heidi smiled as she accepted one of those oversized cardboard checks from a silver-haired man the caption named as the university chancellor. From his spot in my lap, Carl yowled. I leaned closer, my eyes sweeping across the people gathered around Heidi. As soon as I saw him, the answers started tumbling into place, and the niggle in my brain disappeared.

Just behind Heidi, his hand resting on her shoulder in a congratulatory gesture, stood a man I recognized. He'd been staying at the Knotty Pine with a group of so-called philosophers calling themselves Bentham's Progeny. Now I remembered him mentioning that he was a sociology professor—at Prosper University.

The man was Scott Digby.

44

I pointed Scott out to Monika, who remembered noticing him in Mrs. Finney's coffee shop. "I thought he seemed kind of sleazy," she said. "Like he was trying to be all suave and GQ. A pseudo-intellectual, out to prove how smart and worldly he was. Ego wrapped around low self-esteem."

"You got all that from one observation?"

She shrugged. "I had more than one professor just like him. Let me see if I can find anything on him."

Her tongue poked between her lips as she hunched over the laptop. Less than two minutes later, she sat up straight. "Here we go. Scott Digby, born…well, I won't go into all the details. Suffice it to say he was a professor at a Laramie, Wyoming community college for three years before nabbing the position at Prosper University six years ago. On track to achieve tenure in another year. Decent student reviews." She read in silence for a moment and yelped. "Callie, Scott Digby chaired the grant committee that awarded Heidi Forsythe her money."

My nerves vibrated. "So, he's not just a sleaze. He's also a thief."

"We can't be sure of that. She could have conned him, too." Monika kept scrolling. "Looks like he's married. Ten years."

I noticed a small lump in the manila envelope and retrieved a few photos we'd overlooked. My eyes widened. "Married, huh? Not for long, if his wife gets a look at these."

I handed the stack to Monika, who blushed as she flipped through them. I shared her embarrassment. After a lengthy journalism career, not a lot shocked me, but I didn't relish the graphic portrayal of unbridled lust. Along with my peep show at Cabin One, these pictures left me craving a bar of soap and a long, hot shower.

Monika cocked her head. "We're sure that's Scott Digby, right? I mean, we only get a glimpse of his face in profile."

"No doubt about it. There's enough face to convince a wife of her husband's philandering ways—combined with other physical attributes she might recognize."

Monika closed her laptop and pushed it aside. I could see the wheels spinning in her head as she put it all together. "So Desiree…Heidi, that is…or Amy, if you prefer…lures Scott into bed, convinces him to award her the grant, and…what? Blackmails him?"

"Or she just seduced him and kept the photos in case she needed to keep him in line down the road."

Monika nodded. "She bilks the university of seventy-five grand and takes off, leaving Scott with egg on his face and a lot of explaining to do. This scandal might have pushed him off the tenure track. But even if he could salvage his career, his reputation would never recover. I doubt he'd ever chair another committee."

"Not only that, he stood to lose his marriage."

"He must have been incensed." Monika twisted her hair around her finger. "Callie, did you see Scott near the trail after Desiree's death?"

"No. Only Braden. Or rather, Banner." She gave me a puzzled look, but I waved her off. No time to explain right now. "But I ran over to Desiree's body right away. I suppose Scott could've passed when I was busy with the body, though Pamela didn't mention it. Also, there are other paths that lead off the trail into different parts of the village. It wouldn't have been hard for him to escape the scene unnoticed."

I shut my eyes and let my mind wander across the faces of the people gathered on the path before the officers dispersed them. Resort guests. Fran from Quicker Liquor. Mr. Farmington. Weston on the cabin porch. But no Scott.

I snapped my fingers, making a muffled sound through the latex gloves. "Wait a minute. The group of them, the Bentham's Progeny, came into the lodge soon after Dad and I were back inside the lobby. They were being obnoxious, and my father basically told them to get out of our faces. More diplomatically, of course."

"Are you thinking they were all in on it together?"

"That seems like a stretch. Would a group of professors really conspire to commit murder?"

"Seems doubtful." Monika thought for a moment. "Anyway, how does Brian Ratliff fit into all this? Did Scott supposedly poison him before killing Desiree? If so, why? Or did Desiree poison Brian to get his money, unaware Scott was stalking her?"

I stood and stretched. "We don't need all the answers right now. What we have here is enough to get Braden and Banner off the hook. It's time to pack all this up and get it to Raul and Lynn. Let them sort out the details. As Raul has pointed out ad nauseam, it's their job."

We piled the envelopes back into the box the way we'd found them. We'd been careful to keep the documents organized as we read through them, so it only took a couple of minutes. When we closed the lid, the box appeared good as new—if you didn't count the lock Carl had jimmied.

I was almost giddy with relief. It wouldn't take long to explain everything to Raul and Lynn. We'd get a scolding for going through the box on our own, perhaps an idle threat of charges for interfering with evidence, but nothing would come of it. They'd release Braden by the afternoon. With any luck, we'd locate Banner right away and all be back together by dinnertime. I'd drive the boys to Pine Haven to visit their father, then take them to dinner to celebrate the end of this crazy saga.

Monika and I had just exchanged our latex gloves for our winter ones and were putting on our coats when my phone rang. Caller ID showed it was Banner. Hallelujah! I put the phone on speaker so Monika could listen as I gave him the good news.

"Banner, I'm so glad you called. You can come home now. We've found—"

He interrupted, his voice tense. Scared, even. "Callie, I'm in trouble. He has a gun. If you don't do what he says, he's going to kill me."

My heart rate ratcheted up. Monika's hand flew to her mouth. "Who?" I asked, though I already knew.

"He says I should call him Bentham. Says you'll know who he is."

My fingers tightened around the phone. What game was Scott Digby playing?

"Banner, where are you?"

He talked fast, obviously defying his captor's orders. "Callie, don't come. It's not safe. He's going to—"

I heard shuffling. A smacking sound, followed by a yelp of pain. The angry tones of a muted voice. "Banner?" My voice sounded frantic in my own ears, and I fought to control it. "Banner, talk to me."

It was an agonizing minute before he responded. "I'm okay. But he says you need to come. And you have to bring the box."

"What box?" I asked in a strained voice.

A few more muttered words. Then, "He says if you don't know, get in touch with that reporter friend of yours. Weston said he gave the box to her."

"I have no idea what he's talking about."

Another smack, another yelp. I jolted, knowing my words had brought this punishment on the boy. "Okay!" I shouted. "Stop hurting him. I'll come. I'll bring the box."

More mumbled instructions. "Don't call the police," Banner said. "Don't tell anyone where you're going or what you're doing. If you do, he says he'll shoot me. He wants to hear you acknowledge his terms."

"I do," I said, feeling hot tears on my cheeks. "Just tell me where you are."

"In the cabin. The one where Desiree and Weston stayed."

The line went dead. For a moment, I stared at the phone in my hand. Then I grabbed the box and marched toward the door. Monika and the creatures followed close behind.

I spun around and raised a finger. "You stay here. Keep Woody and Carl with you."

Woody barreled past me and pressed his nose to the door jamb. Carl clawed at my calf.

Monika's arms were tight against her sides, her face resolute. "I'm coming with you, Callie. You'll only waste time trying to talk me out of it." She gestured at the animals. "And apparently, they're coming, too."

I shook my head. "Monika, this isn't just some story you're chasing. Banner's life is at stake."

"Don't you think I know that?" Her tone was fierce, but her expression was pained. My words had hurt her.

At that moment, I understood Monika had found more than a job in Rock Creek Village. Like me, she'd found a home. A community. Friends, even. She was no longer simply after a story. She wanted to help save Banner.

I took a deep breath. "Okay. Let's go."

"What's the plan?"

"We'll figure that out on the way."

45

Monika and I pulled into the parking lot of the Peak Inn, down the street from the Knotty Pine. I didn't want my car in the resort lot, knowing my mother's eagle eyes would surely spot my red Honda and wonder what I was doing there and why I hadn't stopped in to say hello. I didn't want her tracking me down in Cabin One and putting herself in danger.

During the short drive from Monika's apartment, I'd fretted about the possibility of collateral damage. Scott had recklessly taken Banner hostage during the middle of the day. What if Felicia or one of her employees walked in to give the place a good scrubbing? Or my father decided it was the perfect time to rid the place of the residual odor of Weston's weed?

When I voiced my concerns, Monika told me it was pointless to worry about things I couldn't control. Still, I parked down the street. A little thing I *could* control.

The plan we'd come up with wouldn't win awards for ingenuity, but it was the best we could create on short notice. After considerable resistance on Monika's part, I convinced her I should go to the cabin alone. It's what Scott had instructed, and I didn't want to start the confrontation by ticking him off.

Besides, I needed Monika as a backup. If ten minutes elapsed without word from me, she'd summon the police, telling them to come with lights blazing and sirens blaring. If I hadn't resolved the situation by then, my agreement to not involve the authorities wouldn't matter, anyway. All I'd have left was the hope of rescue by people with weapons.

But no matter what Banner's kidnapper demanded, I wasn't showing up on the doorstep with the box. No, that item would remain locked in the trunk of my car until I deemed it necessary…or until the cops took possession of it. That box was my only bargaining chip.

As I reached for the car door, Monika put a hand on my arm. Anxiety was written on her face, but to her credit, her fingers didn't tremble. I gave her a confident smile. "Just think, when all this is over, Banner will be safe, and you'll have an award-winning story."

"I don't care about the story," she said. "Just be careful and get Banner out of there."

Carl pressed into my lap, determined to join me on my mission. I handed the squirming cat to Monika. Despite his scratching and chattering, she held on tight. When I got out and closed the car door, Woody barked from the back seat and scrabbled against the window. I steeled myself and walked away without looking back.

Ducking my head, I entered the copse of trees that separated the Peak Inn from the resort property. Sunlight filtered through the branches of the pine trees, dappling the ground with gold. A pair of ground squirrels frolicked in the rays, and a mountain chickadee chirped at me from a branch. Nature seemed oblivious to my plight.

Twenty yards later, I stepped out of the trees and onto the path leading past the Knotty Pine's cabins. I hurried past Cabin Four, then Three, then Two.

When I arrived at Cabin One, the blinds were drawn tight—no gap at the bottom as there had been during my earlier clandestine spying escapade. No way to peek inside and form a strategy. I'd just have to go for it. I climbed the wooden steps, pausing on the porch for a fortifying breath. As I raised my fist to knock, the door swung open. A hand reached out and grabbed my forearm, yanking me inside. I caught a quick glimpse of Scott's frenzied face as he shoved me across the room and slammed the door.

I stumbled over the braided area rug, and my upper body splayed across the bed. At the sound of a muffled groan, I turned to see Banner in a chair near the small dining table. His wrists were bound to the armrests with thick ropes, and his ankles were tied to the chair legs. A wool scarf served as a gag.

I sprang to my feet and crossed the room in two steps. The boy's blue eyes gazed at me mournfully. His sallow skin was the shade of snow as it turns to slush, an unhealthy mixture of white and gray.

I knelt beside him. "Banner, did he hurt you?"

He shook his head, his lips working against the gag. I reached up to pull the scarf from his mouth, but Scott grabbed me by the collar of my coat and dragged me across the wood floor. He swung me around and waved a gun in my face.

"Where's the box?"

I held up my hands. "It's close by, I swear. I only needed to make sure—"

"The boy's fine. For now. But if you're not back in two minutes with that box, he won't be anymore. Got it?"

My heart throbbed in my chest, my neck, my temples, but I forced myself to maintain a calm demeanor. "I'll get it, but first I need an assurance that you won't harm us once I hand it over."

He swiped at the sweat beading his hairline. "You're not in the position to demand assurances, or anything else." He pivoted and pointed the gun at Banner. "You'll just have to do as I say and hope I end up in a good mood."

I moved so I was between the gun and Banner. "Let's be realistic, Scott. You're in trouble. Even if you get what you want, there's no endgame for you."

"Sure there is. I get the box and get myself out of here. I'm sure you took a peek at the contents."

"I didn't," I said, too quickly.

He snorted. "Fine. Let's pretend I believe you. All you

need to know is that the box—or more accurately, what's inside it—might drown me. But if I play my cards right, it could also turn me into an Olympic-caliber swimmer. Heidi—or Desiree, as you knew her—had access to ample funds. Ill-gotten gains, yeah, but who cares? Once we get our hands on it—"

"We?"

"Bentham's Progeny, of course."

"Ah. Your philosopher buddies. They're in on this, too?"

A shadow crossed his face, but he covered it with a smile. "Of course. As long as the four of us stick together, we're indestructible."

I crossed my arms. "Well, it looks like you and your progeny have made some rookie mistakes that are going to come back to haunt you."

Now it wasn't a shadow on his face, it was a full eclipse. "You have no idea what you're talking about. We're no amateurs. This isn't our first…"

He trailed off, then shrugged. I didn't take that shrug as a promising sign. I tamped down the panic that threatened to engulf me, reminding myself that Monika would soon be calling the police. If I could keep Scott talking a few minutes more, Banner and I might survive this fiasco.

"This isn't your first what?" I ventured.

"Let's just say it's not our first rodeo."

I wanted to slap the pompous grin off his face, but a glance at his gun restrained me. "So, Bentham's Progeny have killed before?"

He chuckled. "We don't refer to it as *killing*. Nothing so banal as that. 'Eradication for the betterment of society,' we prefer to term it."

I pretended not to be horrified. "Interesting concept. Care to elaborate?"

I could tell he was eager to expound and pleased to have a captive audience. Literally.

"Of course. I'm always happy to educate the ignorant masses." He smiled at me with condescension. "Our philosophical foundation is utilitarianism. We believe the purpose of life involves the achievement of maximum happiness and pleasure. We promote whatever actions lead to that end. When we run across people who diminish society's happiness and pleasure, it is our moral obligation to eradicate them."

I suppressed a shiver. "You've done this…eradication thing…before?"

He stood straighter. "Heidi makes three. Bernard—you met him—got first crack a year ago with a colleague who previously stole his research findings. A year later, we eradicated the corrupt minister who counseled Judith's husband to divorce her."

He smiled at the memory. The gun dropped an inch, then two. I considered lunging for it, but with Banner in such close range, I couldn't risk it.

"Jerry was supposed to choose next," Scott mused. "But my situation escalated, so we pivoted to Heidi."

"You tracked Desiree…Heidi, I mean…to Rock Creek Village and came here for an *eradication*?"

"Easy breezy." His giggle bordered on manic.

"But why? What did Heidi do to deserve eradication?"

He clenched his jaw. "She didn't deserve to live. She caused irreparable damage to my happiness and pleasure when she took the grant money I'd helped her procure and disappeared. Then she contacted me and said she possessed evidence showing the part I'd played in her scheme. Evidence of our…liaison. She'd kept letters I'd written promising I'd make sure she got the grant. She also had photos that…well, I won't go into the details. Suffice it to say, Heidi could've ruined my career and ended my marriage. And she promised to do just that if I went to the authorities."

He paced around the tiny room, the gun's aim never wavering from me. "When Heidi and I were together, I noticed that stupid storage box at her apartment. Anytime I'd get near it, she'd throw a fit. But one day, just before she took off, she went to take a shower and left it unlocked. So I sneaked a peek. When I saw what was inside, all the cons she'd carried out...I was both appalled and impressed. After she left Cheyenne, I knew she had incriminating evidence on me in that box." He raised a finger. "But there's an upside. There always is, if you look hard enough. I'd gotten glimpses of Heidi's finances in that box and realized she'd accumulated substantial wealth. I knew my happiness and pleasure could multiply exponentially."

Goosebumps broke out on my arms. "I think I understand, Scott. But here's one thing I don't get. If you were after Desiree, why did you poison Brian? Was it intended as some sort of warning?"

He shook his head. "Brian. That stupid oaf simply got in the way. I intended the fudge for Heidi—I even addressed the box to Desiree Bouton. Bernard had prepared the perfect dosage for her body weight, but it wasn't enough to kill Brian Ratliff. In the end, though, everything worked out. Brian's poisoning clued Heidi in that I was coming for her. Watching her squirm was an unintended but gratifying perk."

I listened hard for sirens but heard nothing. I still needed to stall. "She realized you were in town and harbored ill intent. Why do you suppose she didn't run?"

He huffed. "Arrogance, plain and simple. She contacted me after Brian went into a coma. Reminded me she had the goods on me. Said if anything happened to her, her brother would turn the box over to the police. I acted contrite and lovesick, told her how much I was hurting, that I wanted to see her one last time to say a proper goodbye. I promised after that, I'd be out of her life forever. She agreed to meet me, and we settled on a public place—the overlook."

"And that's where you planned to kill her?"

My skin crawled as he giggled again. "That's the beauty of a supple mind like my own. I didn't have a specific plan. I didn't think I'd be able to execute the eradication in such a crowded setting. Fortuitously, the snowstorm started, and the overlook was deserted. Except for us, of course." He held up his hands, as if to say it was fate. "Heidi was too cocky. And now she's dead."

His self-congratulatory tone grated on me. I crossed my arms. "Well, if you ask me, it all sounds pretty self-serving."

He cocked his head. "Self-serving?"

"This whole utilitarianism philosophy you pretend to espouse. You say your group promotes societal happiness and pleasure, yet your so-called eradications result only in personal benefit."

Scott gave me a half smile, like he was dealing with a not-too-bright pupil. "Individual pleasure is the backbone of societal happiness. You can't have the second without attaining the first."

I gave him a cynical look. "If you say so."

The patient-professor facade melted, replaced by a face scrunched up in anger. "I do say so. And who do you think you are to question our tenets? A two-bit photographer who wouldn't know a deep thought if it tap-danced across her skull." He gave himself a full-body shake, like Woody after a bath. "Enough talk. Time to get me that box."

I sighed and shook my head sadly. "And what happens if I do? I mean, you can't go back to work. Back to your wife. You murdered a woman and almost killed her husband. The police will be searching for you, and they won't stop until they catch you."

"Why on earth would the police search for me? I'm just a professor on sabbatical in a little mountain village. It was a mere coincidence that someone died while I was here. People die every day—a number of them right here in Rock Creek Village, from what I've learned. Anyway, by the time we're finished here, no one will be around to tell a different tale."

He winced, having revealed more about his dastardly plan than he'd intended. "No further discussion. Go get that box. Now."

I glanced at Banner, who sat still as death. He was even paler than before, and his breath wheezed around the gag. I gave him what I hoped was a reassuring look before turning back to Scott.

"You just insinuated you're planning to kill us as soon as you get what you want. Why on earth would I cooperate now?"

His smile was so cold it literally made me shiver. "Well, I have an ace in the hole. One I believe you'll find quite motivating. You see, the other members of the Progeny are currently scattered about the village, awaiting my order to carry out a few additional eradications. Your friend Mrs. Finney, for instance. Your boyfriend. Your parents. All I have to do is give the signal."

I sucked in a breath and swayed on my feet. Scott reached out to steady me, and I pulled away from his touch. My repulsion made him smile. "The grim reality, Callahan Cassidy, is that your fate is already sealed, and so is Banner's. Now it's a matter of whether you choose to save the rest of your loved ones."

46

I held my breath and tried to summon sirens. Nothing. Maybe the police had decided to come in silent. They had to be close.

But even if they were, I wasn't sure they could save Banner and me now. Scott was clearly crazed. He was a cornered beast—an insane one. As a journalist, I'd once witnessed that same expression on the face of a man just before he shot his girlfriend, then turned the gun on himself.

As if reading my thoughts, Scott pointed the gun at Banner. "I won't go to jail. I'm telling you, Callie, if you're not back with that box in two minutes, I'll call the Progeny. Then I'll shoot this boy. After that, I'll take my own life. Believe me, if I don't get access to that money, I have nothing to lose. You'll survive, but for the rest of your life, you'll carry the weight of everyone who died in your place."

I looked at Banner. He'd regained his color, and he appeared calm. He stared at me and shook his head. But despite his bravery, I knew I had no choice. "I'll do it," I said to Scott. "The box is in my car, right down the street. I'll go now. It won't even take me two minutes, I swear. Don't—"

Suddenly, a cacophony of noise boomed outside. Not the sirens I'd been longing for, but a flood of barking and yowling. It got louder and louder, then began to fade. Scott darted toward the window. With his gun still trained on me, he lifted a slat in the blinds and peered outside.

"What's happening?" I asked.

He ignored me, rushed to the door, and flung it open.

As he stepped onto the cabin's porch, I followed him to the door, treading lightly.

I couldn't believe what I was seeing. Monika stood at the bottom of the steps, her expression fierce. In her outstretched hand, she held an oversized match, the kind people used to light fireplaces. A flame danced at its tip. On the ground directly beneath the match lay Desiree's lockbox, the lid open like a baby bird waiting for a worm. A nest of manila envelopes rested inside.

"You wouldn't dare," Scott growled.

"Don't worry, I removed the documents that implicate you." She nodded toward a single envelope on the porch railing. "The police will want a look at those. As for the rest, including the bank account information that would facilitate your escape and finance the luxurious life I assume you're dreaming of, I have no qualms about watching them burn."

She dropped the match into the open box and took a step backward as the envelopes caught fire. Scott squealed. "Nooo!" he cried.

The gun dropped from his hand as he leapt off the porch. I hurried onto the porch and grabbed it up. Scott reached into the box and snatched at the burning documents in an attempt to save them from the fire. He screamed and pulled his fingers back as the flames singed his skin.

Then he looked at Monika and roared. The rage in his eyes burned as hot as the fire in the box. I lifted the gun. "Stop right there, Scott. Don't make another move."

He took no notice of me and lunged at Monika. Her face was set in steely determination. As she lifted her arm, I saw that she clutched a shiny object: the pen I'd given her a few days earlier.

Monika swung with all her might. With a squelching sound, the tip of the pen pierced Scott's neck. A stream of bright red liquid spurted from the wound. Scott froze for a split second, his eyes wide with surprise. Then his hands flew to his neck, and he crumpled to the ground. I pounded down the steps and stood over him, aiming the gun at him as he writhed and moaned.

Monika brandished the pen, looking like a red-haired Amazon warrior emerging victorious from battle. Blood dribbled from the nib and splattered in the dirt. She turned her gaze from Scott to me.

"You were right, Callie. The pen is mightier than the sword."

47

I nodded at Monika, but I couldn't celebrate. This wasn't over yet.

With a steady hand, I pointed the gun at Scott's leg. "Call your friends off, or I swear I'll shoot you. First one kneecap, then the other. After that—"

He squealed and rolled onto his back, holding up his hands. "Stop! I lied to you! They all left last night."

Monika stepped toward us, her face pale and her eyes wide. "Callie, what's—?"

I pressed the muzzle of the gun to Scott's knee. "I don't believe you."

"It's true! They said everything was about to hit the fan, and they weren't going down with me. Turns out they're cowards."

Then the barking and yowling I'd heard before recommenced. I turned my head and saw Woody and Carl charging down the path. And behind them…The breath whooshed out of me at the sight of my parents, alive and well and running toward us like track stars.

"Have you seen the rest of the Progeny?" I asked them frantically when they reached us.

Dad quickly assessed the scene and peeled the gun from my hand. "They checked out last night." He looked at Scott on the ground. "All except this one. He said he wanted an extra day."

Sirens warbled in the near distance, growing louder by the second. My muscles went limp. Mom wrapped an arm around my waist, and I looked at her through a haze of tears. "He said…he said…" The story spilled from my lips.

"We're fine, Angelface. We're okay."

"I'm sure Sam and Mrs. Finney are okay, too, but I'll call them to double check," Dad said. He clutched the gun in one hand and hit speed dial on the phone he held in the other.

Relief washed through me. I stared at Scott sniveling on the ground. "I've never been so happy to be lied to in my life."

I looked at Monika and saw tears leaking from her eyes. They were silent tears, stoic ones, but I pulled her into a hug anyway. "You saved us," I whispered. She wrapped her arms around me and buried her face against my shoulder.

Carl and Woody huddled at our ankles, but only for a moment. Once they'd determined Monika and I were uninjured, they paused briefly to growl and hiss at Scott, then headed straight up the porch steps and into the cabin. Mom knelt beside Scott and examined his neck. She pulled off her scarf and pressed it against the stab wound, causing another moan. "Hush," she said. "No arteries punctured. No massive blood loss. You'll live."

"But you may wish you hadn't," Monika added.

"Sam's fine," Dad said, pulling the phone from his ear. "He's on his way. I'll call Mrs. Finney next, but I'm sure she's good, too."

I nodded, relieved, and followed the creatures' lead, hurrying up the steps and into the cabin. There, I found Woody licking Banner's bound wrist, while Carl clawed at the rope around the boy's ankle. I bent and looked into Banner's eyes. "It's over," I said. "He can't hurt us."

He nodded, and relief filled his eyes.

I went to the kitchen and retrieved a butcher knife. When I stepped in front of Banner again, knife in hand, he flinched.

"Don't worry," I said. "I've done this before."

Still, when I noticed a slight tremor in my hand, I took a deep breath to steady my nerves.

I dropped to one knee, nudged Carl aside, and slid the blade between the leg of the chair and the rope. A few seconds later, one foot was free. Then the other. Then the hands.

"See? Told you there was nothing to worry about."

Banner pulled the scarf out of his mouth, spitting out bits of yarn. "You could have started with this thing," he said.

The side of my mouth curled up. "I think what you meant to say was, 'Oh, thank you for coming to my rescue, Callie. You're my hero.'"

He grinned weakly. "That goes without saying." He stood, unsteady on his feet at first, and pulled me tight against his chest, squeezing so hard I almost lost my breath. "I thought I was a goner," he said. "But I was even more scared that you were."

"Remember on the phone, how you tried to keep me from coming? You put yourself in danger trying to save me from it. I guess that puts to rest any doubts you had about your bravery."

He squeezed again, and I wrapped my arms around him. It would take time for us to process the trauma we'd experienced, but we'd get through it. Together. We all would.

Roland, the EMT, appeared beside us, medical bag in hand. "Sorry to break up this lovefest, but Chief Cassidy said I should check Banner for injuries."

"I'm good," Banner said, running his hands over his body.

I frowned at him. "Scott hit you. I heard it on the phone."

"A little punch in the gut. I've had worse messing around with my brother."

"Even so, let Roland take a look," I urged.

Lynn hurried into the room. "Callie? Banner? Are you—?"

"We're fine," I assured her.

Lynn puffed her cheeks and exhaled. "Oh, thank goodness."

At my insistence, Banner let Roland listen to his lungs, check his pulse, and perform a quick examination. When he pronounced the boy "good to go," Woody wagged. Carl sniffed the corners of the room as if he were in charge of the forensic investigation.

I scooped the cat into my arms, and we all headed outside, where a stretcher lay flat on the ground beside Scott. Raul and Frank looked on as Roland's partner, Maddie, tended to the so-called philosopher. Raul held two zip-locked bags, one bearing the gun and the other containing the pen that was mightier than a sword.

Woody trotted toward Monika and nudged her leg with his nose. She crouched down and wrapped her arms around his neck.

I smiled. "Question, Monika: How did you persuade the creatures to fetch my parents?"

She shrugged. "I told them I'd only let them out of the car if they promised to run straight to the lodge to get help. They agreed." She smiled and pulled Woody closer. "They're very special animals."

I hugged Carl, and he responded with a screech of protest. I laughed. "Indeed they are."

Then I turned to Dad. "Mrs. Finney?"

"All good," he said. "Just miffed that she missed all the action. She said to tell you—"

"I know, I know. I'd best deliver a report, in person."

Scott stopped writhing. His eyes were open but glazed, and he wore a blissful smile. "What's with him?" I asked.

"He's fine," Mom said. "Maddie administered a sedative. And thank goodness for that. None of us could tolerate any more of his whining."

Once the paramedics had Scott secured, they lifted the stretcher to its full height and wheeled it down the path. I glanced at the smoldering box and then again to Monika. "Those envelopes were empty, right?"

She grinned. "You know it. The documents are in the trunk of your car, safe and secure."

My adrenaline rush was depleting. I moved to Raul's side, fighting the urge to rest my head on his broad shoulder.

"When will you be releasing Braden from custody?" I asked.

Raul's eyebrows knitted together. "Well, none of this proves anything, you realize."

I stiffened. The adrenaline kicked back in, and I prepared for battle. Then I noticed Raul's sardonic grin. "It was a joke," he said. "Where's your sense of humor?"

I scrunched up my face. "It was a terrible joke. Don't give up your day job in hopes of becoming a comedian."

"As long as you don't give up yours in hopes of becoming a detective," he responded.

"I second that," Dad said. "All in favor?"

I glanced around the small circle. Everyone held up a hand—Raul, Lynn, Frank, Banner, Dad, Mom. Even Woody and Carl appeared to lift paws.

Everyone except Monika.

"I, for one, think you'd make a stellar detective," she said. "You solved this case, didn't you? Rescued Banner? Proved Braden's innocence?"

I studied her. In the short week I'd known Monika, she'd transformed from a rookie reporter to a professional. From an outsider to one of us. She was a villager, through and through.

And she was my friend.

I smiled at her. "You're wrong, Grasshopper. *We* solved it. And now *you're* going to write about it."

48

The next Saturday, our group of friends and family gathered in the Knotty Pine Resort media room. We were ostensibly present to view Braden's photographic montage of Tonya and David's wedding, but we all knew there was more to it than that. We'd shown up to honor friendship, resilience, humanity. To celebrate life and love and the very important philosophies of compassion and empathy. To appreciate the moral obligation—and privilege—of serving each other.

In other words, we'd gathered to stand for everything Bentham's Progeny had stood against.

Champagne in hand, I moved to the back and scanned the room. The space was compact, but we'd squeezed in enough chairs to accommodate everyone. With help from Ethan and Banner, Braden and I had covered the walls with wedding photos. Now, guests circled the room, drinking champagne as they viewed the images.

I turned my gaze to the Ratliff twins. The events of the past week had further strengthened their bond. I recalled the expression on their faces when Frank escorted Braden into the lobby of the police station. It was as if both boys had been granted their deepest wishes. I hadn't snapped a photo, but I knew I'd carry the image in my memory—and my heart—forever. Those boys weren't my blood, but they were my family.

Mrs. Finney, attired in a purple silk skirt and blazer, and Mr. Purdy, in a gray tweed jacket with a purple bowtie, walked toward the boys. *Men*, I corrected myself.

Mrs. Finney gestured to the photos on the wall.

"You've done a lovely job, Braden," I heard her say.

"I'm Banner," he said.

She reached up and pinched his cheek. "Well, of course you are, dear."

Tonya sidled up next to me, along with Jessica, Summer, Renata, and Lynn. Our girl gang, happily reunited. Across the room, I noticed Pamela watching us, and I waved a hand, summoning her to join us. She looked surprised, then pleased, as she made her way toward us.

Resplendent in her new poppy red crepe mini dress from Italy, Tonya scooted over to make room for her. My friends greeted Pamela with warmth, and I thought she might be a good fit for our group.

Then Tonya draped an arm around me. "So, sugarplum, you had quite an adventure while I was away on my honeymoon. Almost got my new employee into some serious trouble."

We all looked at Monika, who stood across the room chatting with Raul and Frank. Or was she interrogating them? The intensity of her expression indicated the latter.

"From what I can tell, your new employee will be churning up plenty of trouble all on her own," I said. "Good trouble, as they say. You found a winner in that young woman. I only hope you can hang onto her. Don't let my former boss get wind of her talents. Preston will lure her to the *Sentinel* if you don't watch out."

"If you keep offering up the same level of excitement as she experienced last week, she'll be here for life," Tonya said. "With plenty of Felden Awards to show for it. We small-town newspaper journalists can make enormous waves of our own, you know."

"Oh, I know." I grinned at my best friend. "You've proven that yourself. Now Monika is following in your footsteps."

Monika's story on the murder of Desiree Bouton had appeared online two days after the events at the cabin, followed by a print version the day after. The story chronicled the events leading to and culminating in the duel in Cabin One, including how Banner had walked into trouble. In an attempt to find evidence that could free his brother, Banner had headed over to the cabin and inadvertently barged in on Scott, who was there to search for Desiree's storage box. Scott had seen Banner as a bargaining chip, and the hostage situation unfolded.

A follow-up story on Tuesday told of Scott's arraignment on charges of the attempted murder of Brian Ratliff and the second-degree murder of Desiree Bouton, along with various other charges spanning from assault to kidnapping. The photo accompanying the story—taken by Monika after a few quick lessons from yours truly—showed Scott just outside the courtroom, clad in an orange jumpsuit, with his black hair combed and his chin lifted in a display of haughtiness. The bandage on his neck was all that remained of his tryst with my—now Monika's—pen.

A third story, published just yesterday, detailed the subsequent capture of the remaining members of Bentham's Progeny, who had indeed left the village just after Desiree's death. They'd soon face charges themselves, once police in other jurisdictions revisited the not-so-cold cases related to Bernard's colleague and Judith's minister. Though sleazy Jerry hadn't scored an "eradication" of his own, he was still on the hook as a conspirator.

Police were still searching for Weston, whose real name turned out to be Gavin Everman. His trail had run cold just outside Colorado, where he dumped Desiree's car. I figured he'd found a beach somewhere and was spending his days either surfing or stoned. Probably both.

Jessica ran a hand through her spiky hair. "So, the poisoning that started all this had nothing to do with Brian Ratliff at all."

"Nope," I said. "A lot of people hate him, but none of

them tried to kill him."

"Not yet, anyway," Jessica said.

Pamela cleared her throat. "I'd like to point out again that the poisoned fudge didn't come from my store."

"That's true," I said. "The Progeny made their own, right there in Knotty Pine Cabin Three. That's where Bernard—a professor of chemistry, by the way—was staying. The group made a purchase from the Fudge Factory so they could reuse the box. They gave a teenager a few bucks to deliver the laced batch to the Ratliffs' porch in case there was a doorbell camera."

"The one I feel sorry for in this whole mess is Trent Wallace," Pamela said. "He's a good guy, and his name got dragged through the mud. I know what that's like."

A pang of guilt pricked me. "I apologized to Trent. He said he doesn't harbor any hard feelings." I touched Pamela on the arm. "I'm also going to keep apologizing to you, for as long as it takes you to forgive me."

She blinked back a few tears. "I do forgive you, Callie. I'm sorry for bringing it up. I promise, I'm moving on." She glanced across the room, and her eyes lit on Willie. Then she leaned toward the group. "Besides, if I'm being honest, I might have poisoned that creep myself, if only I'd thought of it."

We laughed, if a bit uncomfortably. Then Braden headed toward us, excitement nearly bubbling from his pores. "When do you want to start the show?" he asked me.

"You're in charge. It's up to you."

He looked flustered but pleased as he strode toward the projector and consulted with Banner and Ethan on the tech.

"How are the twins coping?" Summer asked, shifting her long blond braid over her shoulder. "They've been through so much."

"That which does not kill us makes us stronger, right?" My friends nodded their agreement. "As brothers,

Banner and Braden are tighter than ever. As for their relationship with their father…" I shrugged. "The jury is out. Maybe this whole experience will give the three of them a new start. But who knows? Brian's recuperating at home now. The twins tell me he doesn't seem especially despondent over Desiree's death. He might be in shock, or still recovering, or…"

"Or more likely, he's just a massive idiot who can't manufacture a single authentic emotion for anyone but himself," Jessica interjected.

I smiled. Leave it to Jessica to put things in perspective.

"And the insurance money?" Renata asked. "Is Brian keeping it all for himself?"

"Remains to be seen. But I can tell you this: Banner and Braden aren't counting on getting a cent. They'll continue with their college courses and their work at the gallery. Que sera sera."

At the front of the room, Banner clapped his hands to get everyone's attention. "Find a seat, please, everybody," he said. "We're about to start."

Murmurs and shuffling ensued, followed by silence once everyone had settled. Sam sat extra-close beside me. He'd been especially affectionate since the ordeal at the cabin. He was always a touchy, huggy type, but he'd taken it up a notch, as if he were afraid to let me out of his sight. Relationship PTSD, I supposed.

Banner proudly introduced his brother. Braden said a few words of thanks to Tonya and David for giving him his first official gig. I beamed when he added a special thanks to me for "being the best mentor anyone could ever have." Then Ethan lowered the lights.

One at a time, the photos faded in and out on the white screen. The happy couple on the altar. The snow through the picture window. Woody and Carl in their homemade tuxes. Tonya straightening David's tie. Sam and I on the dance floor with our arms wrapped around one another. Mom and Dad gazing into each other's eyes as they waltzed. Lydia gazing into Mr. Mob Guy's eyes as they tangoed. Jessica wearing a sarcastic expression as she whispered in Summer's ear. Renata and Ethan with their arms around each other. Elyse's head thrown back in laughter at something Banner said. Mr. Purdy gracefully dipping Mrs. Finney. And Raul and Lynn semi-hidden behind a pillar, sharing a kiss. That one got some oohs from the crowd, followed by blushes from the detectives.

After several dozen more memories, the show concluded. I jumped to my feet and began clapping. "Bravo! Bravo!"

The rest of the small audience rose and joined in. Braden grinned like a schoolboy. Beside him, Woody woofed and wagged while Carl licked a paw from atop a credenza, feigning disinterest.

When the applause died down, Sam called out, "Cheers to the bride and groom." Everyone raised their glasses.

Tonya smiled her red-lipsticked smile, pulled her husband into an embrace, and kissed him hard and long.

When the two of them came up for a breath, David mopped his brow. "*Mamma mia!*"

I noticed my father at the front of the room. I assumed he was going to thank everyone for coming and bid them farewell, but he had something else on his agenda.

"Before we end tonight's festivities, I've been asked to get your attention for one last presentation. A…um…proposal, I'm told."

My heart leapt into my throat. I turned wide-eyed to Sam, who smiled roguishly before shaking his head. *Whew*, I thought. But was my relief tinged with the tiniest bit of disappointment?

I looked around, waiting for someone to make a move. Suddenly, Mr. Purdy sprang up and held out his hand to Mrs. Finney, leading her to the front of the room. He positioned her just so, extracted a small velvet box from the pocket of his tweed jacket, and nimbly dropped to one knee.

"I'm head over heels for you, Dumpling," he said. "Will you marry me and be my ice skating partner for life?"

Her cheeks went pink. She tapped a finger against her chin in mock consideration. "I suppose marriage would mean we could avoid a custody battle over our family of silver cups, which will hopefully grow even larger next month."

"Does that mean…?"

"Yes, Sugarcube. It means yes."

Everyone whooped and hollered and applauded. I smiled, watching my friends and family celebrate another joyful event. Woody trotted to my side and nuzzled my hand. Carl jumped onto the chair I'd vacated and curled his tail around himself, appearing satisfied.

Sam leaned toward me. "Mrs. Finney caught Tonya's bouquet, as I recall."

I nodded. "Guess some superstitions do come to pass."

"Maybe you'll catch Mrs. Finney's."

My heart skipped and fluttered in my chest. It wasn't palpitations. No, I was experiencing happiness. Rightness. Hope.

"Maybe," I said.

This time, I might even fight for it.

Become a Subscriber

Ready for a trip back in time to meet Callie and her friends in their younger years? Subscribe today to receive two free prequel short stories.

It's free to sign up, and you'll never be spammed by me. You can opt out at any time.

www.lorirobertsherbst.com

Acknowledgements

Something I didn't expect when I became an author: the relationships with readers. The kindness and generosity readers have shown me over the course of four (now five) books astonishes and humbles me. When I get bogged down in the not-so-gratifying tasks involved with publishing books, I turn to one of the lovely emails or reviews I've received and feel renewed. Thank you, dear readers. You've made this journey a joyous one.

Thank you to my exceptional group of beta readers for NEGATIVE REACTION: Merrily Boone, Jenny Campbell, Candice Chaloupka, Karin Diskin, Syrl Kazlo, Karen Lakis, Mary Rosewood, Debra Shaw, and my daughter, Katie Shapiro and husband Paul. When I got enmeshed in the book and stopped seeing the story for the scenes, they helped steer the manuscript straight.

In every set of acknowledgements I've written, I've expressed gratitude to my fabulous editor, Lisa Q. Mathews of Kill Your Darlings Editing Services, and I hope to continue that tradition for a long time to come. She's absolutely the best there is. If she ever decides to stop editing my books, I'll simply have to quit writing.

Another tradition that bears repeating is having the covers created by Molly Burton at Cozy Cover Designs. Her talent and vision bring each book to life. I don't know how she does it, but I'm glad she does.

Finally, to my incredible family: thank you for your constant support, your tolerance of my self-imposed deadlines, your willingness to offer genuine critiques, and your ability to make me laugh when I'm stressed. You all make life worth living.

About the Author

Silver Falchion and CIBA Murder & Mayhem award-winning author Lori Roberts Herbst writes the Callie Cassidy Mystery series. A former journalism teacher and counselor, Lori serves as Board Secretary for Sisters in Crime. She is a member of Mystery Writers of America, as well as the SinC Colorado chapter and North Dallas chapter, as well as the Guppy chapter, where she moderates the Cozy Gup group. Lori lives in Colorado Springs, CO, and is a wife, mother of two, and (gasp!) grandmother of four.

Subscribe at www.lorirobertsherbst.com for updates and other fun stuff (including FREE Callie Cassidy prequel stories).